Promise Me

by

Deborah Schneider

Promise Me

First Edition, 2010, Kindle Edition Published by Deborah Schneider October 2012

Edited by Helen Hardt

Published in the United States of America

Discover other titles by Deborah Schneider at Amazon.com

Dedication

In loving memory of my son Garth, who taught me to never give up and never stop believing in myself and my writing.

Table of Contents

PROLOGUE

CHAPTER ONE

CHAPTER TWO

CHAPTER THREE

CHAPTER FOUR

CHAPTER FIVE

CHAPTER SIX

CHAPTER SEVEN

CHAPTER EIGHT

CHAPTER NINE

CHAPTER TEN

CHAPTER ELEVEN

CHAPTER TWELVE

CHAPTER THIRTEEN

CHAPTER FOURTEEN

CHAPTER FIFTEEN

CHAPTER SIXTEEN

CHAPTER SEVENTEEN

CHAPTER EIGHTEEN

CHAPTER NINETEEN

CHAPTER TWENTY

CHAPTER TWENTY-ONE

CHAPTER TWENTY-TWO

EPILOGUE
SPECIAL BONUS SHORT STORY
ABOUT THE AUTHOR…

Prologue

"I think you're getting a little too cozy in this town." Robert stared at him across the expanse of the oak desk. "Have you forgotten why we were sent here?"

"Hardly," Sam responded. "But we knew right from the start this would be a delicate operation. The men we're investigating won't let just anyone into their inner circle. I've worked for months to gain their trust."

"Hrmmp," Robert responded. "Drinking and playing poker don't seem like much hard work."

Sam grinned at his partner. "Not as tough as working for Harriet Parmeter. Your hands must be nearly bleeding from all the dishes the owner of the hotel has you washing every night."

Robert stared down at his boots. "Mrs. Parmeter is a fine woman. I don't mind giving her a hand at the hotel. She treats me fair and is the best cook I ever knowed."

Sam caught his friend's gaze and grinned. "So, you really don't mind staying in this town for a bit longer, do you? You can court Mrs. Parmeter. Maybe settle down and get married.

Robert leaned down to send the chaw he had in his mouth into the nearby spittoon. "Don't get carried away with your imaginin's, Sam. I respect the woman and eating her meals ain't no kinda chore. But you and me ain't the marrying kind. We'll finish up here, get paid and kick up our heels a bit. Then we'll move on.

Sam leaned back in his chair and nodded. "I won't be staying in Willow Creek one minute more than it takes to complete our assignment. But we know this is damned important. I can't take a chance of botching this one. The mine owners invite me to their games, but I've never been to any of their special meetings. If one of the members of the group starts talking about their plans, another guy interrupts him, and they change the subject.

He leaned forward to stare into Robert's eyes. "I need to find out what those meetings are about. They're far too secretive about them.

Robert nodded. "But, if they don't trust you after months of card games and drinking, what's gonna make them invite you into their inner circle?"

Sam drummed his fingers on the desktop. "I don't know. Maybe they need someone to perform a special job for them."

"Murder?" Robert said, his lips thinning and his expression going hard. "That's about the only thing men like that would need. Rich mine owners wouldn't want to get their own hands dirty when they want someone out of the way."

Sam tossed his cheroot over the desk and into the spittoon. "You know I'd never go that far, no matter how important the assignment. I think we both had enough killing in the war."

Robert stood up. "Glad to hear you still got some scruples."

Sam stood and slowly removed his frock coat from the peg. "You know me better than anyone, Robert. There are lines I won't cross." He shrugged into his coat and grabbed his black wide-brimmed felt hat. He set it on his head and smoothed the brim.

"Seems like the last few assignments, those lines are getting thinner and thinner." Robert said.

Sam opened the door and indicated his partner should go out before him. "I do what's necessary, and so do you. I know our superiors in Washington are getting anxious. I'm doing the best

I can to get the information we need."

Robert proceeded out the door but paused to give his friend and partner an anxious look. "I know, but for some reason, you seem more settled and content than I've seen you in years. Might be owning a business in Montana is the thing you been searching for these past few years."

Sam folded his arms across his chest. "You've heard me talk about my dreams, Robert. I want to breed the best damned horses in California. This job is only a steppingstone to getting my own ranch. I do what I have to, but every assignment is just another investigation. We get the information we need and the lawbreakers get arrested.

"Then we move on." Robert said, as he went through the outer door to the street.

"That's right," Sam responded. "We don't settle down, we're just here to get the job done."

Robert tipped his hat with his finger and started toward the Parmeter House to his dinner chores for Harriet Parmeter.

Sam watched him go with a twinge of envy. Despite his teasing, he knew Harriet and Robert had developed a strong bond. She was a good woman, and he wondered if Robert might be seriously considering settling in Willow Creek.

It didn't matter. Once he'd finished his assignment, there was nothing to hold Sam here. Whether Robert stayed or traveled on with him, his goal was to get to California with enough money in his pocket to buy a ranch.

Then he'd settle down. Maybe even try getting married again.

His throat tightened and he swallowed. Maybe not. Marriage was for the young and foolish.

Those were things he'd been once, but a war had burned all the hope and faith he'd ever had to a cinder. Now he protected himself with a sharp wit, as much good sense as he could muster and the ability to use the revolver strapped to his side with cool proficiency.

He gazed down the street to the swinging doors of the Dark Horse Saloon. Truth be told, he'd prefer to go to his rooms and read. A package had arrived for him today, and it included a copy of Mark Twain's newest book about traveling around the world. He was looking forward to reading it.

For now, his job was to find a way to earn the trust of a group of silver mine owners. He stepped off the boardwalk and into the mud of the street. His lips thinned.

God how he hated all the damned mud in this town.

Chapter One

"Seems like an awful lot of stewing over one widow woman."

Samuel Calhoun flicked his gaze across the ample bosom of the saloon girl who set his whiskey on the table before returning his concentration to the cards held in his right hand.

"She ain't just a widder woman. She's the wife of Arthur Wainwright, and the sole owner of the Silver Slipper Mine now that he's dead. I hear tell she got every bit of his property and all his money. Now she's comin' up with these crazy schemes, gettin' the miners together for some kinda association, she calls it." Henry Sanders hurled his wad of chewing tobacco into the spittoon. He missed. "And if she succeeds, well, it's gonna hurt all of us."

Zachariah Dent tossed two cards on the table and raised an eyebrow at Sam. "Easy for you to say, Calhoun. If the rumors are to be believed, she's gonna make you a rich man." He shook his head at his poker partners. "That fella she sent to town, calls himself her agent, he's tellin' folks they're gonna build houses for the miners."

Zachariah picked up the cards Sam had dealt him and swore before throwing his hand down in disgust. "Luck seems to be with you tonight, Calhoun."

Sam let a lazy grin slowly cross his face. "It appears so, gentlemen. But lady luck is as fickle as any woman can be, and she can change her mind in a heartbeat." He threw more chips to the center of the table before dealing himself a card from the deck he held in one hand. Glancing at it, he kept his eyes cast down, never hinting at the fortuitous draw he'd just made.

"I don't like what I hear about this Miners' Benevolent Association. What the hell does any woman want with that kinda nonsense? Why don't she stay up in Helena where she belongs?" Zachariah gulped down the rest of his whiskey and signaled a saloon girl for another drink.

Jack Pruitt studied his cards, his dark, granite-hard eyes giving no hint of his thoughts. He withdrew several chips from his dwindling pile and tossed them to the center of the table.

"Raise you twenty, and call."

Sam gave a slight nod, tossed his own chips into the pile, and spread his cards before him, face up. "Full boat, queens high." His gaze never wavered from the face of his opponent.

Jack stared at the cards, shaking his head as he folded his own hand. "The ladies do seem to favor you, Calhoun."

The other men at the table laughed as Sam gathered his winnings to add to his growing pile. He'd done well tonight. He always anticipated a game with this group of mine owners. They could afford to lose, and they enjoyed the challenge of playing against him. Of course, he hoped they were learning to trust him. In fact, he was counting on the poker games to give him that advantage. He watched the men drink, knowing when they felt the effect of the liquor, they'd talk more. Sam could wait to make his inquiries.

He leaned back in his chair, sipped his whiskey, and studied the group. These were tough men. It would take more than rumors of a lady hell bent on good works to scare them. He wondered how he could use the situation to his advantage.

"What exactly is the good Widow Wainwright up to?" he asked, as Henry dealt another hand. Sam never looked at his cards until all five were in front of him.

"Hell bent on destroying us, that's what the bitch is up to." The venom in Jack Pruitt's voice startled Sam.

Pruitt was a cold, quiet man, not given to emotional outbursts. Sam had once seen him face down an angry miner and plunge a knife into the man's heart with hardly a flicker of concern. Jack clearly considered this woman a serious threat, and Sam knew, in his line of work, there was always a way to benefit when men felt threatened. Especially since he'd learned to always remain calm and unemotional.

"Excuse me for saying so, gentlemen, but a benevolent association hardly seems to be a dangerous proposition. It sounds, very—" He paused to cough discreetly. "Christian."

He picked up his cards, arranged them, and considered his next move. He put two cards face down on the table. "Give me two aces, Henry."

The other men laughed as they each accepted cards of their own. Sam noted that Jack Pruitt took only one.

He folded early, knowing his two fours wouldn't beat Pruitt, who had a tick in his left eye when he held a good hand. Sam had learned to read people, and in more than one instance that skill had saved his life. Tonight it would at least save him some money.

"Christian is right, damn do-gooder women folk." Henry folded his cards and grabbed his beer. He slopped some on his silk vest.

"Let me buy you another beer," Sam said. Henry wouldn't be as careful about what he said if he were drunk.

"Damn kind of ya, Calhoun."

"I'll buy a round for the table, if it's acceptable to you gentlemen," Sam said, as Pruitt laid down a pair of aces, gathered his winnings with one meaty fist, and nodded.

Zachariah lifted his lip and sneered. "You got mosta our money anyhow, Calhoun. By rights you oughta be buyin' fer the rest of the night."

Sam rearranged his chips and flashed a grin. "Well, I plan to retire after a few more hands. I do have a business to run, you know."

The other men made rude noises of objection, but Sam shook his head. "A working man has to pace himself. And if what you say about Mrs. Wainwright needing a substantial amount of lumber is true, I'd best make sure I have a decent stock available."

"Goddamn it, Calhoun, don't tell us you plan to help this woman with her schemes? Refuse to sell her the lumber, and maybe she'll go back where she came from." Henry lifted his glass. "Give her a hard time and send her packin', that's how we should get rid of her."

Jack Pruitt studied the whiskey glass sitting in front of him, but he didn't touch it. He wasn't much of a drinking man, and he nursed a whiskey for hours during a card game. It took real skill to beat Pruitt at poker, and Sam relished the challenge.

"I'm thinking we ought to do just the opposite." Jack tapped one pudgy finger on the deck of cards.

Pruitt's comment intrigued Sam. The man could be a cold, calculating bastard, which was sometimes necessary in a mining town as wild and unpredictable as Willow Creek, Montana.

Pruitt shuffled the cards. "I think we need somebody to court this widder woman, crawl into her bed and then humiliate her in front of the whole entire town. That'd teach the bitch a good lesson— that she ought to be minding her Christian"—he spit the word out as if he were cussing— "concerns back in Helena instead of messing with men's business. We need to run her out of town with her tail between her legs."

Sam raised an eyebrow. "And just who could be cold-hearted enough to take advantage of a woman determined to do good for the less fortunate?" His voice dripped with sarcasm.

Pruitt never looked away from Sam as he finished dealing the cards. "Why, I think you'd be the best candidate for the job, Calhoun. You got all that smooth charm that draws the ladies like bees to a rose garden. You got the looks, too, and you sure enough know your way around a petticoat."

The rest of the men joined Pruitt in laughter before he continued. "Seems you don't have no trouble getting into a woman's drawers, if the gossip can be believed."

Sam slowly sucked in a large gulp of air and then searched his pocket for a cheroot to hold his temper in check. Once, a long time ago, he would have shoved himself from the table and delivered a beating to any man who'd dared to insult his character. Those days were long gone and nearly forgotten. Life had taught Samuel Calhoun some hard and mean lessons; more than anything, he'd learned to survive and to make the most of every opportunity fate threw in his direction.

He lit the cigar and took a deep puff, relishing the rich, slightly bitter taste of the tobacco. He let the smoke circle above his head to form a halo.

Sam pasted the lazy grin back on his face as he took the measure of the man sitting across from him. "I could seduce the lady. There'd be no real challenge to that, gentlemen. My question is, what's in it for me?" Sam balanced the cigar on the edge of the table, gathered his hand together, and sorted his cards. "After all, I aim to make a fortune in Montana territory. That's the reason I came here in the first place."

"Four thousand dollars." Pruitt said.

Sam spread his cards face down on the table and brought the cheroot to his lips again. "Six thousand. The lady might be a pasty-faced bluestocking."

The men placed their bets and Henry Sanders folded.

"Five thousand," Pruitt said.

Sam's mind raced with possibilities. Five thousand dollars to bed a woman. Hell, these men must be desperate to get rid of her. And if he did as they asked, it was possible he'd earn their trust enough to learn what they were planning. He'd worked for several months to get to this point.

"Five thousand and five percent of the profits from each of your mines for the next year." Sam knew it was too much, and he'd never be around long enough to collect, but he loved to bargain.

Pruitt nodded at the other men. "What do you say to those terms?"

Henry belched and shook his head. "Seems to me that's a lotta money for gettin' a woman to do what she might wanna do anyhow. Mebbe I'll take a crack at her myself, and I'd do it fer free."

Pruitt shook his head, and his lips twisted as if he'd tasted something sour. "The only women you can entice into your bed, old man, are the ones you pay cash money for. We're talking about a lady here, and ain't none of us got the know how to court a lady." His voice dropped an octave and he leaned forward. "Most 'specially a Christian lady. I hear tell she's a papist too."

Sam patiently waited for their decision. Dealing with a Christian woman with righteous works on her mind was one thing. Trying to seduce a good Catholic lady was another.

"It just might be, Calhoun, you'll have your work cut out for you. I'll give you the money, because it'll cost me a whole lot more if she starts making the miners think they ain't getting their due." Pruitt leaned across the table and offered his hand.

Sam had a momentary twinge of conscience, but he tamped

it down. He wondered what kind of hellcat he'd be taking on in the form of the Widow Wainwright. Not that he'd actually seduce and ruin her. He'd court her, earn her trust and then find a way to send her back to Helena, her reputation intact. If she *was* a lady the rough mining town would probably do his work for him.

The other men gave in and grudgingly agreed to his terms. Lady luck was indeed with him tonight.

Each man added his chips to the pile and showed his cards. Finally, it was Sam's turn. He carefully flipped each card with a fluent twist of his wrist.

"Four kings and a queen," he said, as the other men stared at his hand in dead silence.

Sam gathered his chips, scraped them into his Stetson, and stood. "I expect I need my rest, gentlemen. Seducing a lady can be hard work." He shrugged into his black frock coat, adjusted his string tie, and smoothed out the wrinkles from his fancy waistcoat.

"I'll be in touch. I don't imagine it'll take long to accomplish the task of getting rid of Mrs. Wainwright."

"We're hoping you can be quick about this, Calhoun. The longer that woman stays in town, the more damage she'll be able to do. Don't lollygag around romancing her." Jack pounded the table.

Samuel Calhoun took offense at Jack's tone, and he turned back to face the poker players still seated at the oak table.

"What we are talking about, gentlemen, is a delicate matter. I take pride in my work, regardless of its nature." He touched the handle of his revolver. "I expect you to let me undertake this courtship in the manner I deem most appropriate."

Jack Pruitt stood, the sawdust on the saloon floor making small clouds as he stomped his foot. "Just remember, Calhoun, we hired you to get rid of her. Don't go getting all soft and feeling sorry for the woman. Be careful you don't go fallin' in love with her."

Sam stood at the bar of the Dark Horse saloon and choked out a bitter laugh. He had learned a powerful lesson years ago. Love ended in disappointment and loss.

"I promise you, gentlemen, I'll make the Widow Wainwright sorry she ever came to town. As for me falling in love, well, there's a better chance of you buying ice from the devil."

Sam folded the money the barkeep handed him and stuffed it into the pocket of his vest. Taking one last draw from his cheroot, he tossed it into a polished brass spittoon and touched one finger to the tip of his hat. "Gentlemen, I'll be talking to you." His long legs carried him across the pine floor, and he pushed through the swinging doors. He stood outside on the wooden sidewalk and grinned when he heard Henry Sanders's voice.

"Damn arrogant son-of-a-bitch. I'm almost hopin' that widder woman keeps her legs shut tight just to teach him a lesson."

Sam brushed a speck of dust from his coat and kicked at the thick mud of the street shining in the moonlight. Truth be known, he wished the same, because resistance from a woman would make the seduction a challenge. Sam loved a challenge.

More likely he'd have to work to woo the widow. Arthur Wainwright had been over sixty when he died. His widow might be near that age herself, which could work in Sam's favor. A more mature woman might be grateful for the attentions of a younger man.

He stood before the mill office and stared at the sign hanging above him. Calhoun Lumber Company. It was simple, and when he was on an assignment, he chose to keep things as simple as possible. His life was predicated upon simplicity and deceit. He constantly re-created himself—no past, no future. He existed for the duration of the job, then disappeared.

On this assignment, he'd discovered he was a good businessman, and several times he'd been tempted to resign from his position and settle down here. But too much was at stake. If he didn't discover more about the mine owners and their plan to turn the country to the silver standard, economic disaster would result.

That was his main reason for accepting the challenge to seduce the much-feared Widow Wainwright. If he could figure out a way to rid the mine owners of this inconvenient woman, there was a chance they'd finally accept him into their inner circle.

His assignment as a member of the United States Secret Service was too important to let an issue like one woman's feelings interfere. He'd already spent months creating his false identity to discover the roots of a massive counterfeiting operation. He was close to gaining their trust, and the information he needed to expose their plot.

Jack's warning echoed in his mind. Sam shook his head. He could protect himself from falling in love while seducing the Widow Wainwright. He no longer possessed a heart to lose.

Chapter Two

"Mud." Amanda Wainwright sighed deeply as she gazed out the carriage window. "This whole town is brown and gray and covered in mud."

She was alone in the carriage, so no one answered her. Lately, she'd taken to talking to herself to fill in the blanks and alleviate the loneliness. People might think her a bit daft, or maybe eccentric, if they heard her. Rich widows were allowed to be eccentric, weren't they?

She touched the black veiling on the hat perched next to her. She hated widow's weeds; each glimpse of herself reminded her she was completely and utterly alone.

Amanda took a deep breath; she needed to prepare herself for the days ahead. She still felt inadequate for the task Arthur had charged to her upon his deathbed. Her dying husband had begged her to make things right for the workers who had sacrificed so much of their lives to make him a rich man.

The stench of sickness had hung over him when he'd extracted the promise from her. She'd vowed to create the Miners' Benevolent Association for the workforce in his mines. It seemed an impossible task. She'd never had any responsibility other than directing servants and being an obedient daughter and wife. What did she know of miners and their problems?

The carriage halted, and Amanda stretched the muscles that had cramped on the long trip into the mountains. Snatching the despised hat, she set it upon her head and spread the heavy veiling across her shoulders to shield her face. The door opened and her driver nodded to her politely.

"We're here, ma'am."

Amanda wrapped the ribbons of her black, beaded bag around her thin wrist and held out a gloved hand. The man assisted her to the ground, and mud oozed over the toes of her boots. Lifting the hem of her bombazine gown, she walked to the steps and into the Parmeter House.

Amanda stood at the polished wood counter and waited patiently. A few minutes passed before a tall woman in a dark gray dress bustled out a doorway and smiled warmly at Amanda.

"Land sakes, you must be the Widder Wainwright."

Amanda felt bitterness sting her tongue as her face grew hot. She hated being identified as the surviving mate of a dead man. It was always followed by looks of pity for the poor widow.

The woman searched a warren of cubbyholes behind her, finally turning to hand a key and an envelope to Amanda.

"My name's Harriet Parmeter, and I own this place. I put you up in the best room I got, but let me know if there's anythin' you need." The woman's smile grew warmer. "That nice Mr. Penny set you up with three meals a day and Lee Chan to do your laundry."

Amanda nodded. "Thank you, Mrs. Parmeter, I appreciate your hospitality." A thick, tight band squeezed her chest as warmth rushed once more to her cheeks beneath the veil.

"Call me Harriet. Your agent's been telling folks what you plan to do for this town, and well—I'm real thankful I can give you a bit of hospitality."

Amanda wasn't sure how to react to this kindness and open gratitude. Her only thought in preparing for this journey to Willow Creek had been fulfilling the infernal promise she'd made to

Arthur.

It was possible Amanda was in Willow Creek to discover if she were still alive. She'd started to imagine she was slowly fading to become a ghost, wandering about the rooms of her hotel in Helena, lost and without purpose.

Harriet pointed toward the stairs. "Last room on the left. Mr. Penny ain't in his room right now, but I'll let him know you got here just fine."

"Thank you. Could you please have my driver bring my things up to the room?" Amanda fingered the large skeleton key.

The woman hurried from behind the counter while fastening a spotless white apron around her waist. "You must be near starved, comin' all that way from Helena. I'll fix up somethin' for you right away. I bet a nice pot of tea would wash some of that road dust outta your throat."

Amanda nodded, grateful for the older woman's kindness. "Tea would be lovely, but please don't go to any special trouble."

Harriet sniffed. "I got biscuits coming outta the oven anytime now, and fresh butter, made this morning. Won't be no trouble 'tall to bring you up a tray."

She scuttled behind Amanda like a mother hen, urging her up the stairs. "Go on and wash up, I had fresh water put in your room. You look pure tuckered out from all that travelin'."

Amanda's legs felt weighted down with lead, and a familiar throbbing pain at the back of her head reminded her she was exhausted. She'd been moving through a thick, white fog for nearly five months. She slowly climbed the stairs, her gloved hand trailing along the banister. What was it Father Mikelson had said to her before she left Helena? That helping others would bring purpose and meaning back to her life?

Amanda hated the endless void that had descended upon

her after Arthur's death. Not that their marriage had been a normal arrangement, with loving partners dedicated to making each other happy. It had been closer to a successful business deal, brokered by her father to expand a financial empire.

Before Arthur had taken ill, she had social engagements, visits to the theater, and her duties as a volunteer with the Helena Library Association. Lately, her only outings were to mass, and her only visitors were sad-faced widows and lawyers paying condolences.

The bright, cheerful, and exceedingly clean hotel room surprised her. A beautiful hand-stitched quilt covered the bed, a small velvet chaise sat in the center of the room, and a brightly painted screen created a private corner for her to dress. The large room also held an oak chiffonier, a washstand, and a matching vanity.

Two windows let plenty of sunlight into the corner room. Amanda uttered a small prayer of thanksgiving, as her one unconquerable fear since childhood had been of the dark. She managed to control the fear a bit, but she always slept with her curtains open, allowing any bit of moonlight into her room.

Crossing the room to see the view out the back window, she discovered a small corral below. A dark black horse stood beneath her, his head lifted regally. He was a magnificent creature.

Excitement surged through her. It would be wonderful to ride again, to feel the wind whipping about her as she raced on horseback. Perhaps she could borrow a horse from the local livery. In a small town, it would certainly be appropriate for her to go for a horseback ride each day. Even a widow should be allowed some fresh air and exercise.

Amanda yanked the long pin securing her hat loose and tossed the offensive head-covering onto the bed with an irritated air. Unfastening the white cuffs of her gown, she threw them down after the hat before pouring water into a large ceramic bowl. It was tepid but splashing it on her face improved her mood. Harriet Parmeter was right; she needed to wash the road dust off.

Her trunk, along with several carpet bags and hatboxes, arrived—a paltry wardrobe for a woman of her wealth. All her dresses were dark black wool or bombazine, the appropriate attire for a widow, and she hated every one of them.

A brisk knock at the door dragged her back to reality. When Amanda murmured her permission to enter, Harriet Parmeter burst into the room with a cheerful laugh, holding a cloth-covered tray before her. An enticing aroma of cinnamon filled the air, and her stomach grumbled in response.

"Enjoy your tea, and I'll be back up in a while to get the tray." Harriet set the tray on the vanity and waved a hand as she exited the room before Amanda could murmur her thanks.

Amanda poured a steaming cup of tea and inhaled the relaxing herbal scent of chamomile. She polished off the food and licked her fingers in delicious defiance. Acting the part of the prim and proper widow exhausted her.

How she wished she could discard her black gown, don a bright riding habit, and take that beautiful stallion in the corral beneath her window for a run. She sighed at the image; she imagined the wind brushing against her face and the hard muscles of the magnificent creature moving beneath her.

A perfunctory tapping on her door shattered her daydream. Mr. Penny, dressed in a dark suit without a wrinkle, stood outside holding his bowler hat in his hands.

"Begging your pardon, Mrs. Wainwright." Amanda shook her head. "Please don't apologize, Mr. Penny. Let me thank you for arranging such delightful accommodations."

The tips of Jacob Penny's ears turned bright red as he adjusted his string tie. "I...I'm..."

Amanda had forgotten how tongue-tied Mr. Penny became whenever she gave him a compliment.

He straightened his shoulders, swallowed, and finally found his tongue. His large Adam's apple bobbed as he spoke.

"Some of the people, the miners and their families, they, um, they want to offer their condolences." He swallowed again, glancing at her face before lowering his gaze to study the floor.

Amanda fought the urge to shut the door and lie down upon her bed to continue her wonderful daydream of riding the stallion. She most certainly did not want to face another room full of pitying eyes and sad expressions of condolence. Not again. Not ever again if she could help it. But, of course, there would be no escaping her duties as the Widow Wainwright. Arthur's employees had the right to express their grief and offer condolences.

"Of course," she said. "Please allow me to make amends to my appearance, and I'll meet you downstairs in the lobby."

Mr. Penny nodded and backed away from her door. Before turning to leave, he twisted his black felt bowler hat in his thin fingers and cleared his throat again.

"I feel I should warn you, Mrs. Wainwright." He set his hat back upon his nearly bald head. "There are some difficulties with your plans for the Miners' Benevolent Association. We should discuss things as soon as you've rested."

Amanda was bone-tired and weary of all the things Arthur Wainwright still demanded of her, even from the grave.

"We can talk tomorrow, Mr. Penny. My husband taught me no problem is insurmountable if considered carefully and thoughtfully." She slammed the door shut before he could respond.

Amanda leaned against the door and pondered Mr. Penny's warning. She'd come to Willow Creek to help people. She planned to build a school and homes for the miners who'd worked for her husband. A sudden flash of pride warmed her as she realized the miners now worked for her. She was wealthy enough to see her plans through, and she didn't understand Mr. Penny's cryptic remark. He always took things so seriously; likely he was seeing problems where none existed.

She crossed the room to peek out the window again and looked down to discover a man standing at the corral. He held something out to the stallion, and the horse gently took it. She examined the man's appearance, from the tips of his knee-high, polished boots to the thick dark hair curling at his collar. He was quite tall, and his shoulders were broad, filling out the dark frock coat he wore with a casual elegance. Amanda wished he would turn to leave so she could catch a glimpse of his face. Then she scolded herself for such a foolish and improper yearning. She was no innocent girl, after all. She turned from the window in disgust. She was a mature, world-weary woman facing yet another round of murmured condolences from sad mourners.

She looked at the bed and decided to display one small act of defiance. Fastening the lace cuffs back on her sleeves, she brushed a few stray curls into her tight coiffure and left the room. The hated veiled hat sat upon the quilt, discarded and lonely in the silence.

∞∞∞

As the Widow Wainwright arrived in town, Sam marveled at the stately way she moved down the boardwalk toward the hotel. Swathed in black from head to toe, not an inch of her was visible to the eye. Yet he admired the way she carried herself with pride and confidence.

Yes, he decided, she must be an older woman. Not as old as her husband, judging by the sprightly way she'd jumped from her carriage. Mature. In his opinion, a woman of maturity was always more delightful because a man wasn't required to play coy games of flirting and courtship. Timid virgins no longer interested him, if in fact they ever had.

He stood on the veranda of the Dark Horse Saloon and ignored the pleas from Sally to come back in and keep her company. He'd paid Sally for the view, not her services.

He climbed back through Sally's window and found her lounging across the pink silk coverlet on her bed, her breasts exposed, and her legs crossed in a provocative display. He tossed her a coin, picked up his black felt hat, and gave her one of his most charming grins. "Perhaps another time, my dear."

He left her screaming obscenities. He didn't have to pay for a woman, but whores made the arrangement clean, without emotion and unrealistic expectations.

He considered his plans to woo Amanda Wainwright using cold calculation and charm. He'd certainly been blessed with an abundance of that commodity. He knew all the right words, the sweet phrases that could soften a woman's heart and make her cling to him. He'd learned the many ways to maneuver his way into a woman's graces, and how to make her feel as if she were the center of his existence. But deep in his heart, it had always been a game.

Sam returned to his office. He still had work to do to keep his business running, and even a sham business needed a leader who could make decisions.

Nearly an hour later, Sam shook his head as he headed toward the corral. He needed to focus, to concentrate on his objective, make his plan and carry it out to the best of his ability. He could create the image of any man he wished; it was his gift, and the main reason he'd been trusted with such an important assignment. If he sometimes felt lost in the deceit, unable to remember who he had been before he worked for the Secret Service, it was an advantage.

He found his horse, Stranger, standing in the corral, waiting for the treat he knew was hidden in his master's pocket. The horse tossed his head at the sight of the apple and gripped it with his lips. Sam brushed his fingers through the dark, silky mane, and marveled that this magnificent animal belonged to him. Stranger held the key to his dreams of rebuilding his family's wealth. Someday he would own a ranch that bred horses renowned for their speed and beauty. He'd recoup all the wealth and prestige that the Boston upper-class snobs had stolen from him, and he'd return to the society that now scorned him.

People gathered in front of the hotel and piqued his curiosity. What was going on so late in the day? Perhaps a medicine show had arrived in town, or mummers. He walked slowly around the building and stopped to see what all the excitement was about.

A small crowd of miners and their families stood in two lines. A familiar looking woman in a dark black gown moved amongst them, and a little rodent-like man followed closely behind her. She took her time as hands pressed into hers, and she listened to each individual with rapt attention.

Auburn hair was piled on her head, and Sam admired the way the late afternoon sun highlighted the color with bright flashes of russet. She had an elegant demeanor, as though she were in a ballroom being presented to royalty.

When she finally turned so that Sam could glimpse her face, a hot flash of desire whipped through him.

The Widow Wainwright was no pasty-faced bluestocking. Nor was she old and decrepit. Sam held his breath. The late afternoon sun peeked out from behind a cloud, burnishing her with golden light, and Sam beheld the face of an angel.

Chapter Three

Amanda paced across the length of her room again and tried to ignore the rumbling in her stomach. It was nearly midnight and she couldn't sleep. Her body ached with exhaustion, yet she had tossed and turned in her bed for hours. She'd hoped she could drift into a dreamless sleep, but here she was, wide-awake and pacing again.

She considered the challenges she faced and wondered if she were up to the task her husband had bequeathed her. Her mind churned, and sleep continued to elude her.

She stood at the window and spied the stallion standing in the pale moonlight. A sense of comfort settled over her, as if he were her guardian, keeping watch and protecting her. She shrugged off the ridiculous notion.

Her stomach growled again. Perhaps if she found something to eat it might help her fall asleep. Pulling on her robe and lifting the candle, she decided to make her way to the kitchen. She left her slippers by the bedside, in hopes her bare feet would mask her movements. She didn't wish to disturb any of the other guests in the hotel or create gossip about the strange widow woman who wandered about in the middle of the night.

She stepped carefully down the staircase and sniffed the comforting scent of beeswax. It reminded her of the convent, the only place she'd ever really considered home, and for a few moments she reviewed her reasons for remaining in Willow Creek.

She'd spent several hours earlier in the day greeting the miners, looking into their faces and listening to their awkward, yet heartfelt, condolences. They were sturdy men, with tinges of desperation shading their eyes. How could she manage to do anything to change the conditions under which these men toiled and suffered?

The pine floor was cold, and she regretted her impulse to leave her slippers behind. She'd warm a little milk on the banked embers of the stove, perhaps find a bit of that delicious pie Harriet had served at dinner.

Amanda swung the kitchen door open and nearly dropped the candle when her eyes clashed with a surprised amber gaze. A man. A strange warmth coursed through her as his gaze moved slowly down her body, lingering on her breasts before rising to scrutinize her face. Her cheeks flooded with heat, and she nearly turned to hurry back to her room, when a deep but gentle voice stopped her.

"I beg your pardon, ma'am, I didn't mean to alarm you."

Intrigued by the handsome stranger, she stepped closer. He was standing now, and she marveled at the way his wide shoulders, long, lean legs, and muscled arms seemed to fill the room to the corners of the kitchen.

She wet her lips, took a deep breath, and stepped even closer. Close enough to notice a gleam of mischief in his honey-colored eyes.

She lifted her chin to peruse him with the same bold look he was giving her. "I couldn't sleep, so I came down to fix myself some warm milk. I didn't expect to find anyone else up at this hour."

He grinned, his eyes challenging her. "You gave me quite a scare, you know. I thought you were one of the Lord's minions come to carry me away. I notice you don't have any gossamer wings, so I suppose I'm safe."

Amanda quickly looked over her shoulder and gave him a flirtatious smile.

"We always take them off at bedtime; it makes it easier to sleep." A shiver of excitement rolled over her as the man's gaze once again flickered along the curves of her body. It was very inappropriate, yet her skin burned as he slowly considered her.

"Besides, are you quite sure when your time comes angels will be the apparition you'll be seeing?"

He held his hand to his chest, as if wounded, and moaned. "I hope with just a glimpse of me you haven't discovered I'm bound for hell. It usually takes at least a short acquaintance before a woman proclaims I'm destined to dwell with the devil."

Amanda laughed. Despite the awkwardness of the situation, she was having fun. It had been such a long time since someone had teased her, and she had missed it.

She knew she shouldn't be talking with a handsome stranger in the middle of the night, but that made it even more delightful. As tempting as forbidden fruit, despite all the warnings to leave it alone.

"Well, I agree, not knowing your identity or character, it's possible you are of good virtue and shall be escorted by seraphim to the hereafter." She gave him a playful grin and narrowed her eyes. "But, I really don't believe so."

He responded with a hearty laugh. The sound echoed in the small room enticing her with its promise of something delicious and secretive. She shivered as warmth spread through her limbs, and the beat of her own heart pounded in her ears. She'd never experienced such a feeling and wanted desperately to explore it.

Amanda enjoyed the sound of his laugh; it was as warm and sweet as maple syrup. She knew she shouldn't be engaged in such outrageous behavior. After all, she was the poor Widow

Wainwright. Of course, he didn't know who she was, and for a just a little while it was fun to pretend she was some other woman. She wanted to be a woman who didn't concern herself with the iron-clad rules of etiquette and propriety. A woman who flirted unabashedly with a man she didn't know.

She glanced down at the table and swept a hand towards him. "Please, do sit down and finish eating. I'm sorry to disturb you, but I couldn't sleep. I'm afraid my restless wandering isn't such a good idea." With some reluctance, she turned to leave.

"My mother had a cure for insomnia. Perhaps you'd allow me to fix you a hot toddy. I guarantee it will make you sleep soundly as a baby."

The sultry tone of his voice mesmerized her.

All the deportment lessons she'd suffered since childhood came back to her in a flash. She should keep going back to her room, but his dark and hypnotic voice promised secret delights, and she didn't want to leave. She wanted to sit down and continue to banter with this mysterious man. If he thought her a brazen hussy, so much the better. For a few moments tonight, she'd be that other woman, the one who didn't care what others thought of her.

Swallowing her apprehension, she tossed her braid over one shoulder and crossed the small kitchen to take a chair at the table. She settled her candle next to the oil lamp and gave him an inviting smile.

"A hot toddy sounds perfectly wonderful. Are you sure it won't be too much trouble?"

The man leaned forward. The corners of his lovely mouth lifted slightly. "It would be my pleasure to assist an angel to bed."

Heat traveled from her cheeks down to her bosom. She had never in her life done anything as brash as this. What would

Father Mikelson say? She didn't want to think about the penance she'd do when she confessed. Flirting wasn't the same as adultery, was it? Could she still be an adulteress if her husband was dead? Good Lord, why was she even thinking about such a thing?

When he turned his back to her, she knew what fueled her illicit thoughts. As he poured a concoction into a cup, Amanda forgot to breathe as she stared at the thick, dark hair curling at the edge of his collar, his lean torso and long legs.

"It's you," she whispered.

He turned back to her, confusion clouding his honey-colored eyes. "I beg your pardon?"

She stood up and hurried to the window to pull back the checkered curtain. She pointed outside. "The stallion, is he your horse?"

He poured hot water into a cup before taking two long steps to hand the steaming mug to her. "Drink this. I guarantee it will help you sleep. And yes, Stranger is my horse."

He was standing far too close to her. Only inches separated them, and she felt a tremor of delight when their fingers touched as she accepted the mug. She was acting silly as a besotted schoolgirl. As she tried not to stare at the chiseled features, golden eyes that sparkled with good humor, and the dark, thick hair that he wore too long to be respectable, she thought perhaps she might discover another use for her bed rather than sleep.

She nearly dropped the cup as she stumbled back a step to remove herself from the enticing scent of tobacco, coffee, and virile male.

She briefly wondered what benefit she'd ever derived from being good and staying out of trouble.

"Beautiful," she murmured.

He raised an eyebrow. “He is a beautiful creature, isn't he?”

She took a sip from the mug and remained focused on him as a delicious ripple of pleasure surged through her. “I'd have to say —magnificent.”

If this were a dream, she'd strangle the person who woke her. She'd take sleeping draughts to stay in this world with just the two of them exchanging conversation in the deep mystery of the night.

“Allow me to introduce myself, I'm Samuel Calhoun.” He bowed slightly, and she gave a brief curtsy in return.

“Amanda Wainwright, expressing her sincere appreciation for this toddy. It's delicious.” She sipped from the cup again, allowing the apple and spice concoction to warm her nearly as thoroughly as the excitement of being alone with Mr. Calhoun.

“Won't you join me?” He gestured toward the table. “I seem to get caught up in my work until very late, and I miss the company of others while dining.” She studied him as he returned to his meal. The brief silence felt comfortable, as if they were old friends catching up.

“Do you eat alone every night then, without seeing your family?” It was bold, but if he had a wife and several children in a little house someplace, she wanted to know.

He sipped his coffee, and for a few moments a profound sadness reflected in his eyes. “My family is...gone. All of them.”

She felt as if she had somehow intruded, that the light banter had dissolved into something else. She didn't know what to say and remained silent while the shadows in the corners of the kitchen grew deeper. What was it about confidences exchanged at midnight? Perhaps it was sometimes easier to confess to a stranger than to talk with a friend.

“I recently lost my husband. He was the only family I had left...” Her voice trailed off, and she closed her eyes to keep the tears from forming as she took another sip of the drink.

When she opened her eyes, he was staring at her. “How do you feel about that, Amanda—about being so alone?”

His easy use of her first name was too personal, but she wasn’t offended. It seemed natural, as if this conversation had taken place many times before. Perhaps it was the anonymity of talking to someone she didn’t know, but for some reason she felt comfortable enough to tell him the truth.

“It’s frightening. I’m terrified the sadness will simply overwhelm me someday, and that I’ll be consumed by it. And if I disappear, who’s going to miss me? I don’t think anyone will mourn my passing or even remember me.” She swallowed a sob, as a tear trickled down her cheek. What was she doing? This man didn’t care how empty and bereft she felt. First, she had flirted outrageously with him, and now she was going to humiliate herself by dissolving into tears in his presence.

She dropped her head, waiting for him to stand up and leave. She didn’t share her deepest feelings with people she knew, much less complete strangers. What had he done to make her feel so vulnerable? Listened? Was she that desperate for someone to talk to?

He moved his pie around on the china plate before dropping his fork. When he made no move to rise and walk out of the room, she swallowed and tried to make her voice sound teasing again.

“What are your intentions regarding that pie?” She wiped away the tear and lifted her face to give him a coy look.

He pushed the plate toward her. “Can I interest you in some?”

She nodded, leaning forward to pick up his fork. It was an intimate thing to do, to use his utensil. It simply wasn’t proper. It would be like pressing her lips to his in a kiss. That thought made her even bolder. She scooped up a forkful of cherries and grinned.

"Harriet Parmeter is an extraordinary cook, isn't she?" She slipped the first bite between her lips and savored the tart flavor.

He leaned back in his chair, pulled a cigar from an inside pocket of his coat, and nodded towards her, seeking permission to smoke. From his impeccable manners, she supposed he came from an aristocratic background. What had he said? That his family was all gone.

They had strayed too deeply into an emotional abyss. She wanted to bring back the teasing tone of their earlier discourse. The pain of loneliness was a frightening topic to discuss in the middle of the night.

"I want to buy your horse." She tried to make her voice nonchalant and businesslike as she continued to eat his pie.

He didn't respond, and she finally looked up to see him scrutinizing her carefully. The now familiar ripple of delight coursed through her as he lazily scanned her face. She gave him what she hoped was a brilliant smile. "The stallion. How much do you want for him?"

He lit his cigar with practiced ease, inhaled deeply, and allowed the smoke to curl up around his head. The raw masculine scent of the smoke reminded her that a virile, sensual male sat across from her.

He smoothed his brocade vest with one thick, finely shaped finger.

"Stranger isn't for sale at any price."

Amanda licked the crumbs from her lips and shook her head. "My dearly-departed husband, Arthur, told me everything is for sale. It's just a matter of establishing the right price."

His mouth twisted into a thin smile and his honey-colored

eyes flickered with amusement. “Do you really believe your money allows you to buy everything you want?”

She considered the question for a few moments, then stood and lifted the candle from the table. She had already stayed longer than was proper, and she didn’t want to tempt fate or destroy her reputation her first night in Willow Creek.

“I’ve been disappointed to learn my husband was right in regard to that assumption. Wealth teaches one that anything is for sale if one is willing to pay the price.” She turned to leave and paused at the door to give him a long, lingering final look. She wouldn’t soon forget her midnight sojourn with the handsome and enigmatic Samuel Calhoun. This encounter would fuel her daydreams of illicit romance for a very long time.

“Tell me, Amanda Wainwright, has all your wealth been able to purchase happiness for you?”

She stood silently as his words washed over her, then gave him a thin smile. “That’s the one thing that is simply unobtainable for some of us.”

Amanda slipped upstairs and found herself leaning against her bedroom door, more troubled by her encounter with the man than she cared to admit. She found him intensely attractive and strangely disturbing at the same time.

She closed her eyes and recalled the warm, golden honey color of his eyes, his dark hair and silky voice. Yes, he was handsome, but he disturbed her because she sensed they both stood in darkness, nearly swallowed up by sorrow and pain. Had she glimpsed a heart nearly as lonely as her own tonight? She took comfort in knowing she wasn’t the only one who suffered. If two souls could find each other in anguish, perhaps they could heal each other with kindness.

The thought surprised her, and spread warmth throughout her body, awakening senses she’d thought dead forever. She blew out the candle and padded across the room to her bed, throwing the quilt back and snuggling beneath the covers.

She wanted to become better acquainted with Samuel Calhoun, and she now had one more reason to remain in Willow Creek.

∞∞∞

Sam sat smoking his cigar in the silence, the only sound a low hiss from the oil lamp. He thought about Amanda Wainwright and the way she'd appeared before him, making him wonder if he'd conjured her with some sort of magic. He'd been thinking about the ethereal Widow Wainwright as he sat eating his late dinner, and suddenly, there she was, standing before him and giving him a bold look.

He'd been shocked earlier to discover she was a young and beautiful woman. He would need to approach her differently. For a moment, his conscience reminded him that he was usually the kind of man who would protect a woman as fragile as Amanda Wainwright. But his mission couldn't be jeopardized for the sake of one woman's reputation. Too much was at stake.

Nevertheless, she intrigued him, and the thought of taking her to his bed excited him. Certainly, the memory of her dark green eyes and perfect mouth made him eager to taste her kisses. And while her widow's weeds didn't favor her fiery hair, her night rail didn't hide the fact that she possessed a full and voluptuous figure.

When she'd appeared in the kitchen, her beautiful face aglow in a pool of shimmering light, her white nightclothes possessed of a magical luster, making her radiant in the dark shadows of the night, he really had thought, for a moment, he was seeing a celestial vision.

Then her frank perusal and vivacious manner had entranced him. He found her amusing, and that was a surprise, as she teased and challenged him at the same time. Amanda Wainwright was an enchanting woman, and he would need to take care he didn't fall under her spell.

He tapped the ash from his cheroot and wondered how he could arrange to see her again. Her inquiry about his horse had pricked his pride a bit. While he'd tried to provoke her about the power of wealth, he agreed with her late husband Arthur's assessment of humanity. One could buy anything; it was just a matter of negotiating the price. After all, wasn't this planned seduction and humiliation of a respectable widow proof of that? Of course, he wasn't really going to seduce and ruin her for the money. He'd simply use her to protect his identity and convince the other mine owners they could trust him.

While it was unfortunate, he was involved in a conspiracy to ruin her reputation, at the moment it couldn't be helped. He pushed the small tug of his conscience back to the depths of his heart. There was more at stake than a rich woman's good name. Besides, from what he'd discovered about her, she possessed enough money to convince people to ignore gossip.

Sam shifted his weight and tried to focus again on his conversation with Amanda. What was it she had said, that for some people happiness was unobtainable? He had to agree, but what made a rich woman with all the opportunities in the world so cynical? She was an enigma—bright and teasing one moment, caught in a web of grief and loneliness the next.

He recalled the single crystal tear sliding down her cheek, and how powerfully he'd fought the urge to reach out and capture it. In fact, he'd been tempted to taste it, as if he could somehow swallow the pain for her, if for only a moment.

But he couldn't concern himself with the sorrows of the Widow Wainwright. His job was to distract her, to take her mind off her efforts on behalf of the miners and charm his way into her life. Eventually, without having to seduce or bed her, he would create some pretense of breaking it off. That would be enough to send her running back to Helena.

Amanda had a unique quality, a force that enticed him, yet made him feel protective at the same time.

Sam crushed his cheroot on his dessert plate and grinned. She hadn't blinked as she picked up his fork and devoured the pie. A hot rush of desire had sliced through him as she licked the sticky juices from her full, red-stained lips, her soft pink tongue making slow circles of invitation. It was too innocent a gesture to be interpreted as a seductive message, and it occurred to him that Amanda might not be aware of her intense sensuality. Her flirting didn't possess a practiced air; it had more of a playful quality, as if she were unaware of her ability to arouse a man. And she had certainly aroused him with her innocent, yet provocative, behavior. Of course, she was a widow, so she would have some sense of what a man desired from a woman.

Sam recalled the way his body had reacted to the surprising Widow Wainwright. When she'd walked into the dimly lit room, with the thin nightclothes hugging her softly curved and womanly body, his cock had responded immediately. By the time she was licking the red cherry juice from her lips, he'd been hard as granite.

Sam was eager to see Amanda again, and he wondered if she'd accept an invitation to go for a ride tomorrow. She'd mentioned Stranger, and her offer to purchase the animal indicated some familiarity with horses. He'd recently purchased a lovely little mare that was stabled over at the livery, and she'd be perfect for Amanda. A long, leisurely ride in the countryside would give him time to learn more about her. Once he understood her needs, her desires, and her dreams, he could use them to plan his attack.

He'd send a note to the Parmeter House in the morning, offering to take her for ride so she could see some of the countryside. It was a bold move, but if he judged her correctly from their encounter this night, she'd accept the invitation.

He turned down the lamp and closed the door behind him, careful to lock it. Meeting Amanda tonight had been a stroke of luck; he'd been trying to figure out a way to wrangle an introduction from Harriet Parmeter. Of course, if he'd happened to mention he found the widow attractive, Harriet would have arranged a not-too-subtle chance meeting.

He crossed town, wandered by the saloon, and considered going in, then a pair of emerald eyes and a brilliant smile came to mind. He could still smell her, recalling the light floral scent that had followed her into the kitchen. He didn't want sawdust, filthy men, and sour beer to wipe that from his memory.

Sam walked back to his rooms over the mill office. For the first time since he could remember, he didn't feel the need for bourbon to help him sleep. His encounter with a midnight angel had lightened his heart and improved his mood. He would have to remain focused on the agreement he'd made with the mine owners; the success of his mission could depend upon it. But pretending to seduce the Widow Wainwright could serve as a pleasant diversion. A very pleasant diversion indeed.

Chapter Four

"What do you know about Mr. Samuel Calhoun?" Amanda asked as she carefully folded the note Harriet Parmeter had handed to her when she arrived in the dining room for breakfast.

Harriet cocked her head. "I know he's a real gentleman, and there's a scarcity of them in these parts, that's for sure."

Amanda sipped her tea and waited, hoping for more information—or some good gossip—about the man she'd met in the kitchen last night.

Waking up from the most restful night of sleep she'd had in months, Amanda stretched like a feline and grinned as she recalled her encounter with the handsome stranger. How could she have acted so witty and coy? She generally wasn't good at that sort of thing, so different from the other women she'd known in Helena. She didn't normally banter and tease. She was usually shy, awkward with strangers, and never comfortable enough to flirt with men. Her convent education hadn't taught her the feminine arts or how to be alluring.

He probably thought she was a wanton woman. The idea should have distressed her; instead, a shiver of delight shimmied up her spine. She'd sat in her night rail in the middle of the night and conversed with a perfect stranger.

Perfect.

That would be the word to use when describing the delicious Samuel Calhoun.

He was tall and broad shouldered, with an air of male superiority that should have repulsed her. Instead, it drew her back to the memory of their meeting with an uncontrollable heat and yearning. She couldn't wipe the image of those golden eyes, with that glint of mischief in them, from her mind. She was attracted to him, and a rush of intense happiness had rippled through her when she opened the note to discover his signature.

"Good businessman. Honest." Harriet tapped her fingers on the table and frowned. "He's not married, engaged, or courtin' anyone, if that's what you want to know."

Amanda nearly choked on her muffin, then recovered as she gave Harriet a look she hoped smacked of indifference. She waved one hand delicately.

"As if *that* would be of any interest to me! I'm inquiring because I'll be doing some business with him." Amanda hoped he wasn't a professional gambler or the town sheriff. Perhaps she should quit badgering Harriet for information and make other discreet inquiries about the man.

Harriet took a seat across from Amanda and leaned forward.

"Sam comes from a good family back East is what I heard. He was a colonel in the cavalry and spent time in a Confederate prison camp. I guess he lost everything in the war. His family, his business." She shrugged. "He ain't the only one to start ridin' west one day, looking for a fresh start..." Her voice trailed off and her face wrinkled into a frown. "I guess Sam came to Montana to build himself a new life."

Amanda set her cup back on the saucer and sighed.

"How awful," she said, realizing the source of the sadness she'd glimpsed last night. He was as alone as she was. She decided to accept his invitation to go for a ride today and apologize for the way she'd acted in the kitchen.

Harriet brushed some crumbs off the oilcloth and shook

her head. "But, the war is over and I keep tellin' Sam he's gotta get on with his life." She grinned at Amanda. "A good woman would do that man a world of good."

Amanda warmed at the insinuation. She twisted an errant curl that had escaped from her chignon as she looked away. "Well, I was considering, he—well, invited me to go for a ride with him." Her words came out in a rush. "And I thought perhaps I would accept." She puckered her brow. "If you think he would be an appropriate escort."

Harriet's laughter boomed through the small dining room.

"I couldn't have planned this any better if I'd tried." She leaned forward, her large bosom nearly covering the surface of the table. "How long you been widowed, honey?"

Amanda traced the blue willow pattern on the saucer with one finger. "Nearly six months."

Harriet stretched out a hand and touched her arm gently. "Well, you still got the hurt inside you, but that gets better as time goes on. I always say, life is for the livin'." She shook her head. "Of course, everythin' is different for a widder woman."

Amanda looked up in surprise. "Different? Do you mean all those dreary hours of prayer for your husband's soul that the church demands of you?"

Harriet laughed again, the sound reminding her of a small, clear bell ringing. "My husband can take care of his own soul, ain't no amount of prayin' down here that can change God's mind, that's my opinion." She sat back in satisfaction. "I mean a woman without a man to tell her what to do all the time can say what she thinks and do what she wants. You don't have to worry about protectin' your virtue or pleasin' a man."

Amanda leaned forward, eager to hear this woman's advice. Harriet Parmeter wasn't anything like the other widows she'd met. All they talked about was how dreary their lives were without their husbands.

"You mean you don't care what other people say about you?"

Harriet shook her head. "I don't care, and I don't pay no attention. I aim to please myself, and I don't aim to please nobody else. Of course, I don't go prancin' down Main Street in my unmentionables." She grinned wickedly. "Or least ways, I ain't done it yet!"

Amanda giggled. Harriet fascinated her. Who would have guessed so many interesting people lived in the small town of Willow Creek?

"As for Sam, well, if that man wanted to take me out for a peek at the countryside, you know for sure I'd get all gussied up nice and go. There wouldn't be no need to ask me twice. That man's so damned handsome, it hurts my eyes to look at him!"

Harriet stood up and waved a finger at Amanda. "Go on out and have some fun, honey, because life's short and before long you'll be an old woman."

Amanda grinned up at Harriet. "You are hardly old, and from the way I saw Mr. Holcomb looking at you this morning, I think you have an admirer."

Harriet blushed and seemed tongue-tied for a few moments. She finally cleared her throat as she picked up Amanda's plate. "He helps me out around here, but don't let your imagination run away with you." She tossed her head, and the silver-streaked pile of dark curls shook. "Now, how about I tell Robert to run back on over to the lumberyard and let Sam know you'll be ready for that ride in about an hour?"

She turned to head back into the kitchen, then whirled back to face Amanda. "I'll pack you two a little somethin' to eat. All that gallopin' around the countryside is sure to make you hungry as bears just comin' outta hibernation."

Amanda nodded. The bright morning sunshine glittered outside, and the thought of once again being astride a horse thrilled her. As she stood to return to her room and change into her riding habit, a twinge of conscience hit her. Father Mikelson's voice droned in her mind about her responsibilities as Arthur Wainwright's widow. He would not approve of her riding about the countryside with a handsome stranger.

She stood outside the door to her room and worried she might be making a terrible mistake. Accepting an invitation from a man she barely knew was bad enough, but she was still in mourning. She shouldn't be going on picnics. She should be going to mass. Of course, Willow Creek didn't have a priest or church. She ignored her anxiety and unlocked the door. Somehow, the fact that she wasn't playing the proper bereaved Widow Wainwright made the entire adventure even more appealing.

She would apply some of Harriet's advice today. Perhaps for the first time in her life, she would ignore what other people said or expected of her and do just as she pleased. She imagined herself a caged bird whose door was left open by mistake. Amanda was ready to try out her wings.

"I really think you should have let me ride Stranger. It would have been the chivalrous thing for a gentleman to do." Amanda gave Sam a sidelong glance as her soft, rose-colored lips formed a pretty pout. Sam nearly laughed at her attempt to be coy. The Widow Wainwright was not the shy innocent he had presumed.

"He's strong-willed and can be difficult to handle." Sam grinned down at her. "Besides, whoever said I have any inclination to be chivalrous or a gentleman?"

Amanda shifted in the saddle and her hat dipped to the side, causing several russet curls to escape from the tight coil at the base of her neck. Sam was briefly reminded of the way her hair had hung down her back the night before, wisps escaping to frame her face like flame engulfing a celestial spirit. A hot flicker of desire whipped through him.

She groaned, and her face contorted in a look of stubborn defiance. "Why is it a difficult horse makes a man proud, but a difficult wife makes him angry?"

Sam couldn't help himself; his grin exploded into a loud, booming laugh.

Amanda made a clicking noise to her horse and took off at a gallop.

Sam let her get ahead of him as he marveled at the way she sat upon her horse. Even on a sidesaddle, her posture was perfect and her poise elegant.

He knew her Morgan was no match for the long strides and stamina of the purebred Arabian beneath him. Still, if he gave her the opportunity, she might prove an admirable challenge.

Sam spurred his horse forward into a run, letting Stranger enjoy the freedom of the level ground and green fields surrounding them. He considered the woman riding ahead of him, an intriguing mixture of innocence and sensuality. Was it natural or contrived?

When he caught up to Amanda, she pulled gently on the reins to slow her horse to a walk. Her forest green eyes sparkled with good humor, and her cheeks were bright spots of scarlet.

"Duchess certainly has spirit to match your stallion. They'll breed fine horses together."

She continued to surprise him. In his experience, no gently reared lady would ever mention horse breeding to a gentleman.

"Tell me, Mrs. Wainwright, do you always speak your mind?"

She sat quietly for a few moments before shrugging her shoulders.

"Nuns don't encourage artifice, and they punish you"—she raised an elegant eyebrow at him— "severely, for dishonesty. I'm afraid I never learned how to be coy or demure. Arthur seemed to appreciate my opinions. He said my wit entertained him."

A shock of surprise struck him like a bolt out of the sky. He wasn't used to women who were so bold or so honest. He shifted in his saddle. It would be easier if he could convince himself they were both playing a flirtatious game.

They rode in silence for a while, the air filled with birdsong, the wind blowing lightly and rustling the leaves in the birch trees. Sam felt at peace, and it was such an odd sensation, he wondered at the source of it. Amanda Wainwright? What was it about this woman that delighted him to such a degree? Why did her presence make him feel younger and more alive?

As they approached a small creek, Sam pointed to an outcropping of rocks. "Shall we take a walk and let the horses rest a bit?"

Amanda nodded. He pulled Stranger to a halt and dismounted, dropping his reins and moving to assist Amanda from her horse. An enticing smile played across her lips.

"I'm not sure if I should trust you, Mr. Calhoun. You've informed me you don't consider yourself to be an honorable gentleman."

Sam wrapped his hands around her waist as he lifted her from the saddle. He kept his hands in place, standing close enough to enjoy the fragrant scent of lilacs surrounding her. The turquoise highlights in her eyes sparkled, the teasing good humor still evident as she looked up at him.

"I'm really quite a scoundrel, Mrs. Wainwright, not to be trusted whatsoever."

Sam finally released her, but from the way the blood rushed through his veins, he knew he wasn't immune to the attractive widow's charms.

She placed a gloved hand on his arm, and he escorted her toward the rocks at the edge of a small stream. She settled on the hard granite outcropping and carefully arranged the dark velvet skirt of her riding habit.

Sam removed the saddlebag from his shoulder. "Shall we see what Harriet has packed for us?" He opened the bag and produced a loaf of freshly baked bread, a wedge of cheddar cheese, and two apples. He held up two canning jars filled with cider.

Amanda clapped her hands. "A veritable feast! I confess I'm starving after that ride."

He handed her a rough linen napkin, then broke off a chunk of bread for each of them. He removed his knife from the pouch fastened to his gun belt and caught her staring at the revolver strapped to his thigh.

"Does the gun disturb you, Amanda?" He sliced a piece of cheese and handed it to her, then began to peel the apple with a slow, lazy motion.

She seemed to consider his question carefully before she replied. "The ease with which some men use guns to solve their problems disturbs me." The corners of her mouth lifted in an impish grin. "But I understand your need to protect yourself. After all, I could be an extremely dangerous woman."

Sam's mouth went dry and he couldn't muster an answer. She was a danger to his mission, because he found himself attracted to her. He couldn't afford to care about Amanda Wainwright, because to do so could destroy any chance of successfully completing his assignment. He needed to keep his emotions under control.

Yet, she captivated him with her unaffected ways and lack of guile. She didn't drop her eyes and giggle at a man, playing the games so many of the women he'd known before did. She expressed her opinions honestly, with a forthright manner he found charming. And for some inexplicable reason, she made him laugh.

He enjoyed the way she took obvious pleasure in her meal. Ladies of his acquaintance nibbled at food, or pushed it about their plates, feigning disinterest. Amanda relished each piece of apple he handed her, closing her eyes as she bit into it, the juice moistening her lips.

Stretching across a large rock, he laid his head on his hand and simply enjoyed watching her.

"I doubt I'll be able to resist you, Mrs. Wainwright, and I suspect there are no weapons I could find to defend myself from your charms."

Amanda threw back her head and laughed, the full throaty sound of it arousing him in a way he never expected. She made him feel alive. No, more than that. She made him grateful to be alive. The sound of the water trickling across the rocks of the creek and the music of birds singing filled him with happiness. Concern nudged him, and he reminded himself that seducing this woman was the key to success. *Or at least pretending to seduce her.* There was more at stake than his happiness. He could enjoy her company, as long as he maintained control of his feelings.

She removed her hat and turned her face to the sun, a soft smile painting her features with joy. "I swear, Calhoun, if you start spouting poetry, I shall simply swoon."

He considered her for a few moments. "Is that a challenge?"

She studied him with a delicate frown. "Don't tell me you're a romantic?"

He remembered the lines of one of his favorite poems and gave her a bold grin.

"My life is like the autumn leaf that trembles in the moon's pale ray, its hold is frail—its date is brief—restless, and soon to pass away." He put a hand over his heart. "Yet when that leaf shall fall and fade, the parent tree will mourn its shade, the wind bewails the leafless tree, but none shall breathe a sigh for me!"

When his words faded into the breeze, Amanda slapped one hand over her own heart and dramatically placed the other on her forehead. "I warned you, sir." She wavered momentarily, lifted her gaze to the heavens then dropped to lie prone upon the rock, her eyes closed.

Sam laughed again as he waited for her to sit up. When she remained stretched across the rock, he became concerned.

"Amanda?" She didn't move. He sat up. "Mrs. Wainwright?" Again, he had no response. Was she playacting, or had she bumped her head on the granite beneath her when she performed her swoon?

He hurried to her side and knelt down. "Amanda, are you hurt?" Her eyes fluttered open, and her emerald gaze captured him. His finger gently traced the side of her cheek, her skin pulsating with warmth.

"I suppose I was just overcome by the power of your oratory." She grinned up at him.

He grasped her chin gently but tried to make his voice stern. "It's not nice to tease a scoundrel, Amanda. I'm going to need to punish you."

"That sounds terribly frightening, Sam."

He saw the invitation in her eyes. And he was seized by an urge he had no power to resist. Leaning forward, his intention was only to taste, to brush his lips across hers, to satisfy this craving to know how she'd react if he kissed her.

He wasn't prepared for her response. Her lips parted, the soft heat of her inviting him into a deeper embrace. She made a delicate, almost purring, sound as her arms wrapped around his neck, pulling him closer. She captured him with her desire.

Sam plunged his tongue deep into her mouth, reveling at the taste of her. She was honey, fruit, and sweet sensuality all in one. Passion seared his blood until he felt as if he were standing in front of a blazing fire. He needed to pull away from her, but the thought was agony. He wanted more, so much more. And he promised himself he would have it, but not here, not yet. If he moved too quickly, he might frighten Amanda and thwart his ultimate purpose.

Finally, he found the courage to release her. He sat back on the rocks, his fingers combing through his hair, and he struggled to catch his breath.

Amanda still stretched across the rocks; the dark black velvet of her riding habit now wrinkled where his body had crushed the fabric. He considered what lay beneath the richness of the velvet—the dainty lace of her undergarments, the delicious satin of her skin.

He closed his eyes and lifted his face to the clouds, silently pleading for help. He needed to gain control of himself. He cleared his throat and opened his eyes to discover Amanda Wainwright studying him with a dark shadow of sadness reflected in the green depths of her eyes. His heart wrenched with fear. What had he done? She was the Widow Wainwright, not some harlot he'd purchased for an evening's pleasure. He had acted too quickly, too thoughtlessly. He needed to win the confidence of this woman, not frighten her with amorous advances.

Pulling to his feet, he offered his hand to assist her. When Amanda stood, facing him, he bowed his head.

“I’m terribly sorry, I...”

Before he could finish the mumbled apology, she placed one of her gloved fingers upon his lips.

Her eyes sparkled, and a smile played at the corners of her mouth. “Don’t spoil a magnificent kiss with an apology, Calhoun, you’ll wound my pride.” She tilted her head and lifted her chin to meet his gaze, then she dropped her hand to her side. “A woman likes to believe she’s utterly irresistible.”

Jumping down from the rocks, she headed back to the horses, but turned again to face him, a hand shading her eyes from the sun.

“I would, Sam.” Her voice was husky with emotion. “I would mourn you.”

Sam swallowed, nearly overwhelmed by her simple words. A flicker of fear slid up his back. He was drawn to this woman.

Resist her? He didn’t know if he could, and that thought terrified him.

Chapter Five

"Why the hell haven't you bedded that widow woman and driven her outta town yet, Calhoun?"

Sam's head came up so fast, the muscles in his neck stretched. His temper rose as he rushed to slam the door shut behind Jack Pruitt, resisting the urge to shove his fist into the man's face at the same time.

He tried to control the anger in his voice when he faced the older man. "Try to remember, I run a lumberyard not a brothel, Pruitt."

Pruitt waved a meaty fist in the air and leaned toward Sam. "We paid you for a job, Calhoun, and from the looks of things, you ain't done the work."

Sam moved closer to Pruitt, working hard to keep the anger from his voice. "I haven't taken a cent of your money yet, if you'll recall. I'll only do so once I've accomplished the task." Sniffing at the sour odor rising from the man, he took a step back to lean on his desk.

"Did you presume she's the type of woman who'd fall into my arms in a swoon the moment she laid eyes on me?" He raised a dark eyebrow to glare at Pruitt.

Jack Pruitt shook his head and waved a balled fist toward Sam. "You've had a week, and everyone in town's seen the two of you together. Lift that woman's skirts and get it over with, Calhoun. The longer she stays in town, the more trouble she makes."

Sam fought an incredible urge to smash the face before him into an unrecognizable pulp. Hearing the man refer to Amanda in such a vulgar manner riled him. But that was the agreement he'd made with the mine owners.

"I need time to seduce a lady, especially one who's been recently widowed." Sam stalked to the window to avoid making eye-contact with Pruitt. "She's still in her damned crepe dresses for God's sake. What do you expect me to do, throw her down in the middle of the street and rape her?"

Pruitt settled his bulk into a chair and slammed his feet on Sam's desk. "I ain't the courtin' type, so I don't know what you need to do. But today she's down at that Miners' Benevolent Association." He spit the words out as if they left a foul taste in his mouth. "And she's handin' out clothes and shoes. You'd think they was rocks she picked up on the side of the road." He removed his dirty boots from the desk to lean forward and point a meaty finger at Sam. "And she don't even care who she hands goods out to. She's givin' to just anybody who wants to come by."

Sam folded his arms in front of his chest and leaned against the casing of the window. "So, she actually opened the doors today, did she?"

Pruitt jumped to his feet to slam a fist on the desk. "Damned right she opened them, and now even my men are down there gettin' a free hand-out. What does that make me and the others when that Wainwright woman is clothin' our miners?"

A bunch of greedy bastards? The thought flickered through Sam's mind, but he didn't respond to the question. He stared out the window again, wishing he'd never made this hellish bargain. At the time it had all seemed so simple. Now that he'd met Amanda, seen that small tear trickle down her cheek, heard her laugh, kissed her... He shook his head to clear it.

Crossing the room, he unrolled his sleeves and fastened the

cuffs of his white linen shirt. He'd been working on his accounts when Pruitt arrived, and he was proud that the business was doing well, despite the fact that it was a sham, set up only to serve as a way for Sam to become accepted in Willow Creek. He reminded himself that Amanda was the key to his mission's success. The President was relying upon him.

He pulled his frock coat from the peg where it hung and shrugged into it. "I suppose I can go down there and see what the troublesome Widow Wainwright is up to this morning."

Pruitt followed him onto the small landing. "Troublesome don't hardly describe that woman. She's got more friggin' schemes than a dog's got fleas." He spit a wad of chewing tobacco over the side of the railing and glared at Sam. "Get rid of that woman, Calhoun, or I'll take care of her myself."

With that, Pruitt thumped down the steps and skulked off toward the saloon. Sam considered the threat still lingering in the air and frowned. Jack Pruitt was a son-of-a-bitch, and he'd do whatever was necessary to protect his own interests. Even kill. The thought chilled Sam to the marrow, as he pictured Pruitt's large fist choking the life from Amanda. He'd have to work faster. There was more at stake now than just Amanda's reputation.

Sam hurried across town, marveling at Amanda's accomplishments. He'd had dinner with her a few nights ago, but their conversation centered on her plans for the Miners' Association and the bid she'd requested for lumber. She'd been cool, precise, and very businesslike. When he'd inquired about the chances of meeting her later in the kitchen for a hot toddy, she'd demurely whispered he didn't need a midnight supper; he'd just eaten with her.

And so he'd sat each night in the lamplight, nursing his whiskey and growing more frustrated while he waited for her to appear. He imagined her copper-colored hair freed from its tight coil, surrounding her, a fiery mane of flame. He recalled the way the thin muslin of her night rail had revealed the delicious curves of her woman's body. But she never appeared, and Sam's desire for her increased each day she remained out of his reach.

Sam brushed his fingers across his chin and tried to clear his thoughts. He'd been too long without a woman. He was never a man to deny his carnal appetite for long. But now, every woman he considered paled in comparison to the vibrant Amanda Wainwright. He was beginning to wish his plan to seduce her could be more than a ruse.

The thought surprised him. For the past few years, he'd felt momentary attractions to women, even some affection for a few, but he'd always attributed it to lust. Once in their bed, the mystery had quickly dissolved into boredom. And of course, there had been his wife, his beautiful, doomed Elsbeth. She'd taught him a painful lesson about confusing lust with love.

Shaking himself, Sam straightened his tie and lengthened his stride. A group of miners gathered at the door of the newly opened Willow Creek Miners' Benevolent Association. He paused to consider Amanda's choice of location and grinned. She'd decided the fanciest parlor house in town would be the perfect choice for her new endeavor and had offered the madam of the place a princely sum to relocate. Sam wondered how many men had arrived at this door to discover the whores had been replaced by a woman intent on good works instead of pleasure.

Several men nodded at Sam when he opened the door. He grinned again as he stood in the vestibule of the house, with its red floral wallpaper, gilt mirrors, and crystal chandelier. Sam's memory flooded with images of the girls he'd been with here. Removing his hat, he brushed his hand through his hair. Too long without a woman, he thought. He'd need to find out where Mrs. Holt had relocated her establishment. Soon.

He heard a murmur of voices from the parlor, and Sam walked across the smooth fir floor to investigate. Amanda sat perched on a stool behind a large counter surrounded by piles of coats, overalls, shirts, and boots. Sam's heart thumped so loudly against his chest, he wondered if she could hear it. The soft cadence of her voice reminded him of their clandestine meeting in the kitchen, and his groin tightened. She was engaged in conversation with the young man standing before her, a thin lad with the long arms and legs of a boy not yet grown to manhood. He held a worn brown hat in his hand and appeared to be shyly asking Amanda for something.

"I ain't too proud to beg, ma'am." The boy mumbled politely.

Amanda bestowed a brilliant smile on the boy that made Sam swallow hard but was lost on her audience. The boy never raised his gaze to look at her.

"That's not at all necessary, Mister..." Her response was gentle and kind. She gave him another smile, and the boy seemed mesmerized when he finally looked up in time to catch it. He didn't speak or respond, just stared. It started to bother Sam. The boy was obviously besotted with Amanda and a prickle of jealousy gave Sam a vicious stab.

"Caleb McQueen, that's his name. Lives over in tent city, I believe." A rush of desire whipped through him when Amanda's gaze found him and lit with warmth that nearly took his breath away.

Caleb turned to stare at Sam, then returned to his conversation with Amanda. "That's it ma'am, and well, I ain't one of the Wainwright folks, but I badly need me some new boots." He hung his head, staring down at the patched and worn leather on his feet. He straightened his shoulders but didn't look at her. "I swear I'd work off a payment to you."

Amanda started to protest, but Sam stepped closer to settle a hand gently on the young man's shoulder. "That's fine, Caleb, and the honorable thing to do. I'm sure Mrs. Wainwright can find some chores around here that need to be done."

Caleb lifted his head, seeming to grow taller beneath Sam's praise. Amanda indicated the pile of clothing surrounding her. "I sure could use some help sorting through all this. And Caleb"—her green eyes sparkled— "why not find the pair of boots you want right now? There's no sense waiting until everything is picked over. I trust you'll earn them."

A grin split the boy's face as he nearly fell over in his rush to find himself a new pair of boots. "Yes, ma'am, and thank you, ma'am. I'll work hard, I swear."

Amanda came out from behind the counter and placed her hands on her hips. "So, Mr. Calhoun, what brings you to the Willow Creek Miners' Benevolent Association?" Her gaze raked his body, lingering long enough to nearly make Sam's blood boil. "It's clear you don't need my help to get dressed."

But I'd love to help you undress, was that what she was implying? Sam shook his head, trying to ignore the heat circling down from his lower belly to make his cock hard as a piece of oak wood. This place gave a man lewd thoughts.

"I heard you were open for business, so thought I'd see what you were up to." He looked around the room and gave a low whistle. "It seems to me you're going to give the dry goods store some stiff competition."

Amanda shook her head. "There are so many things that need to be done. Food, clothing, homes, medicine." She frowned and glanced up at Sam. "Do you know the only doctor in this town is a drunk with questionable qualifications? Willow Creek doesn't have a school or a church, but it has eleven saloons and at least three houses of ill repute." Her voice carried a rebuke in it, and Sam scowled.

"Willow Creek is a mining town. They grow up quick but can fade fast depending upon the ore." He leaned back against the counter and crossed his legs. "There are poor miners up in those hills and scattered all across Montana." He considered his words carefully. "They're all over the west, I suppose. You can't make a difference to everyone who needs help out here, that's for sure."

Amanda straightened her shoulders and pursed her lips. She glanced toward Caleb, who was seated on the floor pulling on a new pair of boots. His face reflected a look of pure joy. She leaned forward to point a finger sharply towards Sam's chest.

"That might be true, but I made a difference to him. Didn't I?"

With that, she turned on her heel and flounced out of the room and toward the kitchen. Sam looked at Caleb and grinned. She was right; she sure as hell had made a difference to someone. Amanda Wainwright was proving to be a force to be reckoned with.

∞∞∞

Amanda was ashamed of herself. Why had she been so irritated with Sam? He'd come to see how things were going for her. She had no reason to be angry with him for telling her the truth.

She sat down at the large pine table in the kitchen and lowered her head. The enormity of what she was trying to do overwhelmed her. Arthur had entrusted her with this responsibility, had wrung a deathbed promise from her, and now she just didn't know if she could.

Yesterday, she'd toured "tent city" with Mr. Penny. He had tried to dissuade her. Later she'd made a note to herself to pay closer attention to the man's advice.

People were living in squalor. The stench of thick mud and refuse had nearly choked her. Sad- eyed children and women with hopelessness engraved on their faces stared at her. Drunken men had called out ribald comments as her horse picked its way through what passed for a street. When she returned to the Parmeter House, the weight of her responsibilities had settled upon her like a heavy wooden yoke on a team of oxen. The visit had left her despondent, aware that her efforts were futile when faced with the enormous challenges of helping so many people.

Then Sam had said the very thing she'd been thinking since yesterday. She couldn't help them all. His words echoed in her heart. What could one foolish woman with no experience do to make life better for these people?

But the look on Caleb McQueen's face made her realize perhaps the way to accomplish her goal was one person at a time. Change one life and hope that would inspire someone to help another person. Like a ripple across a lake, people could help each other and change Willow Creek.

Amanda shook her head. The longer she stayed here, the stranger her thoughts became. She'd wake up in the middle of the night, seized by an idea, and wouldn't be able to sleep again until she lit a candle and wrote in her journal. She'd sit at the vanity table in her room, wrapped in a quilt, her mind straying down the stairs and beyond the closed door to the kitchen. To the man sitting at another table, waiting for her. Night after night, she had resisted the urge to walk down those stairs and fall into his arms again. She craved his touch, the gentle look in his golden eyes, and the fire he ignited when their lips met.

As if she had summoned him with her thoughts, Samuel Calhoun stood in the doorway. "You can't stay in Willow Creek, Amanda. I've heard rumors, and you're in danger." He took a step toward her. "You could get hurt, badly hurt." A flicker of sadness crossed his face. "Go back to Helena and forget about Willow Creek. Leave your agent in charge of this Benevolent Association and get out of town."

Amanda considered his words as she traced a pattern on the worn surface of the table in front of her. "I know about the threats. Mr. Penny informed me nearly the moment I arrived in town." She stood, pulled several china cups from the cupboard, and pointed at the chair across from her.

"Can I get you some coffee?"

Sam sat down. "Don't think the people behind those threats are harmless, Amanda. This territory breeds dangerous men who will stop at nothing to get their own way."

Amanda set the cup and saucer in front of him, poured them each some coffee, and returned to her seat. She stirred cream and sugar into her own cup while pondering his warning.

"How about you, Sam?" She challenged him with a bold look. "What would you do to get your own way? Would you sell your soul for the things you desire or to accomplish a goal?"

His face grew pale, and she briefly wondered if he was part of a conspiracy to get rid of her. What would he gain by running her out of town? No, she was just getting addle-plated, Sam wouldn't... She couldn't finish the thought. She sipped her coffee to distract herself from her own musings.

"I know the kind of men you're up against, and they don't give up, let's put it that way." Sam lifted the cup to his lips, and their kiss a few days ago near the willow grove at the edge of the creek flooded her memories. She closed her eyes, recalling the image of him hovering over her, of his lean, firm body covering hers. Heat coiled through her like flame shooting from a blaze.

She opened her eyes and blinked. "I've hired some men to protect me. Pinkertons." Her voice held a note of superiority. "The best men money can buy. Because you really can purchase nearly everything you want, if you have *enough* money."

He slammed his fist on the table and stood up to lean toward her. "They won't be able to protect you, Amanda. Get out of town. The only way I can know you're safe is if you leave!"

She jumped to her feet to face him and her cheeks heated as he temper seized control of her emotions. "I will not break my deathbed promise to my husband. I'll leave Willow Creek when I'm good and ready to leave. I refuse to be run out by thieves and murderers who sneak about in the dark and send veiled threats to defenseless women. Tell them, Mr. Calhoun, tell them all. Amanda Wainwright has the means to hire a hundred men, perhaps a thousand. I won't be bullied, and I can make any man's life a living hell if he gets in my way."

Sam stared down at her. She'd thrown down the gauntlet, challenging these people to a duel, and calling them out into the street for a shoot-out. She was so flabbergasted at her own behavior she was now speechless.

"Be careful about the bed you make, Amanda, because in the end, you're going to have to sleep in it." Sam donned his hat and stormed out the door.

Amanda let him go with a heavy heart. She didn't know if she could trust Samuel Calhoun, but she knew he'd deliver her message.

She dropped back into the chair. What had possessed her to make such a threat? She was no mythical Amazon warrior; she didn't fight battles. She'd grown up in a convent, raised by the Sisters of Charity, for goodness' sake.

She wanted to put her head down on the table and weep, but tears were useless. She'd instruct Mr. Penny to hire some bodyguards, because despite her boast, she hadn't directed him to arrange for Pinkerton agents to protect her. She would be more careful. What she really needed was a strong man who wasn't afraid to face down danger.

The image of Samuel Calhoun flashed through her mind. Of course, wasn't that the obvious answer? She could hire Sam to protect her. He carried a gun, and she could tell from the way the muscles bulged beneath his jacket when he'd held her that he was strong. He even knew the men who threatened her, so he could provide reliable information about their plans.

She shook her head. He'd never agree because he had his own business to run. And the expression on his face when he left indicated that he considered her to be mad. He'd come to warn her of danger, and she'd spit at him like a wildcat backed into a corner.

Drumming her fingers on the table, she tried to figure out how a woman could entice a man to do what she wanted. She considered the nearly naked woman lying prone across a chaise in the picture hanging above the dry sink. It had been in the parlor, but Amanda thought it was a distraction for the miners who came to visit. She should have discarded it, but the expression on the woman's face reminded her of her mother. The bright green eyes shining with playfulness, the corners of her lips lifted into an impish smile.

Of course.

Amanda stood up, a plan already forming in her mind. She needed someone to run a few errands for her. She remembered the boy in the other room. Caleb. He could do the things she needed to have done. Because for what she had in mind, the proper Mr. Penny would not suffice.

He would not approve of her most improper intentions.

Chapter Six

Amanda tossed her silver-plated brush on the bed and shook her head at the image in the mirror. She leaned forward to pinch her cheeks, then glanced down and wondered if she should adjust her corset a bit lower to expose more of her breasts. Nibbling on her lower lip, she turned her head and batted her eyelashes in what she imagined to be a flirtatious pose. She thought she looked silly, but other women had always assured her men loved a woman who pretended to be coy.

Being raised by nuns and living with her husband's less than stellar performance in the bedroom had not contributed to her knowledge of how to seduce a man. She'd vacillated all day about her plans for tonight.

She was excited one moment, as butterflies danced in her lower belly when she thought of Sam. In the next minute, she trembled as she considered the consequences of her scheme. Though she tried to put thoughts of bedding Samuel Calhoun out of her mind, the idea was far too enticing to dismiss.

She imagined his arms wrapped around her, his rough, callused hands moving over her body, his hot punishing kisses plundering her mouth.

She shifted the rose-colored silk corset. The dainty lace trimmed drawers and the thin muslin dressing gown did little to hide what was underneath. She felt sinful, brazen, and quite wicked.

Taking a deep breath, she grabbed the bottle of port, tossed her head in defiance, and opened her door a crack. She peeked into the hallway, making sure no other guests were wandering about. She paused at the bottom of the stairs to wet her lips and adjust her corset again. She tried to recall the seductive look on the woman's face in the painting at the Miners' Association. Finally, she gathered her courage, took a deep breath, and opened the kitchen door.

When she discovered the room was empty, she wanted to stomp her foot in frustration. All her intricate plans, all of her careful preparations, and Samuel Calhoun wasn't even here for her to seduce. She set the bottle on the table and slumped into a chair. She'd finally found the courage to do something dangerous and forbidden, and circumstances managed to work against her.

She jumped when the door opened, and a cool night breeze swept into the room, stirring the curtains. Sam stood in the doorway, a look of astonishment on his face when he took in her appearance. He quickly slammed the door shut behind him.

"What the hell are you doing prancing around in the middle of the night, dressed in your fancies?" He swallowed, his amber eyes heated and his breathing heavy.

Amanda's cheeks warmed, and although she didn't glance down at herself, she gathered the opening of the dressing gown a bit closer. It was a futile effort. She'd chosen this particular gown because of the deep, wide opening that would allow him to see her corset and view her breasts. She'd taken great pains to arrange for most of her bosom to spill over the top of the silky fabric.

Sam threw his hat on the baking table and crossed the room in two long strides. Towering over her, he eyed the bottle sitting on the table and gave her a lop-sided grin.

"Is this a private party, or can anybody join in?" Amanda didn't let her gaze move from his despite the butterflies in her stomach and the effort it took to keep her teeth from chattering. "It's a private party, but you're invited. If you can find us a couple of glasses." She tried to insert a husky note of invitation into her voice.

His eyes raked over her, and he seemed poised to ask her another question.

The chill dissipated from her skin to be replaced by a hot, steady heat that spread from her fingers to the tender folds of the slit between her legs.

He grinned and went to the cupboard for glasses. He returned to the table to sit down across from her, and quickly pulled the cork from the bottle she'd placed on the table.

"Have you taken to drinking strong spirits in the middle of the night to help you sleep?"

She wanted to fold her arms across herself to keep him from focusing on her exposed flesh. The heat of a blush crawled from her breasts to her cheeks. She tossed her hair and licked her lips, embarrassed when she remembered she'd planned to entice him with this view in the first place. She kept her hands folded in her lap so he couldn't see her tremble. She was discovering that planning a seduction was much easier than the actual execution. His bold looks made her feel naked, and she heated again as her heart raced. Her nipples ached against the silk fabric of her corset.

She licked her lips and took a deep breath to calm herself. "I was bored, and I was hoping you'd be down here."

He poured the burgundy liquid into two glasses and held one out to her. "Then let's drink to boredom and ways to relieve it."

She took a huge gulp of the wine and nearly coughed as the liquid burned its way down her throat. Her eyes watered, and she was tempted to slam the glass back down on the table. Instead, she finished her drink and tried to pretend she was used to imbibing such strong spirits.

Sam smiled, refilling the glass. “You’re supposed to sip port, my dear, not gulp it.”

Amanda shook her head. “I was just enjoying the taste—humble, yet full of body.” She smiled, trying to appear confident.

Sam took his time letting his gaze travel slowly down the length of her body, pausing at her breasts. She shifted uncomfortably in her seat, and his mouth lifted at the corners.

“I’d say that was an apt description. Full-bodied and brimming with innocence yet possessing just a touch of bawdiness.”

The temperature in the room soared. He couldn’t, or wouldn’t, take his eyes off her. A slow, languorous warmth spread through her, and she squirmed under his perusal. She wished now that she had brought a fan with her, but she’d never realized a room could grow so warm and stuffy this quickly. Her breasts felt heavy, and moisture dampened the crotch of her drawers.

“Are you talking about the wine, or about me?” She fought to keep her voice from wavering and struggled to maintain control of her emotions.

His laugh was deep as a bear’s growl, and it resonated through the room. She couldn’t help but join the merriment.

“Do you want to explain your outfit? I thought perhaps you’d taken a job over at Madame Holt’s new place.”

Amanda stopped laughing and frowned at him. “What’s wrong with what I’m wearing? It’s very fashionable.” She lifted her head to give him a haughty look.

He laughed again and leaned across the table to slide a finger beneath her chin and bring her face level with his.

"You look like a woman of loose morals and ill repute. It's possible I might get the wrong idea about you, Mrs. Wainwright."

Amanda widened her eyes. She tried to control herself, but he was making her angry. She shook her head to release his grip and stood up, leaning across the table to confront him.

"I wanted to talk to you, Sam. I thought if I dressed this way, I might manage to garner your undivided attention."

His eyes centered on her décolletage, and she realized too late that her movement had given him an even better view of her breasts.

"Oh, don't worry, darlin', you've got my full and undivided attention." His gaze flickered to her face briefly before returning to her bosom.

Amanda stood, fluffed her hair, and decided to put all that posing in front of the mirror to some practical use. "Good, because I wanted to apologize for the way I acted this afternoon." She took a step around the table toward him. "I realize you were just trying to protect me, and I wanted to let you know how appreciative I am."

Sam's gaze raked over her from head to toe, and his hand shot out to grab her wrist. "Maybe you should just show me how grateful you are, Amanda." Her pulse quickened at his touch, and she wondered if he could feel it, too. He slowly pulled her closer. She knew she should resist or find a way to keep the table between them. But it was too late, because she now stood only inches from him. She wanted this man, yet her conscience fought her every bit of the way. Unfortunately, tonight her body was winning the battle against her better judgment.

Sam moved closer, near enough that she could smell the spicy fragrance of his cologne and see the dark golden highlights in his amber eyes. Close enough to be delightfully dangerous.

Amanda wanted to feel his hands stroke her breasts and she rubbed against him, whimpering with a need she didn't understand. Her body tingled, demanding a satisfaction she craved with a primal hunger that astonished her. It was as if she were possessed by another woman. A wanton seductress who threw off all her inhibitions to explore the depths of desire.

He was playing a game with her, a cat toying with a mouse, holding her captive between his paws. She didn't want to be pursued; her intention this evening was to be the pursuer.

Without pausing to consider the consequences, she plopped herself on his lap, arranged her hands on each side of his face, and turned him towards her. Then she planted a hot, searing kiss on his surprised lips.

But what should have been a flirtatious tease became an amorous embrace. His hand locked behind her head, and she was swallowed up in the ecstasy of the moment. His mouth devoured hers, then his tongue slipped between her teeth and she trembled with delicious sensations. Shivers of delight coursed through her. She responded first with hesitation, then with bravado as her tongue darted forward and explored.

Desire consumed her. When her arms wrapped around Sam's neck, soft mewing noises surrounded them, and she realized they were coming from her. She felt as if she were someone else, observing this embrace, knowing danger hovered, yet so caught up in the moment she couldn't move away.

His hand moved to cover, then gently squeeze, one breast. Fireworks exploded beneath her closed eyelids as hot liquid pooled in the sensitive place between her legs. She thrust herself forward in invitation, begging him to keep touching her, to keep kissing her, to never let this moment end. Every point where their bodies touched made her ache with a craving hunger.

He shifted the fabric of her corset to expose a nipple, moving his mouth lower to suckle her. She closed her eyes to savor the hot needles of pleasure radiating from his lips. His fingers tugged at the fabric again, and she panted as his mouth moved to the other sensitive peak.

She was lost in the moment, unaware of her surroundings, unabashed in her response to Sam. Her breathing was fast when he finally lifted his face to regard her.

"I want you, Amanda. I'm not a patient man, so if you don't want me, get up and walk out of this room right now."

A flicker of fear washed over her at the stern tone of his voice. She swallowed, noting the hot honey warmth of his eyes. She tried to talk some sense into herself. Get up, a small voice within her cried. Get away, leave. You'll humiliate yourself, become a wanton, and destroy your reputation.

But another voice echoed, the voice of a woman denied pleasure far too long. A woman tired of playing by the rules, sick of being the good and obedient little girl. A woman starving for adventure, ready to experience passion.

A rush of confidence in her own sensuality coursed through her. Her hand traced a pattern down Sam's waistcoat, to the top button, and her fingers deftly unfastened it.

"I came down here this evening fully intending to seduce you." Her voice sounded deeper to her own ears, as her fingers moved to the second button. "I'm no innocent maiden, Sam. I want you, too, and I'll be sorely disappointed if we don't make love tonight."

His deep growl was her answer, and his mouth covered hers again in a penetrating kiss that stole her breath. When he finally lifted his lips from hers, satisfaction framed his face. He stood and gathered her in his arms.

He pushed through the kitchen door and headed for the stairs. She flicked her tongue in his ear, and he attacked the stairs two steps at time, his eagerness apparent and arousing.

He stopped at her door. "It's unlocked," she said.

"Good." Turning the knob, he kicked his way inside then used a shoulder to slam the door shut behind them. He headed for the bed and dropped her down upon it, then stood back with his arms folded across his broad chest.

"Now, do you want to tell me what the hell you're really up to, Amanda?"

She froze, stretched across the bed, her clothing all askew. He glowered at her. What had happened to that hot, lusty look he'd been wearing downstairs? And why did he seem angry with her, when he'd been so aroused just moments before?

"I'm...we..." She huffed. "You know damned well what we're doing, Sam. Now, can't we just please get on with it?"

He ran his fingers through the thick dark wave of his hair and swore. His face creased into a frown, but the look in his eyes told her he still wanted her. He swallowed, his fists clenched, his breathing ragged. He took a step toward her. "God, yes..." He swore again. "Hell no!" He paced across the room.

Amanda sat up on the bed and stared at him in confusion. She knew he wanted her, but he seemed engaged in a battle within himself, as if he were fighting the twin forces of desire and honor.

She adjusted the top of her corset. "You said you wanted me, Sam."

He turned to face her, his gaze focused on her breasts, and he closed his eyes and uttered an oath beneath his breath. She was amused by his reaction. She was beginning to realize how much power a woman held over a man, and white heat uncoiled within her. Arthur had never found her desirable, and only made love to her to sire an heir. When it was apparent she was barren, he'd informed her he wouldn't be bothering her with a husband's demands. She had assumed there was something wrong with her. That she was frigid and cold.

Now she was discovering the power of desire. She didn't want to stop here. Somehow, she needed to convince the man pacing around her hotel room that she had no reservations about tonight, even if he did. She had always heard it was easy for men to become aroused. She had no idea it would take this much persuasion to get Sam into her bed. She wondered again if there was something wrong with her, something that repulsed men. She would soon find out.

Drawing to her knees, she started to unfasten the ties that held her dressing gown closed. Sam seemed to panic.

"What are you doing?"

She pulled the gown from her shoulders, the silk swishing as she wadded it into a ball and threw it at him. He dodged, but never took his eyes off her as she stood up on the bed. Her mouth was dry, and her heart skipped a beat as a quiver of excitement danced through her. She didn't care, she wanted to slowly, sensuously strip her clothes off for him.

She shook her head, enjoying the way her hair swirled around her like a crimson cloud, hiding him from her for the span of a few heartbeats.

"I'm getting naked." The words sounded deliciously naughty. He stepped closer. She stretched like a feline waking from a nap, the cool air washing over her skin to counteract the fire building in her lower belly.

"I don't think that's a good idea, Amanda. You still haven't told me what you're up to."

She slowly unfastened her corset, enjoying the way his eyes followed her every move, the small beads of moisture that dotted his brow. She was having fun and beginning to regret she'd never before explored this side of her nature. "I want to be a very bad girl, Sam. Won't you help me?" Her fingers inched their way down the soft, silky fabric, inviting his gaze to follow.

"I'm not sure..." His voice died when she pulled the corset apart, giving him a full view of her nearly naked form. He stood motionless, staring at her. When he finally looked up, she could see that all indecision had disappeared. Her lips curved into a smile of invitation.

"Maybe I'm sure enough for both of us."

Her fingers found the button on her drawers and she dropped them, leaving just her stockings and garters on. Leaning forward, she shook her head, then fluffed her hair and placed her hands on her hips.

"So, are you going to make me stand here all night?"

He crossed the room, put his hands around her waist and lifted her to wrap her legs around him, his palms kneading her flesh where he held her. His lips found hers and his scorching kiss filled her with primal need. She marveled that the two of them didn't burst into flames.

"Promise me," she whispered.

He studied her carefully. "Whatever you want, darlin'. The sun, the moon, even the stars. All yours."

She traced her tongue across his lips, then pulled back to enjoy his response. A quiver of delight sliced through her.

"Promise me you won't hold back, that you'll make love to me as if we're the only two people alive. That you'll make me feel all the things I've never felt before."

He took a deep breath, then kissed her again.

"I promise, Amanda. I'll treasure you tonight, and I'll introduce you to pleasures you've never even imagined."

She shivered at his words. She was acting like a wanton harlot, but for the first time, she felt incredibly, deliciously alive.

Chapter Seven

Sam couldn't believe he'd hesitated for even a moment. This was what he'd wanted since the first time he'd met her. Despite all his noble plans to convince her to leave town and his vow to never touch her, never make love to her, his resolve dissolved in the face of the reality of a naked and enticing Amanda. His blood nearly boiled as it rushed through his body. His muscles tensed and his skin prickled where their bodies leaned into each other.

Her soft lips moved from teasing his earlobe to licking the exposed flesh at the opening of his shirt. He closed his eyes and swallowed an oath. She was sensual and yielding, and God forbid, he wanted her more than he'd ever wanted any woman.

When she squirmed in his arms, Sam knew he could lose control at any moment. His cock was rock- hard, and he didn't know if he could actually live up to the promise he'd just made to Amanda. He wanted to take his time arousing her before making slow, tender love to her until she was weak from the pleasure of it. He wanted to do all the tantalizing things that would satisfy a woman. Yet, his body throbbed with his own need, and he sensed he was barely capable of maintaining mastery of himself.

Amanda's delicate fingers finished unfastening his shirt. She gave him a saucy, heavy-lidded look.

"Sam, wouldn't it be easier if we were both naked?"

Sam gritted his teeth as the image of their bodies entwined

upon the bed flashed through his mind. His erection tented the wool of his trousers, and he couldn't tell if this frightened or excited Amanda.

Her tongue traced a delicate pattern down his chest, and he closed his eyes to savor the sensation. Sam took a step forward to set her back upon the bed, then he fumbled with his clothes. His fingers felt thick and clumsy, and he couldn't get his boots off without stumbling. He took a deep breath and looked up to discover she was laughing.

"You're such a handsome, glib-tongued fellow; I thought you'd be better at this."

Sam growled and tossed his boot across the room and flung his frock coat after it. His waistcoat lay crumpled at his feet and his shirt was fully unbuttoned as he folded his arms across his chest.

"You can't play with fire without getting burned, Amanda. I'll walk out of here right now if you're not sure about this." He swallowed. *And go home and shoot myself.*

She stretched across the quilt, her softly curved female body enticing him with all its secret delights. Her long, copper curls formed a halo of flame on the pillow, and he realized she wasn't going to send him away. He heaved a sigh of relief, because despite his offer, he didn't know if really could have walked away.

Sam fought a war of conscience, his badly tarnished sense of honor reminding him he was a scoundrel for staying with Amanda. He'd never intended to seduce her, despite his agreement with the mine owners. His plan had been to court her, earn her trust and send if back to Helena. When she' was gone he'd let it be known she'd been his lover.

Amanda's golden body shimmered in the light of the candles spread throughout the room. A heavy ache pulsed in his groin. Even the most well- intentioned and honorable man would find it hard to walk away from this angel.

"Are you afraid of me, Sam?" Her voice purred with confidence.

He removed his shirt and dropped down heavily onto the bed next to her. "Terrified, darlin'."

She giggled, then quivered when his tongue started a slow passage from the hollow of her throat, down to suckle each nipple, before traveling farther to her navel. His fingers kneaded the soft flesh at the top of her garters. She panted in small breathless gasps as her eyes closed.

Sam savored the slightly salty taste of her skin. The intoxicating scent of her woman's musk, the unbridled, earthy, and ancient invitation for mating, told him she was fully aroused. His fingers moved up, and he explored the soft petals of her flesh, parting them with a gentle caress.

He stroked the small bud at the apex of her opening with one finger and her hips lifted, as if to draw him closer, deeper within her. His cock was rigid, and he could barely breathe, overwhelmed by the need to plunge into her sweet, soft body. He could bring her to the brink at any moment. But he wanted to give her more, so much more.

He withdrew his hand and she opened her eyes. Disappointment flickered there. He adjusted his position to lean over her, and his tongue found the place his fingers had deserted. Her legs spread wider and his fingers continued to knead her flesh.

She lifted her head from the pillow to reach down and gently push a dark lock of hair that had fallen forward to obscure his face. He lifted his chin and grinned at her. Her eyes glowed bright as twin emeralds.

"Now Sam! I want you right now." Her brazen command fired his blood even more.

Sitting up in the bed to face him, she slowly unbuttoned his trousers. He followed her movements with tension stretching his nerves to the limit. Finally, she unfastened the opening, and her fingers found his erection.

He gasped when she slid her soft hand up and down his throbbing flesh. His blood bubbled as it whipped through his veins. It took all his self-control not to lose himself in the rhythmic movement of her fingers gliding over his skin. His heart hammered and his cock throbbed. He grew heavier and thicker.

She released him and leaned back upon the pillow and spread her legs wide, wrapping them around his thighs. Sam shook her loose to climb off the bed, then quickly peeled the trousers from his body. She observed him with curious abandon.

She gazed up at him, licking her lips, looking as if she were anticipating a delicious meal. "I believe I said it before, Sam, you are a magnificent animal."

He grinned. "I thought you were talking about my horse."

She laughed softly. "Was I?"

Sam looked down at his engorged cock and he lifted his shoulders with pride. He'd seen his stallion set out to stud, and it was a generous comparison.

Covering her with his body, his lips sought hers and his tongue gently explored her mouth. She welcomed him eagerly.

Her legs wrapped around him again as her hips lifted, inviting him to penetrate her. He shifted his position and discovered she was hot, wet, and ready. He plunged deeply into her and couldn't breathe as her slick heat enveloped him. He'd never been so enticed or aroused by a woman. If desire were a hunger, he'd be a starving man.

He slowly withdrew, then drove into her again. She encased him in heat, bringing him to the brink of ecstasy with her urgency and her need.

Their bodies moved in a dance as ancient as the moon glowing high above them, its soft light reflected in the window. Bodies shifting, with a languid, sensual rhythm, they were unbridled in their need for one another. Every stroke brought him closer to the abyss, but Sam didn't want this excruciating pleasure to end. He held onto the shambles of his control with the thinnest of threads.

Finally, Amanda gasped, and her body trembled against him. She reached her climax, and a look of pure ecstasy flashed across her beautiful face.

"Sam," she gasped, her head twisting on the pillow, "oh yes, Sam!"

Sam covered her mouth with his own, wanting them to be fully joined when he finally released the iron control he'd fought so hard to maintain. Liquid heat poured out of him and stars flashed across his vision as he thrust hard, releasing. He gave a final roar of completion, satiated beyond his wildest dreams, and collapsed next to her.

Their hearts beat in unison. He didn't budge, afraid he might spoil the mood with even the slightest movement. It took several minutes to regulate his breathing. Finally, he lifted himself on one elbow to gaze down at Amanda.

"Did that fulfill your expectations, madam?"

She frowned, as if considering his words carefully. "I'm not sure; I think we should do it again. Perhaps this time you could put a bit more effort into it."

Sam fell back onto the bed. "My God, woman, you're insatiable."

Amanda turned on her side to tickle the soft down of hair on his chest. She formed her lips into a pretty pout. "What's wrong, Sam, are you afraid you can't live up to my standards?"

"You'll kill me with these demands of yours. I'm not a

young man you know."

Amanda traced her fingers across a nasty scar that created a jagged path near his right shoulder.

"Perhaps I should seek out a younger replacement for you."

He touched her cheek with one finger. "If you do that, I might be forced to shoot the man. Let me prove my mettle before you replace me."

Amanda narrowed her eyes. "Just remember, you made a promise."

Sam closed his eyes and grinned. "Even if you do kill me, I'm sure to die a happy man."

"What if you burn in hell for all the sinful things we've done together?" Her words were measured, and he sensed that beneath her worldly banter lurked a shamefully guilty woman.

He pulled her to him, wrapping his arms about her. "Then let's not waste any more time. We might as well enjoy our sinful ways." He kissed the top of her head. "I'd trade one night of delight with you for playing a harp for eternity."

"I don't really think you need to practice any harp playing, Sam."

He laughed and closed his eyes. "I believe you're right about that, darlin'".

They lay in silence. The warmth of their bodies entwined together made the quilt unnecessary.

Finally she spoke. "Did this happen in the war?" She touched the scar on his shoulder, sorrow evident in the emerald depths of her eyes.

He didn't answer for a long time, carefully considering what he would say. He tried to shield his thoughts from memories of the war, and he never spoke of it. Not even to Robert, who had shared so much of the pain.

If he told Amanda about it, trusted her with his secrets, she might turn away from him. Yet, for the first time in more years than he cared to ponder, he wanted to talk about his past. He'd start with a small piece of his past and see how she reacted.

"I was wounded at Chattanooga. Taken prisoner and ended up in a Confederate prison camp." He kept his voice cool and controlled, reciting the facts as if they held no emotion for him.

She studied him, patiently waiting. He wanted to tell her more, to talk about the hopeless days that had followed one after another in that hellish place. Perhaps that was why the devil held no sway over him. He'd faced the cruelty that men could heap upon each other, been to the depths of despair and survived the landscape of hopelessness. It was easier to keep the lid tightly shut on the part of his life, old battle scars were better left alone. Especially when the worst scars were on his heart.

"It was a long time ago," he said.

She touched her lips gently to the scar and kissed it. "I know, but the pain is still there, isn't it?" He was swept away by a feeling of loss. He struggled within himself, wanting to tell her more, to release the pent-up loneliness and sadness. But he remained silent, closed up, attempting to nail a "No Trespassing" sign across the memories.

"It's over." He shifted position and gathered her closer into his arms. She snuggled against him, and he covered them with the quilt that had slipped to the floor during their lovemaking.

They lay together, and he fought with his emotions, knowing he could use their tryst to destroy Amanda and achieve all of his goals. Yet also understanding that despite his agreement with the mine owners, and the possible threat to his mission, he couldn't hurt her.

"You still have to go, regardless." He tightened his jaw. "Maybe even because of this."

Her head shot up, the expression on her face reflecting her confusion.

"So, is that what this was about, Sam? You wanted me, but now that you've made it into my bed, you'll get rid of me as soon as possible?" Tears shimmered in her eyes and she brushed them away.

His arm tightened around her. It was painful to say the words, and he regretted what he was forced to do. It was for her own good, he kept repeating to himself, to protect her.

"I care about you, Amanda. Too much to let anyone hurt you." He let one finger gently trace down her cheek. "But, you're still in danger. There are men determined to stop you and your Miners' Benevolent Association."

"I told you before, I'm not afraid of hooligans who try to scare me with veiled threats."

Sam frowned. "You have your Pinkertons, right?"

She blushed and tried to hide her face. He wasn't going to give up.

"When does your agent expect them to arrive from Chicago?"

Amanda didn't answer. Finally, he lifted her chin gently to force her to look into his eyes.

"There are no Pinkertons, are there, Amanda?" She remained silent, and a flush of dark color slid across her cheeks.

He swore under his breath before releasing her. Climbing out of bed, he gathered his clothes. "I'm going to make arrangements for you to get out of Willow Creek, today if possible." He searched for his other boot, swore again, and leaned over to look under the bed.

"I'm not going anywhere until I've finished what I came here to do. I made a deathbed promise to Arthur, and I refuse to be run out of town." Amanda folded her arms and cocked her head.

Sam stood up to stare at her. A muscle near the edge of his cheek began to throb. "You will leave in the morning if possible. The day after at the latest."

She shook her head and held out one hand to study a cuticle carefully. "I don't believe I will."

"You can't stay here. I told you, it's dangerous." Waving the lone boot around, Sam exploded in anger. "These men are killers. You can't protect yourself."

"I know—that's why I need you." She thinned her lips and twirled a lock of copper-colored hair as she waited for his reaction.

He stared at her in silence and wondered if he should simply storm out of the room. Why was she being so disagreeable? He was only trying to protect her by getting her to leave town. Did she expect him to become her bodyguard? To spend each day dogging her steps and every night exploring the boundaries of desire in her bed? His mind filled with images of those possibilities. He shook his head to clear it.

She seemed to know she had the advantage now, and she didn't waste any time considering the consequences. Flinging the quilt aside, she stood in front of him, naked and vulnerable.

"Please, Sam," she begged, "I need you." Her fingers slid up his chest. He swallowed, but he knew he was softening.

"You don't know what you're asking, Amanda. I'm not the kind of man a woman can rely on, believe me."

"If you send me away, there won't be any more passionate, sweet nights making love." She placed her lips on his skin and her tongue skimmed across the exposed flesh. Heat sizzled through his veins.

That's good, because if I continue behaving like this with the Widow Wainwright, I'm a doomed man. But he couldn't form the words to send her away when her arms were encircling his neck, pulling him down toward her.

Her body leaned into him, and the places their bare flesh met seared him. "I can't," he protested, thinking he should push her away, yet aware he couldn't muster the courage.

She kissed him eagerly with a confidence that swept away all of his illusions about sending her anyplace she didn't want to go. Her tongue moved from the center of his chest toward his navel, and the power of his desire increased with every inch. Her fingers traced the outline of his erection as she lingered at the top button of his trousers. She lifted her eyes and arched a well-shaped eyebrow.

Blood rushed through his body and pooled in his nether regions.

He needed to say something, do something, but the tension, the waiting, the wondering if she would...

He had his answer and his bones melted along with any resistance. Amanda drew him into her mouth, and he knew in an instant he could never send this woman away. He was her captive in a prison constructed of his own passion and need. It was terrifying and exhilarating at the same time, and he fell into an abyss of sensual pleasure.

Chapter Eight

"I can arrange it easy enough, Amanda," Harriet Parmeter said, raising an inquisitive eyebrow. "But are you sure about this? It's a small town. The people who live here love to gossip. It's about all the entertainment we've got."

Amanda brushed crumbs off her lap and gave the hotel owner a smug smile. "I want them to talk, it's the key to my plan." She spread raspberry jam across the muffin she held in her left hand, then waved the knife to punctuate her words.

"If people know Samuel Calhoun is protecting me, they'll think twice before interfering with my work." She dropped the knife and took a bite of the muffin, savoring the sweet flavor.

Harriet tapped her fingers on the oilcloth. Amanda wondered at the woman's reluctance to assist her. After all, it was Harriet who had informed her that widows were not given the intense scrutiny conferred on virgins. Nor were they expected to adhere to the rigid rules and expectations of society. Losing a husband gave widows permission to ignore some of the silly rules that governed women. A fair trade-off, in Amanda's opinion.

She knew Harriet struggled with the concept of moving Sam into the room next to hers. The room with the connecting doorway. It was the perfect means for turning Sam into her protector. Once she arranged all the details with Harriet, she'd hurry to the lumberyard and tell him. She sipped the rich, dark coffee and tried to imagine his reaction. Sam didn't seem to be a man who would enjoy being told what to do.

She had discovered a way to manipulate him though, with soft, silky caresses and blazing desire and need. But she'd only just awakened her sensual side and had no idea how long lust worked on a man. Perhaps he'd quickly grow tired of her and she'd lose her advantage. She wished she could ask Harriet about the powers of sensuality, but even though the woman was becoming a friend, those kinds of questions were too intimate.

She dabbed at the corner of her mouth with the linen napkin, then folded it carefully and settled it next to her plate.

"Tell your boarder I'll pay his rent for the next month if he'll move to another room." Amanda stood and brushed the soft dark silk of her gown before picking up her bag.

"I'm sure Sam will want to move in right away, so could you have the room cleaned as soon as possible?"

"You discussed this with Sam, right?" Harriet held the tray of dirty dishes on her hip and waited for Amanda to answer.

Amanda adjusted her lace cuffs and avoided eye contact with Harriet. "Sort of. I mentioned that he would be the best choice to provide protection from the men who have been making threats against me." She raised her gaze to the ceiling, trying to look innocent. "I simply need to convince him he's perfect for the job."

Harriet started to clear the dishes, shook her head, and snorted. "You'd best not count your chickens before you talk to him about it. Sam ain't the kind of man who welcomes anyone makin' decisions for him. He's strong-willed, and it takes a tender hand with his sort."

Amanda winked at her friend. "I've used all the tender persuasion I can muster. Now I'll try to appeal to his heroic side."

"Good luck, but don't be too disappointed if he refuses to move. Sam likes his freedom to come and go. Movin' in here to take care of you could look like the first step to gettin' hitched, and he's one fella who doesn't fancy the idea of bein' tied down."

Amanda tossed her head. "I have no intention of ever tying myself to another man. Marriage is for women who think they need a man to make decisions for them." She adjusted her hat and gave Harriet a confident smile. "I'm beginning to discover I like making my own decisions and taking care of myself. Most of the time, anyway." She laughed and gave Harriet a sly look. "Men do have their uses."

Harriet's laughter trailed behind her as Amanda strode out onto the boardwalk. Several people nodded in greeting, and she realized she was becoming someone of importance in Willow Creek. The dry grocer stopped sweeping the front stoop of his store to inquire about her day. Amanda smiled at the good nature of these folks.

Apparently, not everyone was opposed to her efforts to improve the town and the plight of the miners. Good, honest people welcomed her. She couldn't give up because a small, ugly contingent didn't approve of her benevolence. After all, didn't the Bible bless her for seeking to care for the poor and the forgotten? She needed to remember that, in her good works, she served the Lord.

Lifting her nose proudly, she tried to ignore a rough element hanging out in front of the saloon. Several men lounged against the wall in chairs. She stepped around them and kept her eyes focused forward.

"Well boys, take a gander at this. A real, honest-to-goodness lady." One of the men leaned his chair forward and stood up, blocking her way. She straightened her shoulders and refused to look away, even though her stomach lurched.

"I would appreciate it if you would allow me to pass." Her voice squeaked, and her cheeks heated.

The man bowed, but when he raised his head, an evil glint flashed in his eye. "The cost to pass is just one lil' kiss."

Amanda raised herself up to her full height, which put the top of her head at the level of his chin. “How dare you suggest such a thing? Can't you see I'm recently widowed? Please, just let me pass.” Amanda tried to brush past him, but one thick-fingered hand stretched out to grasp her upper arm. She fought the urge to scream and pound her fists against him.

“From what I hear, pretty young widows can be real fond of kissin'”. He pulled her toward him as she struggled to escape the unwanted embrace.

“Unhand Mrs. Wainwright, or I'll deposit a bullet in that space beneath your ribs where your heart should be.”

Amanda whipped her head about to find Robert Holcomb staring down the men accosting her. She dropped to her knees and relief washed over her.

The ruffian released his hold and stepped back. His eyes measured Robert, the man who helped Harriet out around the hotel. He tipped his hat at Amanda.

“Beggin' your pardon, ma'am. Guess seein' such a pretty lady walking down the street dulled my good sense.” He sat back down with the other men and allowed her to pass.

The other men teased her tormentor as she continued down the street.

“Thank you, Mr. Holcomb.” She smiled up at him.

He bowed to her. “Please, call me Robert. I'm glad I could be of assistance.” He offered her his arm. “Would you allow me to escort you to your destination?”

Amanda nodded. “I would appreciate your company. I didn't realize I might be troubled by the tough element in this town.”

Robert nodded. “Willow Creek is a bit rough around the edges, and all sorts of folks wander in here. You might want to have an escort when you're walking about town.”

They arrived in front of the Calhoun Lumber Company and Robert backed away, lifting his hat.

Amanda breathed deeply, inhaling the fresh, clean smell of pine. She heard the sharp whine of saws cutting trees into board lengths. From all appearances, Sam operated a profitable business. Workers bustled about, loading lumber onto wagons.

Arthur had indulged her interest in business by teaching her the intricacies of commerce. It had amused him to solicit her opinions, and he'd even confessed to instituting some of her suggestions. Of course, he'd never admitted to anyone that she had originated them. She opened the door to the offices and walked in with as much confidence as she could muster. Sam probably would not appreciate her coming to his office to speak with him. But she'd created the perfect ruse, and she didn't think he'd cause a fuss in front of his employees.

A young man in a threadbare jacket stood up from his desk and nodded at her. "May I help you, ma'am?"

Amanda stepped forward to thrust one gloved hand toward him. "I need to speak to Mr. Calhoun regarding a lumber purchase. Could you announce that Mrs. Wainwright is here to see him?"

The young man swallowed, a flush rising from his shirt collar to his forehead. He twisted his head to frown at the closed door, then turned back to awkwardly extend his own hand.

"He's got, um, some business associates with him right now, ma'am. Would you care to wait?"

Amanda looked around but didn't see an extra chair. She tried to make her smile friendly.

"I can wait, but would it be possible for you to find me a place to sit?" She leaned forward and gave him another playful smile. "I confess, these boots are new and they give my big toe a terrible cramp."

The young man stumbled back, then grabbed his own chair and brought it forward. She gathered her skirts and settled onto the oak surface with an air she hoped suggested she wandered into lumber offices every day to conduct business.

"Do you think the wait will be long, Mister..." She waited for him to fill in the blank.

He blushed again and hung his head. "Walter Abbott, ma'am." He lifted his gaze from studying the floor and gave her a boyish grin. "I'm real pleased to meet you. My pa's one of the Wainwright miners, and well, we all, I mean my whole family and all, we appreciate the things you're doin'. My ma says you're a real fine Christian woman."

Amanda nodded. "Thank you and tell your mother I look forward to meeting her."

Walter Abbott puckered his brow. "But, ma'am, Ma ain't the type to go to fancy socials or tea parties and such. It ain't likely the two of you will be meetin' up."

Amanda considered his statement. This very thing had been bothering her for days. She would see the miners at the association if they needed something, but there was so much more she needed to do. She must meet with some of the women to discover what they needed to make their lives better. "I would enjoy meeting your mother, Walter. But"—she lifted her eyes to plead with him—"I don't know how to get to know the wives of the miners.

Perhaps you could help me?"

Walter shifted his weight to his other leg and looked uncomfortable. "The rich women of this town just look down their noses at our kinda folks. They think they're better'n us. Fact is, Mr. Calhoun took a chance takin' me on." He brushed at a lock of sandy- brown hair that had fallen into his eyes. "But he said I had potential. I didn't rightly know what that was, but he caught me stealin' boards to fix up our shack and instead of turnin' me in to the law, he gave me a chance to work for him."

Walter straightened his shoulders. "I'm learnin' a trade. That means I don't have to live underground twelve hours every day. I'm proud to say I can read and write, and I'm right clever at cipherin'. Rich folks don't have no right to look down on me and my kin."

Amanda stood and clapped her hands. "I absolutely agree with you, Walter. That's why I want to meet with the women. I need to talk with the wives and daughters of the miners. I want to make Willow Creek a better place for them to raise their families, and I need their help to do it."

Walter blinked at her. "I can talk to my ma and see what she says. She's got some influence with the other women, 'cause of Pa bein' a foreman and all."

Amanda thrust her hand forward again. "It's a deal, thank you, Walter. And if she decides she would meet with me, tell her to come to the Benevolent Association, it's..."

She didn't finish because Walter was laughing. She pulled her hand back and frowned at him. "I'm sorry, ma'am, but everyone knows where you located the Miners' Association. Fact is, most of the womenfolk in town have been curious to see the inside of that parlor house for years. That alone should be enough to bring 'em callin'."

Amanda laughed with Walter until they were interrupted by the bang of a door being thrown open. Sam's voice bellowed as several older men exited his office.

"I said the deal is off. I can't be expected to do something that goes against my own conscience."

One of the men turned back toward Sam and shook a fist. "You led us to believe you didn't have a damned conscience, Calhoun. There ain't no going back on a deal once it's made."

All three older men stopped suddenly when they discovered she was sitting in the outer office. They glared at her with angry eyes and such malevolent expressions of dislike that she cringed. Without another word, they donned their hats and marched out into the street.

Sam started to stomp out after them, then came to an abrupt halt when he caught sight of her. Amanda?" He glanced toward the outer door, seemed about to say something, then shook his head.

He clenched his fists, heaved a deep sigh, and turned to her. "How long have you been here?"

She bestowed her sweetest, warmest smile upon him. "Only a few minutes, and this nice young man, your clerk..."

"Walter," the young man mumbled, as if she were so dense, she couldn't remember his name.

"Walter"—she made her voice cheerful despite a sinking sensation in her belly— "has been kind enough to help me solve a little problem I've been having."

Sam's mouth twisted in a grim smile. "You came over here to see Walter?"

Amanda's confidence faltered at the harsh tone of his voice.

"No, that was just lucky happenstance." She stepped toward him, curving her lips in the provocative manner that had made him melt in her arms earlier this morning. He didn't seem to notice as he leaned around her to slam the front door shut.

"Did you want something, then?"

Amanda was growing irritated. Instead of looking happy to see her, he looked annoyed. And he seemed distracted by his fierce encounter with the men who had just exited the building. It was clear a business deal had gone sour. Perhaps timing was everything, and hers couldn't be worse.

"I... wanted to discuss something with you, but perhaps it

can wait." She shifted her position and backed toward the door in an effort to beat a hasty retreat. His words stopped her.

"No point in wasting the trip. You might as well come in." He held open the door to the inner office and she slowly made her way past him, berating herself for not planning this better. Manipulating an aroused, passionate Sam was one thing. Dealing with an angry, irritated one was quite another.

"Sit down." He gestured to a chair before sliding down into his own at the large solid table covered with papers and maps. His fingers drummed against the oak surface while he waited for her to compose herself.

Butterflies flittering through her belly made her too nervous to sit still, and she wandered the room to study several large maps nailed to the wall.

"These are interesting. What are all those areas outlined in red?" She pointed to several large tracts of land.

"Did you come here to discuss my leased land holdings, Amanda?"

She tried to hide her surprise and turned back to investigate the maps. "Are all those parcels yours, Sam?"

He picked up a glass pen and tapped it against the inkwell. "Yes. Or at least that's land I have options on. Now, does that satisfy your curiosity?" He tossed the pen on the blotter and sat back in his chair with his arms folded in front of him.

She moved to a large table covered with papers and tried to hide her nervousness by shuffling some of them. Instead, they flew in several directions. "Oh my," she muttered.

"Amanda." His voice was sharp. "Sit down this minute and quit destroying my office."

She tried to comply, but her skirt caught on a paperweight as she brushed past, and it nearly toppled to the floor before he caught it.

He stood, walked around the table, and pushed her into the chair. "What the hell do you want, Amanda?"

She stared up at him in horror. Where was the tender lover she'd been with this morning? The man who'd said he worshipped her and that she was a goddess? She wanted to ask this cold, angry stranger what he'd done with the body of Samuel Calhoun.

"I..." She couldn't cajole this Sam into being her protector, to move into the hotel, into the room adjoining hers. She didn't even think she liked this man very much, with his rude behavior, unkind attitude, and sharp words.

"I've made a terrible mistake, please forgive me." Standing up again, she worked to keep a quiver out of her voice.

She turned to hurry out of the room, but he stopped her by putting his hands on her shoulders. Moving closer, he lowered his lips to the back of her neck, kissing her gently and sending shivers down her spine.

"I'm sorry, Amanda. It's been a helluva day." He took a deep breath and shook his head. "I shouldn't take it out on you, though."

"I thought you were already regretting last night." She couldn't keep the note of sadness from her voice.

His lips moved to the side of her throat, just beneath her ear. "God, no. Why would I regret that? It was wonderful."

Warmth exploded deep within her. She turned to face him, lifting her gaze to meet his. "Then you're not angry that I came to the office to see you?"

He wrapped a curl around one strong, thick finger. "I didn't say that. Coming here in the middle of the day was a foolish thing to do. You're a respectable woman, and you can't be visiting men in broad daylight."

The corners of her lips lifted into a smile as she trailed her hands down the fabric of his vest. "But it's perfectly respectable to cavort with a man in the early hours of the morning, is that what you're saying, Mr. Calhoun?"

Sam closed his eyes at her sensual assault. "This is hardly the time or the place to discuss such things, Amanda."

He caressed her arms and pulled her closer. Desire smoldered in the depths of his eyes.

"But that's exactly the reason I came over here, to discuss some important details about our arrangement." She stroked his cheek and marveled at the way her touch transformed him. Already he was more relaxed, his voice calmer, his demeanor softer.

"Amanda, we don't have an arrangement. Quite frankly, it would be better if you just waltzed out of this office right now and never looked back." He tried to step away from her. She refused to release him.

Her heart plummeted and her words stuck in her throat. He still wanted to send her away, even after all the things they'd done together. Even after their night of passion, a night he had just referred to as wonderful. She backed away to give him a scrutinizing stare. Maybe she needed to use more persuasion.

"I want you to move into the hotel." She lifted herself on her tiptoes to plant a kiss on his chin. It didn't seem to distract him.

"I have rooms right above here. Why would I want to move into the Parmeter House?" He tried to release her, but she still refused to let go.

"To be closer to me, of course." She gave him a look that should have curled his toes. Instead, he managed to free himself and step back. Calmly, he sat upon the edge of his desk, crossing one leg over the other. He pulled out a cheroot, but he didn't ask her permission to smoke.

"I think you'd better sit down and explain yourself,

Amanda. I have no intention of moving into the Parmeter House, even if it means being closer to you."

The finality of his answer convinced her she'd been right. Arousing a man appeared to be useful for a very limited time. She couldn't accurately gauge what the exact amount of time had been, but not nearly long enough for her purposes.

"I thought you'd want to be closer to me, so that we could, well, you know."

He tapped some ash from his cigar and gave her a mischievous grin that lit his eyes with touches of gold. "Judging from last night and this morning, don't you think I'm close enough to manage just fine?"

Her face grew hot, and she wished she could reach that big glass paperweight; it would be the perfect thing to smash his arrogant skull.

She stood abruptly, brushed at her skirts, and arranged her petticoats before tossing him a cold glare. "Please forgive me for interrupting your important business. I can see I'm wasting my time, so I'll just leave you alone, Mr. Calhoun."

"Tell me what you want, Amanda." The chiseled features of his face were set in hard planes, and his eyes snapped bright amber flashes. "The truth, without any tricks or deception. Just tell me what the hell you want."

She stomped her foot and shook with anger. "I want you to move into the hotel, into the room adjoining mine. I want you nearby so I can feel safe. I want you to protect me from the men who want to hurt me."

Her tears shamed her, and she truly wanted to whack this man with a sturdy object. Then she could slink out, humiliated.

He rubbed his hands across her shoulders and the smoldering heat in his eyes hypnotized her. "That's all I wanted, darlin'. Tell me the truth. I hate all the lies and deceit, and the one true thing in my life right now is you. Always be honest with me, can you promise that?"

His breath, warm and soft, caressed her as he moved closer. "I promise," she whispered, instantly forgetting his earlier bad temper.

His lips crushed hers, and she was lost in a whirlpool of sensation before she could demand the same of him. By the time they stepped away from each other, she was too breathless to ask him for anything else. Too grateful for her success to wonder if she should demand honesty from him, also. Her own sensuality captured her, and she didn't question his sudden change of heart.

"I'll move in tonight, but Amanda..." She didn't let him finish before she silenced him with another kiss.

She was walking back to the hotel before she recalled the words he'd whispered before they'd become lost in a sea of desire.

"I'm no good for you, Amanda. I'm not the man you think I am."

Her intuition demanded she examine that phrase, to think about those words of warning. Instead, she ignored them. In her opinion, goodness was a highly overrated quality, anyway. What had being good ever gotten her? Years of Father Mikelson's sermons echoed in her ears, but she shut them out.

Being bad with Samuel Calhoun was more fun than being good with anyone else had ever been.

Chapter Nine

"Sweet Jesus in the morning, Amanda, what the hell happened in here?"

Sam stood in the doorway, taking in the clothing strewn about, the unmade bed and open trunks with shoes, corsets, and various women's accouterments piled haphazardly within.

Amanda turned from the dressing table mirror where she was arranging her hair and frowned.

"Happened? I was just getting ready for dinner." She turned back to the mirror to tuck a few glossy red curls into an arrangement on top of her head.

Sam picked his way carefully through the chaos of the room to stand behind her. She smiled at his reflection. It was a lazy, inviting, seductive smile, and heat shot through him and pooled in his most sensitive parts. It bothered him a bit that she could arouse him so easily.

"I wish you could wear your hair down, it's beautiful when it shimmers in the lamplight." He touched one errant curl gently.

She shook her head and frowned. "It wouldn't be suitable for a widow to pretend to be a maiden." She wrinkled her nose. "I'm supposed to be devastated by my recent loss, remember?"

Sam nodded and walked across the room, carefully stepping over clothing. He tossed enough items into a trunk to clear a spot, then settled himself on the bed.

"I've been meaning to speak to you about that, Amanda. For all your talk about keeping your promise to Arthur Wainwright, you don't exactly appear to be..." He coughed politely. "Overwhelmed by grief."

Amanda stood and adjusted her black crepe skirts. "I'm not devastated, if you must know the truth." She crossed her arms and stuck out her lower lip. "Arthur Wainwright married my money. He and my father were business partners, and when I turned eighteen, I was informed that I was to be wed." She gave him a thin smile.

"No one suggested I might have any choice in the matter or asked me if I wished to be married. It was simply a matter of doing what I was told."

Sam looked up at her, amused by the petulant tone of her voice. "And it never occurred to you to argue, or to run away?"

Amanda nibbled at her lower lip. "I was raised to be an obedient Catholic girl, to do what my father and the church thought best for me. I didn't argue because I'd been in the convent so long, I believed one simply did what one was told to do."

She slammed one of the trunks shut and sat down heavily upon it. "I was miserable after our wedding night. Arthur was rather perfunctory, shall we say, about the whole thing."

Sam stared at her. He knew some men didn't care if women were pleasured and simply saw to their own needs. But the thought of having a partner as passionate as Amanda in bed, then wasting the opportunity, disgusted him.

Amanda shrugged her shoulders. "I know it's not good to speak ill of the dead, but Arthur was, well, very dull. He certainly lacked your imagination." She gave Sam a dimpled grin. "He never seemed very interested in me, and then, after a while, when he realized I wasn't going to produce he son he wanted, he never entered my room. I had to give up on the idea of having children."

The depth of her loss shone in her emerald eyes when she lifted her gaze to meet his. A shimmer of tears appeared, but she took a deep breath and continued.

"I learned to accept things as they were, a marriage that lacked emotion. But Arthur took care of me, and we made the best of the situation."

Sam fought a sudden urge to stand, pull her into his arms, and kiss the pain away. He pictured her then, an innocent young woman, filled with dreams of babies and happiness.

He knew only too well the painful loss of such dreams. He had once been young and filled with plans for his life. A war and prison camp had changed all that. For many years, he had been content to live each day as it came, without hope. But lately, he'd started to look towards the future with a new sense of purpose. Something profound had changed in his life, starting that night in the kitchen when he first met Amanda Wainwright.

She smiled. "Arthur encouraged me to learn and to try new things. In many ways, I was his protégé. He trusted me, and that's why I must honor the promise I made to him."

Sam stood and approached her. He brushed a finger across her cheek. "So it has nothing to do with a stubborn streak about a mile wide that I've observed?"

Amanda tilted her head and fluttered her lashes. "Stubborn? Why, how could you even insinuate such a thing Mr. Calhoun?"

He leaned back on his heels and laughed. "I seem to remember a certain amount of—ahem— persuasion was used to encourage me to move into the Parmeter House."

Amanda's eyes turned dark and sultry. She licked her lips and that flash of heat surged through him again.

"I have an idea that I didn't need to persuade you nearly as much as you pretend I did." She stood up and rubbed his chest. "In fact, I hardly had to say a thing other than please."

Sam grasped her chin, turning her face up toward him. "Maybe it's just the lovely way you say please." He crushed his mouth to hers and reveled in the softness and immediacy of her response. Her lips parted and she invited him in. He wrapped his arms around her, and for a few moments, their hearts beat in cadence. Her body molded against him. She felt so right in his embrace.

He knew he could carry her to the bed, and without a word of protest, she'd allow him to make love to her. The primal need they experienced for each other tantalized and terrified him at the same time. He craved her touch, the sound of her voice, even the sweet lilac scent of her. A warning sounded deep within him.

His own desire was nothing compared to the mission with which he'd been charged. He needed to focus on the conspiracy of the mine owners, not be sidetracked by the comely Widow Wainwright.

Releasing her, he swallowed and stepped back. "We'd better go down to supper before we get distracted." He adjusted the cuffs of his shirt and smoothed his hair back, trying to calm his enflamed senses.

Amanda picked up a shawl and gave him a playful smile. "I'm really not that hungry, perhaps Harriet could simply leave us one of those midnight suppers."

Sam considered her words. He wanted to stay in this room and make love to Amanda. Yet he also wanted to prove to himself that he could resist her.

"We have a long night ahead of us. Let me help you with that and let's get downstairs to eat. If memory serves me correctly, I'm going to need the sustenance to survive another night with you."

Amanda batted at him playfully, and the ugly black shawl fell to the floor. She grimaced when she retrieved it.

"I'm so tired of black. I swear this year will be the longest of my life. Widow's weeds are so depressing, it's no wonder women wearing them don't want to go out unless they have to."

She wrapped the shawl around her shoulders and picked up her gloves.

"Why don't you just dispense with them? After all, you've admitted you're not exactly in mourning for good ol' Arthur. Why not exchange them for some bright colors and get on with your life?" He stepped over several petticoats piled in front of the door.

Amanda made a disparaging sound and shook her finger at him. "As if that wouldn't make people talk. Women are expected to follow strict rules of mourning. There are very specific wardrobe requirements. Black, to gray, to blue, to colors."

Sam opened the door and followed her into the hall, offering her his arm gallantly.

"Well, you don't always have to do what other people want you to. Isn't it time you learned to defy the expectations of society and do what you want? Don't wait for someone else's approval, Amanda, because you might have to wait a very long time."

Maybe a lifetime, and then you discover what you wanted wasn't worth the price you were forced to pay. For a moment he wanted to tell her about Elsbeth, his beautiful aristocratic wife. The woman who had deceived and nearly destroyed him. But not yet. A tiny door slammed shut inside him. If he told her about Elsbeth, she'd know the worst of him. He couldn't face the possibility of Amanda backing away, shocked and frightened. He wanted a few more precious days of believing in happiness.

They descended the stairs together, and Sam noted all talk ceased when they entered the dining room. They faced curious glances from the other diners, and a few whispered comments swirled around the room. It was already common gossip that he'd moved into the hotel and taken the room next to Amanda Wainwright. He expected a visit from Jack Pruitt, who was probably awaiting a public boast from Sam about bedding the widow.

As he pulled her chair back and inhaled her scent, he faced the reality of his situation. One simple comment at the bar of the saloon, and his mission would move forward. He'd earn the trust of the other mine owners, and he'd discover if they were stockpiling silver in an effort to force up the value.

An offhand remark about the talents of Amanda Wainwright in bed, a bit of bragging about his successful seduction, and everything he'd worked so hard for would finally be his.

But, at what price?

Amanda looked around the room. A touch of strawberry color tinged her cheeks, proving she wasn't immune to the gossip or the stares. Despite the hard veneer she tried to project, a gentle, vulnerable woman lay underneath. If he ruined her reputation, she'd leave Willow Creek. It was probable she'd leave Montana altogether, considering the way sensational stories spread across the territory.

He imagined her in San Francisco as part of the wealthy social whirl. She'd meet another man and become his wife, bear his children, and be happy. He frowned. He didn't like the picture of her holding another man's son in her arms.

He didn't like it one bit.

"The chicken and dumplings, I think. I know Harriet's dumplings are probably light as a cloud."

She peered at him over her coffee cup. "Are you all right? You look angry enough to fling that menu across the room. Has it annoyed you in some way?"

He drummed his fingers on the table, unnerved by his own thoughts. He should get Amanda out of town, and he had the means at his disposal. At the same time, he didn't want to humiliate her, and he really didn't want her to leave.

"That's fine, I'll have the same." He knew he sounded abrupt, and both Harriet and Amanda stared at him before exchanging glances.

"I'm thinking of having a dinner." Amanda's voice wavered.

"Some folks call it supper, but I predict you're right." His voice was sharp. The thought of losing Amanda filled him with melancholy, while at the same time he knew he should get her out of Willow Creek. He ran his fingers though his hair. Ultimately, he didn't know what he was going to do. But for tonight, he wanted to recapture the warmth of their embrace upstairs. He touched the tips of her fingers.

"So, do your plans include eating all of your dinner and some of mine too?"

She looked at him with her mouth open. "I do seem to enjoy eating your food, don't I? How impolite of me." She blushed a pale rose color. "I apologize. Can you ever forgive me for being so rude?"

Sam relaxed and settled back in his chair. Teasing Amanda served as a tonic for his tender nerves.

"You also mess up any place you're in for more than five minutes, become a small tyrant when you boss people around, and can be a bit of a spoiled child when you don't get your own way."

Amanda's face turned a shade pale and her eyes widened. "How awful of me, Sam. Why didn't you mention these things before? I'm appalled to discover I've behaved so badly. I've just simply lost all my manners."

Sam placed his hand over hers and leaned forward again. "Despite these faults, you're kind, loving, beautiful, and immensely entertaining." He sat back again. "Not to mention you possess a variety of special talents that have not gone unappreciated."

This time she blushed a deep scarlet which Sam found most appealing. Just sitting at dinner with her aroused all his senses, not to mention made his private parts jump to attention. She was the only woman he'd ever met who could be so profoundly sensual and innocent at the same time. When they made love, she had no inhibitions, but afterward, she'd confess to being embarrassed by her own lack of modesty.

She nodded her head to indicate the people scattered around the room. "My behavior is already under scrutiny here in Willow Creek. I believe people are quite scandalized by your move into the room next to mine. I might be considered a fallen woman."

She didn't sound as devastated by the idea as he thought she'd be. Amanda was always a puzzle to him. She could be a feisty do-gooder one minute and a naughty vixen the next.

"People will talk, Amanda. You're rich and powerful, and there are folks who resent that in a woman. Are you tough enough to handle it?"

Holding her coffee cup gently between her hands, she shook her head. "I don't know..." Her voice trailed off into a whisper. "I pretend I don't care what people say, or think, for that matter. But as you so carefully pointed out upstairs, I'm too bound by society's expectations to discard a practice I consider stupid and impractical." She sighed. "I've always been jealous of men. They don't seem to ever care what anyone thinks of them. If I were a man, I could simply do what I please and the devil take the high road."

Sam shook his head. "It might seem that way, Amanda. And I agree—men aren't constrained by the rules of society in the ways women are." He stared off into space for a few moments, remembering the beautiful houses, the parties and balls, and all the spiteful, jealous gossip. He'd wasted years of his life trying to live up to the standards of others. He'd married a woman he didn't love because of his family's expectations.

"We may have different rules, but they can be just as unforgiving." He rubbed her hand, enjoying the softness of her skin and the warmth of her touch.

He looked into her eyes. "I've done a lot of things I'm not proud of, and sometimes I've even forgotten what I stand for or believe in." He glanced away; her eyes were too trusting, too full of...love? God, he hoped not. Falling in love with him would be the worst mistake Amanda Wainwright ever made.

"We can all sometimes forget who we are, Sam." Compassion softened her voice. "After I married Arthur, I forgot about my dreams, my hopes." She caressed his fingers and closed her eyes for a moment, then opened them.

"But I'm beginning to remember some of those dreams." She straightened in her chair. "That's why making the Miners' Benevolent Association a success is as important to me as it was to Arthur." Her voice grew stronger. "I want to succeed at managing a charity that I've created. I want to prove I'm capable of taking care of myself and making my own decisions."

Their supper arrived and the creamy chicken and dumplings smothered in smooth, tasty gravy melted in his mouth. A companionable silence enveloped them for a while before Amanda finally set her fork down.

"That's why I'm planning a dinner. Well, actually, a ball."

Sam nearly choked. "A ball? In Willow Creek?"

Amanda nodded. "A Miners' Ball, with all the families of my miners invited. I want to have the best food, beautiful music, and gifts." She warmed to her subject. "Wonderful gifts for everyone."

Sam raised an eyebrow. "Isn't it a bit early for Christmas,

Amanda?"

She picked up her fork and waved it. "I want a magical evening, an opportunity for the people who work for me to feel important." She studied him. "Don't you think everyone has the right to feel important, even if it's only for one night?"

Sam wanted to argue with her, to tell her this was just another crazy idea. But he agreed with her. He knew many of the men who worked in the mines, who spent long, hard hours beneath the ground, digging ore. Their lives could be dark and dismal, and when he considered it, he figured every man was entitled to at least one night of feeling rich and important.

"I guess you could be right about that, and I'm inclined to think this is going to make you more popular than ever with the miners. But remember what I told you, you have enemies."

Amanda gave him a smirk. "With you to protect me, Sam, I'm not afraid of anyone." She returned to her meal, but Sam pondered her response for a few moments.

"Don't put all of your trust in me, Amanda. I'm afraid at some point I will fail you, and you're going to be disappointed." He glanced down at his meal which no longer held any appeal. He pushed his plate toward her. "Would you like another dumpling?"

She raised her shoulders in a delicate shrug. "If you're sure you aren't going to eat it."

He grinned. It was difficult to remain in a foul mood when in Amanda's company. "I'm sure, darlin'. You won't offend me if you eat it."

She stabbed at the dumpling with her fork and popped it onto her own plate. "I will never be disappointed in you, Sam. You're a good man, even if you don't think so." She brought her fork to her mouth, then set it down again. "I understand you've done some things you're sorry for, but Sam, believe me, we all have." She nibbled at her lower lip.

"Maybe that's why I need to do these things for the miners, because I know I never loved Arthur the way I should have. Maybe I could have tried harder. I think the one thing I learned is that you can't make your heart do something it simply doesn't want to do. You can't choose love, Sam. Love chooses you." Her eyes brightened and her beautiful face glowed.

"Even when it's inconvenient, or tragic, or just not supposed to happen, people come together. And if it's only briefly, we need to grasp love with both hands and hang on for dear life." Amanda sat back and gave him an understanding smile.

"No more promises, Sam. No tomorrows. No yesterdays. Let's just enjoy today and we'll pretend that's all there is."

Sam felt the room tip sideways when he finally grasped what she was saying. Amanda didn't expect any promises of forever from him. She didn't need that. She just wanted to enjoy what they had, while they had it. His heart danced as he absorbed her words.

"You keep that crowd of rowdies away from me so I can do the things I need to do. We'll be happy and together for as many moments as we're given." She stared into his eyes, then stood abruptly.

"I need to meet with Mr. Penny at the Miners' Association. There are some papers to sign, and he told me an old friend of my father's is in town. I should see him before he leaves." She adjusted her skirts and wrapped the shawl around her shoulders.

Sam nodded, then he stood up to offer her his arm. "If you don't mind, there's some business I need to attend to also. I'll leave you with your Mr. Penny and come back for you later."

Harriet waved at them then she turned her attention back to Robert, who shot an angry look at Sam and shook his head. Robert Holcomb was his best friend and partner, and it didn't bode well for Sam if he'd done something to upset the man.

Settling his Stetson on his head, he slowed his pace to match Amanda's smaller steps. The spring evening was mild and there hadn't been any rain for several days, so the streets were fairly dry with only a thin covering of mud. Sam inhaled the fresh air and his spirits lifted.

He'd made a decision tonight. He wasn't the kind of man who could destroy a woman's reputation for his own purposes. Amanda wasn't expecting much from him, but he didn't intend to disappoint her, or to use her for his own gain. In the morning, after breakfast, he'd tell her about the arrangement he'd made with the other mine owners. He'd confess his role, and he'd do everything he could to convince her things had changed. He had no intention of hurting her. Amanda Wainwright was a woman worth having, and he wanted to keep her in his life, no matter how briefly the happiness lasted.

He stood at the door of the Willow Creek Miners' Benevolent Association and shook his head. The former parlor house still aroused his senses. He wished he could convince Amanda to move to a more appropriate location, maybe to build near his mill. He'd be sure to talk with her about it. Tomorrow.

What had Amanda said, not to think about yesterday or tomorrow? He wasn't inclined to examine his past too closely, and it had taken him years to find the courage to imagine a future. But now he had an urge to share his hopes and his dreams. And he wanted to share them with the woman standing beside him.

He kissed Amanda gently. "I'll come back for you in about an hour, I promise."

She laid a hand on his waistcoat, over his heart, and lifted her face to him, good humor reflected in her eyes. "Just don't get caught up in a game of poker at the saloon and forget about me, Sam."

He backed down the steps and bowed. “I could never forget you, darlin’. I’m counting the minutes until we’re back together.” He gave her a sly grin. “And I’ve got some interesting plans for later. Trust me.”

Amanda threw him a kiss. “I do trust you, Samuel Calhoun.”

Sam walked away and he felt good, really and truly good. It was a heady feeling, one he hadn’t experienced in a very long time. He had a sense that, after tonight, everything would change for him and Amanda.

Chapter Ten

It took every ounce of self-control for Amanda not to vomit her supper onto the floor that seemed to be rolling beneath her. She used her anger to maintain the slightest thread of control.

"I don't know if it's true, Mrs. Wainwright, I'm just telling you what I've heard around town. The gossip." Mr. Penny dropped his gaze to the surface of the desk in front of him, and dark red rose from his neck to color his entire face.

Amanda wanted to break something, anything. Glass. That's what she needed, something that would shatter and break into a thousand crystal pieces, just like her heart.

"You said it was the talk of the town, didn't you?" Her voice sounded cold and detached, and she couldn't believe her words hadn't come out as a scream. She wanted to lose control and succumb to an angry, spiteful tirade against the man who had betrayed her.

Mr. Penny twisted his hands into a knot and kept his voice so low she had to lean forward to hear him.

"It's been said your Mr. Calhoun was paid to..." He avoided making eye contact with her, feigning interest in a spot just above her head as his neck turned crimson. "To take advantage of you. The other mine owners banded together and hired him, to...um..."

Scream, a small voice said. Don't worry about making a fool of yourself or what Mr. Penny will think of you. Just throw things and scream, and maybe you'll feel better. But she knew it wouldn't help, because the ache deep within her insisted she'd never feel better again.

Shaking her head sadly, she crossed the room to stand before the large marble fireplace. She glanced down at the log crackling at her feet. "I don't understand." She turned back to Mr. Penny, almost expecting him to be able to explain what had happened.

Why had Sam done this to her? Why would he plan to seduce her, then humiliate her by ruining her reputation? It didn't make any sense. Yet from what Mr. Penny had told her, it was all part of an arrangement. A scheme concocted for money. Sam had been paid to destroy her, and that hurt more than anything else.

She straightened her shoulders and took a deep breath. "I suppose there's nothing I can do except confront Mr. Calhoun and ask him if these rumors are true."

Mr. Penny's eyes popped wide at her announcement. He swallowed hard and shook his head. "I don't think that's a good idea, Mrs. Wainwright. I've heard he's a dangerous man. If only part of what I've heard is true, it's enough to convince me you're in peril. Maybe you should speak with Father Mikelson. He'll know what to do."

Amanda shuddered at the thought of telling Father Peter Mikelson about her misadventures with Samuel Calhoun. The old priest was a harsh, cold man who'd been a great friend to her father, but a disapproving judge and tyrant to her. He was the executor of her husband's estate, and he managed to find fault with everything she did. Amanda had no intention of asking for his opinion or his help.

She lifted her chin and gave Mr. Penny a haughty look. "I'm a grown woman, for heaven's sake. I believe I'm capable of questioning a man about his intentions without a chaperone or caretaker." She adjusted the white lace cuffs of her gown and worked hard to stretch a thin smile across her face.

"It's my opinion this whole thing is a terrible misunderstanding, or just malicious gossip." She picked up her bag and backed toward the kitchen. "In either event, it's my business, Mr. Penny, and I would appreciate it if you would remember you work for me."

She slammed the door and stood frozen for a moment, afraid if she moved even a hair, she'd dissolve into a fit of tears. How could Sam do this to her? She had believed in him, wanted him, and more than anything else, trusted him. And he had betrayed her. What had he said earlier? Not to trust him, that he didn't deserve it and eventually he would disappoint her? How profound and true his words seemed now.

She considered her choices. She could leave town, return to Helena, and forget all about Willow Creek, its problems, and its people. She didn't owe anyone in this town a thing. All she had wanted to do was help some of the people who lived here. Instead, she'd been dragged down to the lowest level, made to feel cheap and used.

Brushing tears from her cheek, she crossed the room to the small pantry. She rummaged through the shelves for a few minutes until she found what she was looking for. A Smith and Wesson Colt .32. The cowboys called it a suicide gun, because if you didn't hit what you were shooting at, you'd probably be dead before you could reload. It was small, easy to handle, and she had stored it in a crock in the pantry in case of trouble. Well, there was trouble tonight, she thought, sliding the cartridges into the chambers.

She slipped the gun into her bag, stood tall, and stiffened her spine. Her throat felt parched and her face felt warm, almost feverish. She didn't know if she could shoot a man. Up until this moment, she'd never had the inclination. But stepping out onto the boardwalk, she thought perhaps she could pull the trigger. If Sam had planned to seduce her, use her, and then destroy her reputation for the sake of money. If he had schemed with other men to betray her, she thought she could do him harm. It would certainly teach him not to trifle with a woman's emotions.

Her pace was measured as she walked toward the Dark Horse saloon. Tinny music and loud, bawdy laughter echoed from inside. She pulled out the gun and leveled it, then swung through the doors.

The noise died abruptly as faces turned to gape at her. The piano went silent and laughter and conversation dwindled until the people in the room sat spellbound, waiting. She stepped toward the bar where Sam stood, watching her in the mirror. "You're a low-down, sneaky, son-of-a-skunk, lying coward, Samuel Calhoun."

Sam let out a deep breath when he turned to face her. A deep, tortured sadness haunted his eyes, and he shook his head.

"Don't do this, Amanda. It won't solve anything. I know I've hurt you but killing me won't change what's happened. Don't make this any worse for yourself."

Amanda held the gun steady, aimed at his heart. She had to use her other hand to help keep from shaking. Her knees wobbled, and despite the heat of her temper, she was chilled to the bone.

"It will rid the earth of some low-down, lying vermin, and that should be worthwhile. It will prevent you from taking advantage of another woman, hurting her and breaking her heart after you ruin her." She struggled to keep her voice under control when she felt great, earthshaking sobs swirling through her chest.

The amber highlights in his eyes darkened, and she knew her words wounded him. Good. She wanted to hurt him as badly as he had hurt her. She wanted him to know how sordid and abused she felt.

He stepped toward her. "I didn't want this, Amanda. You've got to believe me. I wasn't going to go through with it." He stood still as she leveled the gun and pulled back the hammer. The click echoed through the saloon.

"Stay back, Sam. You can't sweet talk your way out of this one. Everything you've ever told me is a lie, isn't it?" All of her dreams crumbled to dust, again. "You planned this, didn't you? All those chance meetings in the kitchen? The romantic gestures? Even the rumors about me being in danger. It was all part of some plan, wasn't it?"

Sam shook his head and took a step back. "Can't we go someplace more private to talk about this, Amanda?"

She laughed and waved her hand at the crowd of people who listened avidly to their confrontation. "Everyone in town knows about us, Sam. We're the main topic of conversation from the dry goods store to tent city. They're all laughing at the foolish Widow Wainwright, deceived by a glib tongue and a handsome face." She stepped boldly toward him. "I've been so gullible, but I'm going to get even now, Sam. I'm going to—"

"Amanda Rose Dumont Wainwright, what in God's name do you think you're doing?"

Amanda's heart leapt into her throat. She froze, as the attention of the people in the room shifted away from her and Sam to the tall man looming in the doorway.

She wanted to run away, escape to her hotel room, throw the covers over her head, and weep until she was drained of tears. Instead, she turned slightly, gave the man a nod, and waved the gun in Sam's direction.

"I have a dispute with this man, and I'm settling it in a manner he can understand."

Father Mikelson took two long steps into the center of the room. With his pure white hair, piercing blue eyes, and large, lanky frame clothed in dark priestly garb, he held the crowd enthralled.

"Shooting him might be the method he best understands, but it is the least productive means for settling an argument." The priest's voice boomed through the room. "I demand you give me that gun."

Amanda's arm wavered, and she nearly succumbed to the priest's authority, until she caught the small gleam of triumph in Sam's eye. She leveled the gun toward him again.

"I can't do that, Father." Her voice sounded weak to her own ears, but she gained strength with every word. "He has humiliated me and destroyed my reputation. I believe shooting him is my only recourse."

"Is this true, sir?" Father Mikelson demanded in a booming voice that was meant to echo through a sanctuary when he gave a sermon. "Did you publicly humiliate her, and is she a ruined woman?"

Sam shifted from one leg to the other and gave Amanda a look so tender and filled with regret she nearly melted.

"I made a deal with some other men in town to seduce her and spread rumors about our relationship." There was an audible gasp from the on-lookers and a low murmur of disapproval at his confession. He turned to face the priest.

"I never intended to go through with it, Father. I haven't said anything about her, and I'd swear to that on a stack of Bibles."

He turned to Amanda. "I didn't betray you. I truly care about you, and I didn't start these vile rumors. I'd never want to hurt you." His shoulders slumped, and she noticed his golden eyes held dark shadows of the truth.

Amanda wanted to believe him, but she couldn't afford to make another foolish mistake. Even as her head told her to be cold and calculating, her body responded to his plea with a rush of heat that made her nipples tingle, and her pantalets feel too tight and confining. She'd trusted him once, accepted all the beautiful promises he'd made, and he'd taken advantage of her. She wouldn't ever be so naive again.

"I've been seduced and ruined, Father. He planned it all for the sake of money." Her voice trembled. "Now I'm forced to shoot him, even if I hang for it and burn in Hell for an eternity."

The room was silent, everyone waiting. Emotion played over Sam's face—guilt, sadness, and finally, resolve.

"She's right, Father. I have taken advantage of her. Nothing I can say or do will ever be able to atone for that. She has no choice. Amanda darlin', aim for my heart." He opened his frock coat and pointed to a spot on his vest. "Right about here should mean a quick, painless death."

Amanda was stunned. He was inviting her to shoot him. She couldn't tell if he was serious or if he was teasing her.

"What makes you think I'd be that kind to you, Sam?" She lowered the barrel of the gun. "I was thinking of making it as slow and agonizing as possible. I'd enjoy imagining you suffered a great deal before you went to the devil."

His face blanched as he caught the aim of the weapon. He stumbled backwards a few steps. "Maybe this vengeance thing isn't such a good idea, Amanda. Listen to the priest. You wouldn't want to be joining me in purgatory, would you?"

She gave him a wicked grin, re-aimed the small gun, and slowly pulled the trigger.

A woman screamed, and Sam yelped in pain. "God damn it, woman, you shot me in the foot!"

Amanda tossed her head and walked away from him. He hobbled about behind her.

"You're lucky I'm such a poor shot, I was aiming higher." She rubbed her hands together; they were still stinging from the recoil of the Colt.

"Lucky? You just shot me." Sam sat down in a chair and looked at his boot, which was leaking blood.

"I wanted to do more damage, but I've never been good with guns. Here Father, you can have me locked up now." She handed the gun to Father Mikelson and stood patiently, waiting for the sheriff to come and arrest her. Glancing back at Sam with his face contorted in pain, she didn't experience the sense of satisfaction she had imagined she would feel. She'd thought a tiny spike of happiness would follow pulling the trigger. She'd craved revenge, and she should be enjoying it. In fact, watching Sam remove his boot, seeing how much agony it caused him, her head started to ache and the smell of gunpowder, sweat, and stale beer nearly made her gag.

The priest grabbed the gun and scowled at her. "What kind of damned foolishness have you got yourself into here, Amanda?"

Amanda closed her eyes and put her hand to head. "I have a headache, Father. Can we discuss this tomorrow when I make my confession?"

Father Mikelson pointed toward Sam. "Did you say that man has taken advantage of you?"

Amanda groaned, her patience with all men, even those who represented God, nearly at an end.

"That's what I said. He seduced me, Father. Knows me, in the biblical sense. We had carnal relations." Cold seeped into her bones and her heart thundered. She was out of patience and wanted to shock the old man. "He's been in my bed and we have engaged in fornication!" She took a ragged breath in a futile attempt to regain her composure.

The crowd exploded into loud speculation. Amanda

thought this night would never end.

Father Mikelson narrowed his icy blue eyes as he glanced around the saloon. "Quiet," he boomed again, and the crowd silenced.

"Amanda, you've done some foolish things in the past, but this is beyond my comprehension. I'm just grateful your father isn't here to witness these events." He drew himself up to his full six feet, three inches of height. "But he expected me to take care of you, to protect you as if you were my own daughter, and that's exactly what I'm going to do."

"Can't we please talk about this in the morning? Shooting a man is exhausting." Her legs felt heavy as trees and her teeth were starting to chatter. She turned to leave, deciding she could go to the sheriff herself, perhaps in the morning, after she'd rested a bit.

"Stay here." The priest demanded, waving his hand at the gathered crowd. "Be silent, the lot of you." He pointed at Sam. "Are you confessing to fornicating with this woman, outside of the bonds of holy wedlock?"

Sam looked horrified at the question, and Amanda felt the blood drain from her face. Just when she imagined the humiliation couldn't possibly get any worse, by some uncanny force of nature, it did. She wondered if she could wrestle the gun from Father Mikelson so she could shoot herself.

The priest grabbed Amanda by the arm and dragged her to the table where Sam sat. He'd removed his boot and had a dirty, blood-stained cloth wrapped around his foot. Someone had poured him a tall glass of whiskey and left the bottle nearby.

Sam glared at her. "Are you crazy, Amanda? You didn't really have to shoot me."

Amanda glared back at him, her hands planted firmly on her hips. "Beware a woman scorned. You know the saying, don't you, Sam?"

The priest stood in front of them with arms outstretched.

"Dearly beloved, we are gathered here today in the sight of these witnesses to..."

Blood turned to ice in Amanda's veins. "What are you doing, Father?" Her words came out in a high-pitched screech.

"I'm performing a marriage, because I feel compelled to bring you two sinners back into the fold. You have both participated in fornication." He seemed to relish saying the word. "It's my duty to make sure such a sin is purified by the sacrament of marriage."

"The hell you are." Sam tried to struggle to his feet, then fell back into the chair.

Amanda turned to race out of the saloon. Before she could escape she felt the priest's iron grasp on her arm. His face hovered over hers, his cold blue eyes snapping. "I will not have you traveling about the territory a ruined woman, Amanda. You will become this man's wife and behave in a decent manner from now on."

Amanda tried to pull away. "You can't make me marry him. I won't!" She balled her fists and stomped her foot. "I'm tired of doing what everyone else says I'm supposed to do. I refuse."

Father Mikelson didn't release her; he simply plopped her down in a chair next to Sam.

"You'll do what I say, and so will he. Or I'll have the law after both of you. There is such a thing as common decency and standards of behavior to consider. I'll haul you both before the justice of the peace. You could go to jail."

Amanda crossed her arms and turned away from Sam. "I'd rather rot in jail than become his wife."

"I'd rather hang than become that woman's husband," Sam

snarled.

"Well, if that's the way you want it. Sheriff, get over here." Father Mikelson waved toward the swinging doors. "Arrest this woman for lewd behavior, and this man for fornication. Slap them both in jail, in fact"—a wicked gleam twinkled in the old man's eyes— "put 'em in the same cell, then throw away the key."

Sam and Amanda both turned back to face him. "You can't do this," she said.

"Put me in jail, but leave her alone," Sam said. Father Mikelson shook his head. "I can't punish one and not the other, because you know how the old saying goes, it takes two. Justice and grace demand that since you both got yourselves into this mess, you both must perform the penance. The only solution I can see is to marry you to each other. From the looks of things, that should be a satisfactory punishment."

"That's an idiotic solution." Amanda stood up. "Let him go, and I'll return to Helena. I'll join the Sisters of Charity and become a nun."

Sam waved a hand in the air. "Wait, that's not necessary." He leaned toward Amanda. "Don't do this. You can't lock yourself away from the world forever."

Amanda glared down at him. "I can't believe you care what happens to me. This is your entire fault in the first place. If you needed money so badly, why didn't you just ask me? I've got more than I'll ever need."

Sam shook his head. "I'd never take a penny of your money, Amanda. It wasn't about that, not after I met you." His shoulders stiffened and he raised his chin.

Amanda paced across the room and tried to ignore the staring crowd.

"If I had me a chance to get hitched to Sam Calhoun, I'd do

it in a heartbeat, honey," a blonde with a large bosom urged her. "Shotgun weddin' or no, he's a catch."

"Marry me instead, widder woman. I'd take care of you." A grizzled prospector with no front teeth leered at her.

Amanda didn't know what to do. She didn't want to go to jail, and she didn't think she wanted Sam to, either. Her thirst for revenge had slackened, and now she knew they needed some time to talk things over. Her heart ached at the truth of his deception; all her dreams for helping the miners had vanished in one ugly ruse. And her fantasy of building a life with Sam disappeared at the same time. But she also needed to give him a chance to explain why he'd made the bargain with the other mine owners. Despite his confession, she knew deep inside that Sam would never intentionally betray her. Or was that just what she wanted to believe?

She wished she could go to bed and sleep for a few weeks. Maybe she'd find this had been a bad dream, and she'd wake up in Sam's arms in the morning.

More voices joined the melee, some urging her to marry Sam, others telling her to shoot him again, even others offering a different solution. Her head ached and her stomach churned at the combined stench of unwashed bodies, sour beer, and filthy sawdust.

She turned to Father Mikelson. "Can't you give us until tomorrow to work this out? We shouldn't be forced to make this kind of decision under these circumstances." She nodded at Sam, hoping he'd agree. "It's going to affect the rest of our lives."

Sam nodded back. "We need to talk, and we can't do it here, Father." He stood up, grimaced, but managed to step forward. "I give you my pledge of honor I'll make things right with Amanda. I'll do the honorable thing."

Amanda made a sound of derision and rolled her eyes. "You can certainly trust him, Father. I did."

Father Mikelson cleared his throat. "I've given it some thought, considered the circumstances, and taken all the particulars into account."

Amanda held her breath.

"I believe I've made the right decision."

Amanda gulped, but stood poised for his pronouncement.

"Dearly beloved, we are gathered here together in the sight of these witnesses to join this man and this woman in the state of holy matrimony."

The floor slipped from beneath Amanda as she fainted.

Chapter Eleven

Sam wiped the sweat from his forehead as he limped across the street. He stumbled several times, favoring his wounded foot, but he refused to ask for help.

A tight-lipped and pale Amanda walked ahead of him with the priest. They'd passed smelling salts beneath her nose to bring her out of the swoon. She'd been so horrified at the proceedings she'd barely been capable of uttering a word. Her eternal vows to love and obey him were repeated in a hoarse whisper, and then only at the stern insistence of Father Mikelson.

Sam grimaced in pain when he crossed the threshold of the Parmeter House. He found Harriet staring at them from behind the desk. A look of sympathy crossed her face when Amanda passed, but open loathing replaced it when he halted at the bottom of the stairs to take a deep breath.

"I can explain everything," Sam closed his eyes for a moment, wounded by his friend's apparent disgust with his conduct.

Harriet pursed her lips and glowered. "You don't owe me an explanation, nor any apology." She pointed toward Amanda. "But you'd better have a powerful good reason for what you did to her."

Sam trailed up the stairs, favoring his right foot. He understood Amanda's fury and her motive for shooting him. Even if he wasn't responsible for the rumors that had destroyed her good name tonight. The fact that he'd entered into the agreement in the first place proved he was a lying, deceitful bastard. He deserved to be shot, and worse.

It wasn't the shooting he regretted; it was the wedding. By forcing her to become his wife, even through circumstances beyond his control, he knew he'd manipulated her. And the one thing he'd learned about Amanda was how much she despised lies and manipulation.

Father Mikelson conversed with Amanda before opening the door to her room, and Sam tried to avoid eavesdropping.

"I'll deal with this, Amanda. You needn't worry," the priest promised, before turning his back on her. He seemed surprised to discover Sam standing so close. "I thought we should find someplace a bit more private than the center of a saloon to discuss our business." There was no sympathy in the older man's eyes, and ice in his tone.

Sam produced a key and unlocked the door next to Amanda's room, then nodded for the priest to enter. Father Mikelson couldn't disguise the look of fury crossing his face as he realized the arrangement. Once inside the room, Sam collapsed on the bed, grateful for the opportunity to finally rest his aching foot. He didn't open his eyes until Father Mikelson cleared his throat. It took all of Sam's self-control to pull himself back up to a sitting position.

Father Mikelson had settled himself into a chair closer to the bed. He knotted his thick eyebrows, and a thin smile revealed several deep dimples in his still handsome face, despite his age. His expression appeared to hold a little compassion, and it shocked Sam. Years of serving as an altar boy had taught him how rigid and uncompromising a man of God could be.

The priest crossed his arms and cleared his throat again.

"I suppose you wonder why I would force Amanda to be married to a man who seduced her then sullied her reputation by boasting about it."

Sam pulled off his hat and flung it towards the foot of the bed. He slowly combed his hand through his hair. "It has crossed my mind there might be some ulterior motive to your actions. Considering that a lying, dishonest bastard might not be your first choice as a suitable husband for Amanda. Nor hers for that matter." He narrowed his eyes and gave the priest a hard look. "I never said anything about seducing her, despite what you might think."

Father Mikelson surprised him with an understanding smile that softened the hard planes of his face somewhat. "Actually, I believe you, Samuel. But I'm hopeful we gave folks a good show tonight."

Sam couldn't form a response. *Show?* Was this entire ugly incident something Amanda had cooked up to humiliate him? Maybe she wasn't an innocent victim after all.

"I've heard from my contact here that there have been serious threats against Amanda since she arrived in Willow Creek. Apparently, you know something about them?" The priest folded his hands into a tent that made him appear to be pausing to pray.

Sam considered the question for a moment. "There's a group of local mine owners opposed to her Miners' Benevolent Association, and they did approach me. They offered me a substantial sum of money to seduce her and destroy her reputation."

Sam pulled his legs over the edge of the bed and leaned forward to gauge the reaction of the good father a bit closer.

"Why do I have a feeling there's more to the story than you're letting on?"

Father Mikelson stood up, casting a long shadow, and paced across the room. "So you did what you were paid to do?"

Sam's spine stiffened and anger shot through him. "I've been protecting her, and I never told a soul what transpired between us." He took a deep breath. "It wouldn't take a genius to figure it out though, and I never should have moved in here with her."

Father Mikelson studied him carefully, frowning before giving a sigh and slumping his shoulders. "Then you do care for her?"

Sam swallowed, trying to buy time to compose himself and come up with a reasonable story. His life depended upon subterfuge. The future of his country might depend upon how well he played a role. He didn't want to divulge his true feelings for Amanda. He'd only just come to terms with them himself. Yet the priest obviously trusted him, so he would have to confess. This was a time for total honesty. He met Father Mikelson's brilliant blue eyes.

"I love her."

The words freed him the moment he uttered them. His heart felt lighter and the darkness of his soul brighter. Why didn't he have the courage to tell Amanda how he really felt?

"Good, that will make this easier." Father Mikelson sat back down in his chair. He didn't appear startled by Sam's declaration.

"I've had a man keeping an eye on Amanda these past few weeks. He's given me regular reports, including his observation that she appeared to be, um"—his face went red— "involved with a gentleman."

Sam briefly wondered just how close the scrutiny had been, and he frowned.

"The impeccable Mr. Penny, I suppose?"

Father Mikelson shook his head. "He's employed by Amanda, and he refused to divulge any information about her daily affairs." The priest blushed. "Well, her *activities*. Penny wouldn't say a word. He's a little weasel as far as I'm concerned, but apparently a faithful weasel. We couldn't even drag your name out of him and ended up having to pay someone for information about you."

Sam shook his head and scowled; the priest wasn't making any sense. "You knew about me before tonight?"

Father Mikelson placed his hands on his knees. "I wouldn't have performed that ceremony if I'd believed you were taking advantage of my girl. Despite what Amanda thinks, I'm very fond of her." His eyes went misty for a moment. "I've known her since she was a child."

"Then why did you force her to become my wife if you don't believe I attempted to destroy her reputation?" His voice was harsh with anger, but for Amanda's sake, not his. She had been manipulated by more than one person tonight. He rubbed his aching foot and wondered if priestly vows would be sufficient to protect Father Mikelson from Amanda's wrath.

The older man laughed deeply, and the sound couldn't have shocked Sam more if he'd let loose with a string of profanity.

"Amanda is a poor judge of what's good for her. I allowed her to make a terrible mistake once when she married Arthur Wainwright. I tried to talk her father out of that arranged marriage. Arthur was too old and too debauched for an innocent young woman, but all Adam could see was the cementing of a great dynasty." He stared off into space and slumped in the straight-backed chair. His bright blue eyes clouded over, and the wrinkles on each side of his face seemed to grow deeper.

"I would never allow her to sell herself again." He shook his white head. "I performed that marriage ceremony tonight to protect her, and now"—he leaned forward again— "I'm going to beg for your assistance."

Sam wanted to fall back on the pillow, close his eyes, and digest this last tidbit of information. If Amanda's life were still in danger, he'd find a way to keep her safe.

"I don't know how you're going to get Amanda's permission to let me near her again."

"Amanda chose you, for reasons I can't know. She'll come around, as women do. But, since you're in a position to be of assistance to her, I thought I'd make you a handsome offer."

Offer? Was he trying to buy Sam's services the same way the mine owners had? Hell, he was getting tired of being set out to stud.

"I doubt I'd be interested in anything that would involve lying to Amanda again." He cocked an eyebrow at Father Mikelson. "I believe I've learned my lesson on that one. She might not adjust her aim the next time."

The priest laughed. The sound was full, vibrant, and oddly comforting to Sam's ears.

"Let me just tell you what I have in mind, Sam." He made that prayer tower with his hands. "Stay married to Amanda and pretend that, although things aren't what you expected, you're going to make the best of the situation. Act the perfect husband in public. Maybe you could even soften her attitude a little. Be attentive. From the things I've heard about you, you're a man who knows what a woman appreciates."

Sam raised an eyebrow. "Everyone except Amanda seems to think so, anyway."

Father Mikelson bent closer, his voice softer, as though he thought someone might be trying to listen in on their conversation. Sam's attention shifted to the door dividing his room from Amanda's, and he wondered if the priest might be right.

"The only thing I'll ask is that you not assert your..." He glanced down at the floor, clearly embarrassed. "Husbandly rights."

Sam coughed and tried to keep the grin off his face. He wanted to remind the priest that if he hadn't been asserting those same rights, he wouldn't be in this predicament right now.

"Let me get this straight, you forced me to marry Amanda because I was involved in, what did you call it?" He pretended to search his memory for the words. It wasn't likely he'd ever forget the scene in the saloon. "Oh, *fornicating* with her. But now that I'm her husband, you're asking me to abstain from having relations and to keep my hands off her?"

The priest blushed, then nodded his head. Obviously, a man who was celibate had no problem making such a request. It irked Sam though, and he had no intention of making such an agreement.

"She's my wife and I have every intention of living with her within the bounds of a normal marriage." He drew his hand through his hair in agitation. "And that certainly means making love to her, when I finally manage to convince her marrying me isn't the biggest curse ever thrown upon her."

"You can't." Father Mikelson was adamant.

"The hell I can't, she's my wife." Sam wished his foot didn't hurt so badly. He'd get up and stomp right out of the room.

The priest shook his head, any previous good humor dissolving as his skin turned ashen. "It's possible we can get the marriage annulled if you don't, well, you know, with her, again." He coughed into his hand. "Stay out of her bed, Sam, and I might be able to release her from her marriage vows when I know she's safe again."

Sam frowned. "I've already been with her, Father. She confessed that in front of you and half the town tonight. I don't think an annulment is going to be the solution to our dilemma."

Father Mikelson's body sagged, and suddenly he seemed ten years older. "I know it would be a lie. But I'm willing to atone with time in purgatory so Amanda can be happy. She deserves some happiness." His mouth dipped. "Do you really think, my son, that you can do that? Do you believe you can make her happy?"

The old man's words burned their way to Sam's heart. Could he? What kind of sacrifices would he be willing to make to see Amanda truly happy?

The question haunted Sam through the long, lonely night.

∞∞∞

Amanda tossed her boot across the room and swore. How had she allowed this to happen to her again? Circumstances had swallowed her up and drowned her in events seemingly beyond her control. But she knew better. She was just too weak and afraid to resist.

Now she found herself married against her wishes to a man she despised. It was worse than becoming Arthur's wife, because in her innocence, she'd held illusions about that union, and while they later were dispelled, at least the truth hadn't spoiled her wedding night.

She flung her other boot across the room and leaned back against the pillows. She wondered what Father Mikelson was saying to Sam. Maybe her husband was kneeling in front of the priest repeating a litany of his sins and offenses and begging for mercy. She hoped the old priest gave him enough *Hail Marys* and *Our Fathers* to keep him kneeling there until next week.

She supposed it would be her turn in the morning. *Forgive me, Father, for I have sinned. I tried to murder my husband last night, but since he wasn't my husband until after the attempt, could I be exonerated?*

It was all Sam's fault. He lied to her, deceived her with all his pretty words and slippery charm, then dragged her name through the mud with his male bragging. She should have aimed for his heart.

She had a nagging suspicion though, when she replayed events in her mind, that some of the responsibility could be shuffled onto her own shoulders. Of course, planning to seduce her for money was a horrible thing to do. But, when she finally made her confession to the priest, she'd need to be honest and admit the seduction was as much her fault as his. She had wanted Samuel Calhoun with a fierce, hungry desire that frightened her even now.

Seduction could only be successful with a willing accomplice, despite what she wanted to believe to maintain her rage. She should hate Sam with every fiber of her being. But—if she were truly honest with herself, she'd been a compliant partner in the lovemaking. Even now, the door between their rooms was a lovely temptation. She knew the pleasures that stood beyond that portal, and it took all of her self-control to keep it locked.

She was going to keep the door shut and Sam out of her bed, despite their marriage vows. In her opinion, they were meaningless unless uttered with complete conviction. She'd been forced to marry Sam, but no one on earth could make her act like a wife.

It was a desperate measure, and she could only imagine Sam's reaction. At first, disbelief. Then, he'd try to charm his way into her bed again. He'd ply her with soft words and gentle caresses. She stiffened, and her bones began to melt at the memory of Sam's kisses. But she would remain a bastion of virtue. This time, she promised herself, there would be no surrender.

She closed her eyes and tried to forget the pleading in Sam's eyes when he'd begged her to believe him. What had he said? That he'd never hurt her? More empty promises and sweet words from the master of lies. She clenched her fists. He had destroyed her life, taken her autonomy, and changed everything because it suited his purpose.

Revenge burned in her soul. She wanted him to suffer, to agonize, and to come crawling to her on his knees, begging for forgiveness. A weak plea in front of witnesses would never suit her; she wanted to inflict heartache and pain. She wanted him to feel all the hurt that spiraled up from her belly to encase her heart in ice.

She sat up with a jerk and twisted her hair in panic. How could she make him suffer if she never let him near her? How could she get revenge if she ignored him? And would she be able to resist him if she did allow him to cross that threshold?

She stood up and paced across the room, leaning her ear against the door to eavesdrop. There was only silence. Sam was over there, his lean, muscular body stretched across the bed the way he once stretched across her naked body. She wet her lips and wondered if she should knock. Perhaps he'd passed out from the pain of the gunshot? Although the doctor had simply declared it a flesh wound, dumped whiskey on it, and continued his quest to drink himself into oblivion.

Still, she was responsible for his injury, and she was his wife. Despite the fact that she wasn't inclined to fulfill her obligations in that arena, shouldn't she at least discover if he were conscious?

She reached down to unlock the door and a knock startled her. She jumped back.

"Amanda, open this door."

Obviously, Sam was cognizant enough to believe he had a God-given right to order her around.

"Go away, Sam. I have nothing to say to you." She made a face when she realized he'd know she'd been hovering on the other side, waiting for him to call out to her. There was a moment of silence, then she heard a shuffling.

"Please, darlin'. Let's talk. I promise I won't do anything to hurt you."

Amanda took a deep breath. "I don't think I could ever believe another promise you made. Leave me alone, Sam." She turned away from the door, determined to go to bed and pretend this horrible night had never happened.

"Darlin'"—his voice was gentle and persuasive— "I need to explain some things to you. We're married now, and you have the right to know the truth about me." He paused. "I'll never touch you again unless you ask me to. You can trust me on that, Amanda. Now please open the door."

She considered her options. She could just climb into bed and ignore him. Then again, he was right about one thing—they were married, and she would have to deal with that reality sooner or later.

She turned the key and swung the door open. He stood, framed by the soft glow of the lamp, his dark hair tousled and his face grave with pain and worry.

She fought the urge to run forward and wrap her arms around him. She wanted to place her ear against his chest, to listen to the cadence of his heart beating, a sound that never failed to comfort her.

His amber eyes reflected sadness as he met her gaze. "Honey, you've got to believe me, I never planned for this to happen."

Amanda backed away from him. Her entire body felt broken from the pain of his betrayal, and her head throbbed. "Well, at least you had some kind of plan, didn't you, Sam?" She turned to face the bed. "But the question is, what in heaven's name are we going to do now?"

Chapter Twelve

Amanda sensed him standing behind her, the warmth of his body reminding her of the long, intimate nights they had shared. She wanted to stay angry at him, but her heart fluttered and her skin tingled. She needed to gain control of herself. Spinning on her heel, she stepped close enough to jab a finger toward his chest.

"How does it feel to become one of the richest men in Montana with just a few empty promises and lies? You'll never have to sell yourself again, Sam. In fact, you can buy everything you've ever wanted." She took a step back in disgust, her eyes flickering to his face to catch his astonished expression. "But wealth is a two-edge sword, *darlin'*, and it'll buy you more pain than you can imagine." She crossed the room and settled herself onto the bench at her dressing table.

Sam seemed frozen to the spot. She waved a hand toward the bed.

"You'd better sit down before you pass out. You're looking a bit pale."

Sam limped his way to the bed. She should have offered to help him, but her anger kept her rooted to her seat, waiting for his response. He grimaced before settling himself onto the bed, and she averted her eyes. She'd be damned if she would summon even one ounce of sympathy for this man. He'd deceived her, used her for his own purposes, and she intended to remain furious with him.

When she finally looked at him, he wasn't quite as pale, and the lines of pain had eased a bit.

"I never planned to marry you, Amanda. And I certainly don't want any of your damned money."

She pursed her lips. "Why thank you, Sam. That certainly makes me feel so much better." Folding her arms across her bosom, she gave him a cold glare.

His golden eyes clouded, and he shook his head. "I'm not doing a very good job at apologizing, am I?"

Amanda tossed her head and frowned. "I suspect you don't have much experience with apologies."

A slow, sad smile crossed his face. "You're right about that. I've always considered an apology to be a waste of time. It doesn't fix what you've done, and it can't really make the other person any happier about the circumstances."

Amanda stood up and turned to confront him, anger quickening her heart.

"I never asked for anything but protection from you, Sam. I expected you to keep me safe, but you used me as if I were a cheap whore, then told everyone in town about us. You forced me into a marriage I never wanted, and if you can't manage a simple apology for that, then get out of my room right now."

Sam dropped his head and a dark lock of hair fell forward to obscure his face. When he lifted his gaze, a pleading look illuminated the depths of his eyes.

"I truly care about you, Amanda." His voice was soft, the tone begging her to understand. "I didn't brag about being with you. I told you before, our time together holds some of the best memories of my life. I wouldn't share them with anyone."

She wanted to believe him. The tone of his voice, the look in his eyes, they all begged for her forgiveness. Her breasts ached for his touch as warmth cascaded through her body, the heat pooling to moisten the place between her legs. Yet how many times had she believed his lies? Did she really even know the real Samuel Calhoun?

"But you did agree to seduce me for money, didn't you, Sam?" She trembled with the question because the answer terrified her.

He never blinked. He just rubbed his chin with one hand. Finally, he shrugged.

"I agreed to bed the Widow Wainwright, then ruin her reputation by boasting about it. The hope was that you'd go running out of Willow Creek and forget all about the Miners' Benevolent Association."

The heat suffusing Amanda's body exploded into a flash of anger so overwhelming it sucked the air from her lungs. Fury blinded her. She picked up the first item she could find, which happened to be her silver hairbrush. She flung it at him. He dodged, but that increased her wrath. She reached for a bottle of lilac water.

"Wait a minute, Amanda."

She flung the crystal container and he caught it, but the stopper had come loose, soaking his shirt with the scented liquid. He took a quick step sideways, moving in time to avoid the porcelain hair receiver, which whizzed by his head and splintered against the wall.

Amanda searched for something heavier, something that could inflict some real damage on Sam's thick skull. She rummaged through a trunk and pulled out her beautiful china doll. For an instant, she considered tossing it at Sam. But she looked at the toy and realized she was acting like a spoiled child. Grown women did not indulge in temper tantrums.

Turning, she was startled to find Sam standing directly behind her. His hands snaked out to grasp her wrists, and his face was flushed, almost feverish looking.

"I said my plans involved the *Widow Wainwright.* I didn't know anything about you, Amanda. I thought you were some snooty rich woman, hell-bent on changing this town to make yourself feel better. But after we met in the kitchen, after you told me about your sham of a marriage to Arthur—"

He stepped closer, his lips brushing her hair. She struggled, but even though he was in a weakened state, she was no match for Sam's strength.

"After I made love to you and started to care about you, Amanda, I knew I couldn't go through with the plan." He released her, and she took a stumbling step back, falling onto the bench and staring up at him.

He fell to his knees in front of her and took her hands gently in his. "You were in my office the day I told the other mine owners I refused to go along with our agreement. Remember how they stormed out of there?"

"I saw some angry men leaving your office, but..." She closed her eyes. Sam's words echoed in her heart. *After I started to care about you.* Her heart wanted to accept his words, to imagine that after they had become friends, then lovers, he wouldn't deceive her. Her head reminded her she couldn't trust her own judgment. She had been wrong before.

He touched her cheek, and she opened her eyes. "I want to believe you, Sam, but there have been so many lies." Tears prickled at the back of her eyes, but she fought for control. She refused to cry in front of him.

"I don't know if I can ever trust you again. I don't think I even believe what you're telling me right now." She studied his expression, then shook her head at him.

"I don't know what to do, Sam. I need some time." She rubbed her throbbing forehead. "Please, can't we talk about his tomorrow? I'm so tired."

Sam stood up, a painful grimace crossing his face. A small surge of pity jolted through her, but she pushed it away. She did need to sort out her feelings regarding Sam, but not tonight. She was too emotionally overwrought to make any decisions about their future. Too torn about what she felt for him. "You'd better get to bed yourself; you've had a rough day." She purposely inserted a sarcastic note in her voice.

Sam hobbled toward the door separating their rooms and glanced over his shoulder. "You don't have to believe anything I've told you but believe this. I won't let anyone hurt you. Ever. I can promise you that, Amanda."

Amanda followed him to the door and slammed it shut behind him, turning the iron key in the lock, then leaning back against it. Tears silently slid down her cheeks as she realized the only person who could truly hurt her was standing on the other side of that doorway.

∞∞∞

Amanda refused to play the dutiful wife and did everything in her power over the next few days to humiliate Sam. She spurned the offer of his arm when they entered the dining room. She ate her meals in pained silence. And whenever she had the opportunity, she needled him with a sarcastic remark or a short, curt answer to his questions.

People stopped to offer congratulations or sympathy, depending upon their mood. One grizzled old man walked up to them, shook Amanda's hand, and told her he was "damned pleased you shot that son-of-a-bitch, 'cause I been wantin' to do it for months." At night she slammed the door in Sam's face and ignored his pleas to discuss the state of their marriage. She threw herself into the management of The Willow Creek Miners' Benevolent Association, and often returned to her office to work with Mr. Penny until nearly midnight.

It irritated her to leave the association, only to discover Sam quietly smoking his cigar on the other side of the street, maintaining a vigil. He escorted her back to the hotel, begging her to talk to him with each step. She maintained a tightlipped silence and tried to ignore his pleas for forgiveness. Yet, her attitude grew softer. He patiently waited upon her, gently abided her rudeness, and quietly endured her bad humor. She fought an ever-growing battle within herself, wanting to maintain a cold indifference, yet yearning to give him a small bit of encouragement.

Today was no different, and she drummed her fingers on the maple counter while considering her dilemma. What was she going to do about Sam? It was a constant source of concern and trepidation.

The ringing of the doorbell startled her out of her revelry. It was a rare sound, since the men who now came to the Miners' Association felt welcome enough to enter without the need to request permission by pulling the bell.

Caleb's dark head bobbed up from behind a stack of clothing. "You want I should get that, ma'am?"

Amanda smiled at her young assistant. Despite all of the trouble in her life, her success with Caleb McQueen was one bright note. He had become her faithful companion, good friend, and adept student. The growing warmth of their relationship a bright spot in an otherwise dreary emotional landscape.

She smoothed her dress and nodded. "Perhaps it's a new miner, someone who doesn't understand this building belongs to everyone and there's no need to stand on formality. Do invite him in, Caleb."

She stared at the ledger in front her and frowned. Mr. Penny had brought the figures to her this morning, telling her it appeared the Silver Slipper Mine was producing less ore than last month. The large vein could be petering out, and he suggested letting some of the men go. The decision haunted her. How could she take a man's job away? How could she fulfill her pledge to make the lives of these miners better, then snatch their very living from them?

A group of women entered the room behind Caleb, and Amanda's jaw dropped in surprise. She had asked many of the miners to invite their wives, daughters, and sisters to the association, but up to this point, none of the women had presented themselves. She didn't know if it was because of the building, or her own questionable reputation.

An older woman stepped forward, offered her hand to Amanda, and gestured toward the others.

"Good afternoon, Mrs. Calhoun, we've been told you wanted to meet with some of the womenfolk. So we come to offer you our best wishes on your recent marriage." She smiled tentatively. "We come to give you our thanks, too, for the things you're doin' for our menfolk."

A flash of triumph rippled through Amanda. This was the very thing she'd been hoping for, an opportunity to talk to the women of Willow Creek.

Bustling from behind the counter, she removed her apron and offered her hand to the woman who had spoken.

"I'm so pleased you've come. Won't you stay and have tea with me?" She signaled the young man standing behind her. "Go put the teakettle on, Caleb, then run over to the hotel and tell Harriet I have some special guests. Ask her if she could please send over a pie."

The spokeswoman looked horrified. “Oh, Mrs. Calhoun, you don’t need to go to all that trouble.”

Amanda took the woman’s rough hand in hers. “Please say you’ll stay, I’ve hardly had any female visitors since I’ve been in town, and I do so miss talking with other ladies.”

“If you’re sure it won’t be no trouble, I guess we can stay.” She grinned at the other women. “We ain’t the sort who get invitations to fancy tea parties everyday, that’s for sure.”

Several of the other women giggled, and Amanda gave them all a warm smile. “You know who I am, now please tell me your names.”

The leader looked mortified. “I’m so sorry, that sure was rude of me to come bustin’ in here and never even mention who we are.”

Amanda pulled her toward the dining room and waved her other hand. “Please don’t worry about that, we can take all the time we need to get acquainted. I’m so hungry for female companionship, I could just cry sometimes.”

After uttering the words, Amanda realized the truth of the matter. For the past week, she’d been shutting herself in her room or trying to forget her troubles by working all of the time. She had brushed off Harriet’s offers to talk, and refused any real conversation with Sam. She was lonely.

The women stood around the huge mahogany dining table and gawked at the furnishings in the room. Amanda was keenly aware of the bright red and gold flocked wallpaper, the gaudy beaded trim on the burgundy velvet drapes, and the overabundance of gilt. She was about to apologize for the state of the building when the woman she had escorted into the room cleared her throat.

“I’m Margaret Abbott. You’ve met my son, Walter.” A bright look of pride shone in her eyes. “He works for your husband over at the lumber mill."

Amanda's cheeks grew warm at the reference to her *husband*. She never thought of Sam as her husband. At the mention of the word, her first reaction was always to think of Arthur.

"A very nice young man." Amanda tried to keep her expression and voice nonchalant.

"This is my daughter-in-law, Sarah." Margaret indicated a very pregnant woman who looked younger than Amanda. For a moment, a flash of jealousy jolted through her. The desire for children reminded her of the cruel twist her life had taken, trapping her in another loveless marriage. But she gave Sarah a bright smile. "It appears congratulations are in order for you."

Sarah dropped her head and blushed, and the other women giggled.

"Sarah didn't think it was proper for her to be callin' on a new bride, but I said, best you know what you're in for."

A petite woman with carefully arranged dark curls offered her hand to Amanda. "My name is Lydia Brown, my husband is Sherman. Perhaps you've met him?"

Amanda nodded. "Perhaps, there are so many..." Lydia interrupted her. "You'd remember my Sherman. He's so handsome, so very charming."

"Don't mind her," Margaret said, "she's only been married a month. She's a new bride, just like you, and we know how starry-eyed you ladies can get." She waved a finger at Lydia. "Mrs. Calhoun is likely saying all them things about her Sam, too."

There was more laughter, and Amanda felt trapped. Handsome? Sam was surely that. And he had more charm than any man should legally be allowed to possess. That was the problem. Of course, she could also add deceitful, arrogant, and manipulative to the list. She suspected Lydia harbored warmer feelings toward her Sherman than she did toward Sam.

Disconcerted by her own bitterness, Amanda changed the topic of conversation. "And the final member of your entourage, who might this be?" She turned to a stately older woman, dressed in black.

Margaret made the introduction. "This is Katherine Foley, her husband was killed in a cave-in not long ago."

Amanda dropped her gaze. A cave-in, one of the most feared events in a miner's life. Crushed by rock, or smothered due to lack of air, it was a horrible way to die. Bright tears shone in Katherine's eyes, and a warm rush of sympathy coursed through Amanda. She couldn't relate to the loss of a lover, but Arthur had been a companion. She reached out to touch Katherine's glove gently.

"I asked to come, because I wanted to say how much I appreciate all the things you've done for my family." Katherine's voice trembled. "You've made it possible for us to stay on here in Willow Creek. The food, the clothing, the money you gave us..."

Amanda's backbone stiffened. How foolish she was, to waste so much time on the petty issues of her life. Women like Katherine Foley didn't know where their next meal was coming from, or if they'd have a roof over their heads tomorrow.

She touched Katherine's shoulder. "Let's be seated, ladies." Amanda nodded at the chairs placed around the table. "I'm glad you've come to see me, because to be honest, I desperately need your help."

"I want to do everything possible for the people who work for the Silver Slipper Mine. My late husband, Arthur Wainwright"—she took a deep breath and crossed herself— "may his eternal soul rest in peace, made me give him a deathbed promise." The other women were silent, raptly listening to her story.

"I came to Willow Creek to fulfill that promise, and despite everything that has happened, I plan to carry out Arthur's wishes. I have sufficient funds in an account for the Miners' Benevolent Association to provide for homes, a school, and a church."

Caleb entered with a silver tea tray. The young man was clean, well fed, and had a glow of happiness about him. When Amanda had discovered his father was a drunk who beat him several times each week, she'd allowed him to move into a room upstairs. Every afternoon she gave him lessons, and she'd discovered he had a quick, resourceful mind.

Settling the tea tray on the table, he pointed at the plate of biscuits, dish of clotted cream, and apple pie.

"Mrs. Parmeter said if this weren't—" Caleb stopped for a moment and blushed a beet red from the tips of his ears to the edge of his shirt collar. "*Wasn't* good enough, to send me back for more."

Amanda gave his shoulder a friendly pat. "This is wonderful, Caleb. Why don't you take a treat for yourself, then go ahead and finish what you were doing. Our lessons will be a little late today."

He gathered a handful of biscuits and ambled out of the room as she started to pour the tea.

"You've surely done wonders with that boy," Margaret said. "If I didn't hear you call him by name, I might not have knowed who he was."

Offering each of her guests a china cup and saucer, Amanda nodded. "He's a very special young man with immense potential. It's made me incredibly happy to be of assistance in helping to shape such a keen mind."

She handed a long silver knife to Margaret. "Would you mind serving the pie?"

Margaret visibly puffed up with pride. "Why, I'd be right honored." She lifted an eyebrow at Amanda. "Just hope I do it right. I never been around rich folk before."

Amanda lifted the cup of tea to her lips and blew gently. "Just remember, rich folks enjoy their pie just like everyone else. Make the pieces generous."

Her remark put the other women at ease, and before long they were lost in conversation, as Amanda outlined her plans for the town of Willow Creek. She caught their looks of relief when she mentioned recruiting a new doctor and the need for a hospital. Katherine clapped her hands at the announcement of a school and murmured that she'd been a teacher before she married. Amanda offered her a job and was thrilled when the widow accepted.

By the end of their tea party, the five women had mapped out a plan for transforming a rough, rollicking mining town into a small island of civilization in the wilderness of the Montana territory. With their promises of support, Amanda assured them she would pay for all of the improvements. She promised them nothing would stand in the way of the Miners' Association, because all of the money had been left in trust. She didn't mention Sam, but knew they'd surely heard the tale of his betrayal.

Finally, the women pushed back their chairs, and Margaret coughed discreetly and blushed. She twisted her hands, and Amanda couldn't imagine what was distressing the woman.

"There's just one more thing, Mrs. Calhoun."

"Please, call me Amanda." She stepped forward to grasp one of Margaret's hands. "We're all friends now. Don't be afraid to ask me for anything you need."

The other women giggled, and Katherine tried to hide her face behind her hand. "It's such an awful thing to ask, Margaret. Let's just be on our way."

Sarah pushed herself forward and placed her hands on her hips. "It's the main reason we came here in the first place, Mrs.—um, Amanda. And now that we got to know you, we're sorry, because you're not snooty or nothin'. But, well..." She turned pink.

"For heaven's sake." The shy Katherine shook her head and pursed her lips primly. "We all wanted to see the whorehouse."

Amanda stared back at them dumbstruck, then burst out laughing.

Katherine relaxed and laughed along with her, until finally the other women joined in.

"I would be happy to give you a tour, but I should warn you. Some of the pictures I left hanging upstairs are pretty risqué. I don't want to offend you."

Margaret gave her a gentle push toward the dining room arch. "We won't take no offense, we promise. But as God is my witness, I been so curious about his place, I could nearly burst."

Amanda held her hand to her lips to keep from dissolving into a fit of giggles again. Winking conspiratorially, she leaned towards her new group of friends.

"If you promise not to tell, I can share some of the stories about this place. I found a diary that belonged to one of the previous residents."

Amanda raised an eyebrow. "That is if I won't offend any of you ladies."

They dissolved into another fit of laughter, then plied her with questions about the furnishings in the hallway and the wallpaper, and she realized how much better she felt. Talking with other women had served as a balm for her soul.

Willow Creek was her home, at least for a while. She was going to make the best of her circumstances.

And maybe it was time to start talking to Sam again.

Chapter Thirteen

Amanda was in better spirits than she'd been since before her wedding. She cringed at the word wedding; it was a farce she and Sam had participated in. She still couldn't believe Father Mikelson had performed a marriage ceremony under such odd circumstances. She considered writing to the bishop to complain but found herself reluctant to get the priest in trouble with his religious superior. She had discovered a soft spot for the old man.

She briskly walked along the boardwalk to return to the Parmeter House, deciding she'd finally break her silence and speak to Sam tonight. For the first time in days, she was experiencing a warm, pleasant mood. She would deign to give him a few simple words. Nothing extravagant, because the man must be made to suffer for the humiliation he'd caused her. But a small phrase or comment wouldn't do much harm. She would offer him something that would make his eyes glow and his heart beat a bit faster. Then he would certainly double his efforts to enter into her good graces.

Amanda smiled to herself, imagining how grateful he would be for such a tidbit of her attention. He would probably beg for her forgiveness, or at the very least, for a kiss. She touched her finger to her lips and recalled how hot and eager one of Sam's kisses could be. A shiver of delight rippled through her.

She requested her mail at the large reception desk and found Robert studying her carefully, a frown creasing his usually friendly face.

She wrinkled her nose and grinned at him. "Have I acquired an outrageous growth on top of my head while I walked over here, sir?"

Robert stepped backward and fumbled with some papers stuffed beneath the counter. "Sorry, ma'am. I meant no offense."

Robert had always been gentle and most considerate when in her presence. She liked him. "I apologize, Robert. I was just teasing you."

"Unless of course there really is a growth upon my head, then I hope you'll tell me." She winked at him.

Robert smiled at her, then shot a worried look upstairs. Amanda frowned as she waited for him to say something. He returned to making a bigger mess of his papers.

"Yes ma'am, I mean, no—. He took a deep breath. "But, well..." He blinked at her. "Sam ain't a bad sort. He just seems kinda stuck in the past, and he's gotta hard time trustin' folks. He was a regular hero in the war, saved a bunch of men in his company and got captured for it." His voice took on a soothing tone as a glimmer of light reflected in his dark eyes.

Amanda was shocked. In their brief conversation about the war, Sam had never mentioned being heroic or saving anyone's life. Then again, Sam wasn't the type to brag about such things. He was an intensely private man. She really didn't know much about Samuel Calhoun and his life before they met.

Straightening her shoulders, she gave Robert a thin smile.

"I have no doubt Sam can be very heroic when it suits his purposes". She lifted the hem of her dress to climb the stairs.

"There are many things I don't know about my husband, Robert. I suppose it's time I learn more. We *are* married.

Amanda fumbled in her bag, searching for the key to her room. She listened carefully for any movement from the room adjacent to hers, wondering if Sam had returned yet. If he discovered she was back, he would probably start pounding on the door and insist upon speaking to her.

She smiled. Perhaps it was time she opened that door and listened. She'd been too angry with him before, but her good mood today tempered her rage. She needed to stop being so childish and accept her responsibilities as a wife.

Swinging the door open, she tossed her bag on the bed, unpinned her hat, and hung it on the bedpost. She leaned forward to examine herself in the mirror of the dressing table. She didn't much care for the image staring back at her. Dark smudges beneath her eyes illustrated her long, restless nights. She tossed and turned throughout the night, tortured by dreams of Sam. She imagined his strong, muscular arms tight around her, his hands caressing her body, and she woke up feverish and out of sorts.

She pinched her cheeks to force some color in them, then glanced back into the room reflected behind her. The view made her freeze. Turning slowly, she couldn't believe what she was seeing. Or rather—not seeing.

Sam's room was clearly visible to her. She could see the pitcher and bowl, the small oak dresser, and the large brass bed with a quilt stretched across it. Everything was neat, orderly, and perfectly in her view because there was no longer a door separating the two rooms.

Her good mood dissolved in a cloud of fury. She stalked to the threshold and stood, folding her arms across her bosom, as she examined the details carefully. There were clearly hinges on the door frame, but no wooden expanse or doorknob.

"God damn you to purgatory for a million years, Samuel Calhoun." She paced into the next room, ignoring the man's privacy. He'd given up that right when he removed the door. Not that there was anything in the room to disturb. A few clothes hung on pegs, a razor and shaving cup stood on the washstand.

This wasn't home to Sam, it was just a place to sleep. And a place to torment her, it seemed. She paced back into her own room.

Amanda turned slowly to stare at the open doorway again, and it fueled her anger even more. She was furious with Sam, nearly as furious as she'd been on the night she'd shot him. Their wedding night.

He was robbing her of all privacy. Just who did the man think he was? Did he imagine he could simply lie in there on his bed and enjoy the view of her disrobing every evening? Her nipples puckered against the fabric of her chemise at the thought of standing naked in front of Sam again. She tossed off the arousal. The man was an arrogant mule if he thought she would stand for this outrage. Her temper jabbed at her like a red-hot poker.

She marched out of her room, stomped down the stairs, and slapped her hands firmly on her hips as stood at the reception desk glaring at Robert. He swallowed, tried to avoid looking at her, and stuck his hands in his pockets.

"I seem to be missing my door, Robert." The man frowned.

"Are you missin' the outside door to the hallway, or the inside door, between the rooms?" He didn't seem very worried, either way.

Amanda narrowed her eyes. "I'm missing the interior door, the one that separates my room from Sam's room. I want it replaced immediately." She pitched her voice as threatening as possible.

Robert shook his head. "Can't be done."

Amanda thumped her fist on the counter. "I demand you return the door to my room." She glanced around the lobby. "And where is Harriet? I need to speak with her right away."

Robert studied the guest register. Apparently, he'd never seen it before. His expression was so serious, Amanda wondered if Generals Grant and Lee had signed in together today.

"Harriet had to go to Crooks Corners, and I don't expect her back for a few days." He gave Amanda a charming smile. "I'm in charge while she's gone." His chest puffed out a bit.

"Fine," she said, with as much patience as she could muster, "then please put the door in my room back on the hinges." She smiled. "I'm sure now that you and Sam have had your little amusement, you can fix my door. While I don't find your boyish prank very funny, I will play along. Ha, ha, the joke is on me." She pointed a finger at Robert. "Now give me back my door!"

"Sorry, darlin', but you'll have to deal with me to get your door and your privacy back."

A chill curled up her spine. Turning slowly, she faced Sam. Not the affable, charming Sam, but a cool, stone-faced Sam with hard eyes and an icy voice. He didn't look like he intended to budge one inch on this issue.

Amanda didn't care; she wanted her door back right now. It also occurred to her that she didn't need to spare this man any humiliation. She tossed her head, and a hot flash of anger rushed through her and warmed her cheeks. Her chest felt tight, as though a band were slowly choking the breath from her lungs. She swallowed the huge lump in her throat.

"Is that how you intend to exercise your conjugal rights, Sam, by ripping the door off the hinges so you can force your way into my bed?" Crossing the small space between them, she nearly spit in his eye. She glared up at his imposing form when the toes of their boots touched. He might be cold and angry, but she shook off a shiver rippling down her spine. She wasn't afraid of him. In fact, her body once again betrayed her when she caught the familiar scent of cigars and male musk that identified him.

Robert sputtered behind them, "I gotta get going!"

Light hit Sam's eyes. It was a signal that his cold disdain was turning to a white-hot anger. Good. She wanted to manipulate him. It would be good for him to find out how it felt to have someone else seize control of your emotions.

"If I intended to force myself upon you, madam, the deed would already be accomplished." He leaned down and whispered, "And despite what you think, there are some women in this town who appreciate my attention."

Amanda's cheeks turned hot and she was composing a scalding response when he raised his hands in surrender.

"Let's not make another scene for the town folk to witness. Would it be possible for us to argue in private for a change? I'll even loan you my weapon so you can shoot me again. But upstairs, if you don't mind."

She wanted to slap the sneer from his face, but Sam grasped her hand in his vise-like grip.

"Don't," he warned tersely, his manner formal. "We have to clear some things up between us. I think it's time you stopped acting like a spoiled child and talk to me."

"How dare you," she hissed, trying to move her hand toward the side of his face. But he was too quick for her and held tight to both her hands in one large fist.

Grabbing her elbow with his other hand, he guided her toward the stairs. Amanda tried to resist him, but he ignored her efforts, and her temper came to a full boil.

She twisted and fought against him, until he finally released her hands and she whacked him as hard as she could on the shoulder. He barely reacted to her assault. Instead, he leaned down and slipped his arms beneath her, sweeping her into his embrace to carry her up the stairs.

"Put me down!" She tried to squirm, but his arms wrapped her tight as leather cinches, holding her firmly.

"I seem to recall that on another occasion when I did this, you didn't protest whatsoever."

The shock of that memory silenced her. She recalled the fierce, passionate embrace in the kitchen and the eager coupling in her room that followed. Fire rushed through her limbs, making her blood boil. His hand cupped her bottom and she squirmed at the pressure of his touch, liquid heat pouring through her like lava to moisten the center of her womanhood.

Pausing in front of his door, Sam set her on her feet while he maintained a firm hold on her arm to prevent her from escaping. He opened the door and pushed her into the room. With one quick movement, he entered behind her, then tapped a booted heel against the door to slam it shut.

He tossed his hat on the bed and drew one hand through his hair.

"I know you're angry with me, Amanda, but this silent treatment has got to stop. We are married. Whether you like it or not. And there are issues that need to be sorted out." He paced across the room and pointed to the empty doorway.

"I took the door off the hinges so you would be forced to talk to me. I won't let you shut it in my face and ignore me any longer."

Amanda tossed her head and turned away from him. "I think you're wrong about that. Even if I can't keep a door between us, I can still refuse to speak to you."

His strong fingers gripped her shoulder firmly, and he forced her to turn toward him. His handsome face was a blaze of fury. He leaned forward, and the scent of tobacco and whiskey warned her to tread carefully.

"I can make you forget you're even mad at me, if I choose to."

Amanda laughed up at him. "You're so arrogant, so sure of yourself aren't you, Sam? Perhaps I'm now the one woman on God's green earth who is immune to your charms."

A flicker shot through his amber eyes—wild and a little bit frightening—reminding her of his stallion and the way the horse could keep the world at bay with his haughty attitude.

"Don't tempt me to prove that's a lie, Amanda."

She moved closer, the heat of their bodies now entwining, wrapping them both in a snare of anger and desire. "Is it a lie, Sam? Are you *that* sure of yourself?"

With one swift movement he pulled her closer and the warmth of his mouth found hers. She wanted to resist, attempted to pull away, but the dark, sultry taste of good Irish whiskey and pure male animal lust hypnotized her. The heat of his body turned her bones to liquid. He traced along the edge of her lips with his tongue, and in eager anticipation, she opened her mouth. She couldn't struggle; she wouldn't wrench herself from his arms, even though a small inner voice whispered a warning. The sweet agony of this kiss was too powerful, too intoxicating. She surrendered to the exciting, sensual magnetism. With a whimper, she wrapped her arms around his neck, eager to extend the moment.

When he finally lifted his lips from hers, he trailed them down to the soft crevice behind her ear. He gently licked along the length of her neck to the hollow of her throat. Throwing back her head, she invited him to explore further. She thrust her breasts forward, her body melting into his.

"Tell me you want me, Amanda. Say the words, or I'll stop right now. I promised I would never touch you again unless you gave me permission." His voice was husky with need. "Say it darlin' and let me make love to you."

His words jolted Amanda from her trance. She pushed hard against him and stepped back. She was ashamed of the way her body had just betrayed her. She wanted him to make love to her, desperately. It was a wild hunger, insatiable, uncontrolled, and destined to devour her if she didn't learn to govern it.

Backing away, she shook her head and waves of hair tumbled down around her shoulders. She didn't remember losing her hairpins. She'd been too caught up in the sensuality of the moment with Sam.

"No. I won't make that same mistake again, Sam. I won't let passion override my good judgment or common sense."

He took a ragged breath, letting one finger gently slide down her cheek. "God damn your good judgment and common sense, woman."

Amanda tried to smooth her disheveled appearance and cool her tender nerves. When he was this close, it took all of her self-control to keep from flinging herself back into his arms and begging for more kisses. It alarmed her that he had this kind of effect upon her. She took several steps away from him.

"You said you wanted to talk, remember?" She considered sitting on the bed, then thought of how vulnerable that might make her. She'd be defenseless against another caress, more kisses, and surely that would lead to a long, enchanting night of lovemaking. She took several more steps in the opposite direction, ending up at the now open doorway between their rooms.

"I want my door back. If talking to you will achieve that, then let's get on with it." She took a deep breath and made her voice as cool and composed as possible.

She glanced into her own room. Compared to Sam's neat and tidy abode, hers appeared to have been hit by a cyclone. She briefly wondered what he thought, then she pushed the concern away. Sam's opinion was no longer important. Lately, she'd become used to doing things her own way, and she'd made a momentous decision. She would never again change who she was to suit a man.

Sam paced the length of the room, glancing at her uneasily before he cleared his throat.

“Would you at least let me get you a chair?”

She nodded, and he placed a straight-backed maple chair in the doorway. It was neutral territory, a space for negotiations between warring factions. She smoothed her skirts and tilted her head up, signaling her willingness to give him her undivided attention.

The dark shadows reflected in his eyes nearly took her breath away.

“When I tried to apologize to you the other night, I made an even bigger mess of things. I want you to know how very sorry I am about this forced marriage. I know the priest was trying to do the right thing, to salvage your reputation.” He paced to the window and straightened his shoulders. “I can imagine how much you must hate me right now, and I don’t blame you a bit, Amanda.”

He moved to the bed, sat down, and placed his elbows on his knees, letting his hands drop between his legs. Warmth crept up Amanda’s face as she recalled the image of his powerful naked body sprawled across that same bed.

“I wouldn’t say I hate you, Sam.” She licked her lips and avoided meeting his eyes. “I’m just very angry about the way things have turned out between us. I believe I made it very clear to you that I never considered myself to be an exemplary wife.” She twirled a lock of her hair self-consciously. “I’m afraid you’re learning that lesson the hard way.”

Sam hung his head, avoiding her gaze for a few moments.

“I think you’re wrong about that, under the right circumstances, I believe you’d be a wonderful wife. But, if it makes you feel any better, darlin’, I discovered long ago what a rotten, miserable husband I am. Just ask my first wife.”

His words echoed in the silence. *First wife?* What in the world was he talking about? He’d never mentioned being married before. And where was this mysterious woman right now?

"I...um..." She sat with her mouth gaping in confusion.

Sam stood to cross the small room and lean upon the window casing. Finally, he turned to Amanda, who sat patiently waiting, her interest piqued by this new revelation.

"My first wife, Elsbeth"—he put his hand on the back of his head and grimaced, as if the memory pained him. "She died, right after the war ended. There are some people who blame me for her death. Her sister has called me a murderer."

Amanda stood up so quickly the chair fell over. Her petticoats swished in defiance as she crossed the room to take one of Sam's hands in hers.

"I've thought you were despicable, unprincipled, and vile, but there's one thing I know about you, Samuel Calhoun. You couldn't murder an innocent person. Most especially not your wife."

He closed his eyes for a moment. When he re- opened them, relief clearly reflected in his gaze. "Thank you, Amanda. You'll never know how much I appreciate your faith in me."

He gave her a sad lop-sided grin. "Although my character still does seem to be in question, what with the despicable and vile part."

Amanda dropped his hand and backed a few inches away from him.

"There's a difference between doing something for monetary gain and doing something truly evil. While it appears you are capable of being selfish and calculating, I don't think you're a cold-blooded killer." She raised an eyebrow. "Of course, perhaps I'm not a very good judge of character." She turned and sighed deeply. "You wouldn't be the first person I've misjudged. I seem to have a habit of marrying the wrong men."

He gently placed his hands on her shoulders. "I'm going to

try to prove to you that you can trust me. I appreciate your honesty, even though it does raise some serious questions regarding my good character." He squeezed her gently. "Such as it is."

He lowered his hands to wrap them around her waist and she had that same urge to resist the embrace. She wanted to fight her hunger for Sam, but every moment near him made her want him more. She wondered if she was destined to suffer the torture of desire for this man for the rest of her life. She was tired, and so weary of battling against her own emotions. Her breathing grew ragged and her pulse throbbed.

She closed her eyes and leaned back into the comfort of his body. It felt good to be this close to him again, to inhale the combination of good Virginia tobacco, Irish whiskey, and bay rum that marked him in her mind. She didn't want the moment to end.

His lips brushed close to her ear. "I could make love to you here, right now, and never regret a moment of the pleasure."

She shivered. She wouldn't regret it, either. Why was she acting such a fool and resisting this man? Her body knew what it wanted. Why couldn't she simply shut down her mind and enjoy the sensual interlude he was offering? Could she trust him and believe the words that tumbled so easily from his lips? So what if she succumbed to his charm? Wasn't it possible that the only moments of real happiness for either of them might be found in each other's arms? And wasn't she a fool to squander them?

He released her and stepped back, putting distance between them and making her heart plummet.

"I want you to know the truth about me, Amanda." He shrugged his broad shoulders. "Up until now, I haven't cared what anyone thought of me, so I've been silent." His eyes pleaded with her for understanding. "But it's important to me that you know the truth."

She understood suddenly that he was giving her a precious gift. His honesty, even at this late date, was what he offered.

Tears pricked her eyes, and her heart slowed to a measured beat. The heat of passion cooled, and she struggled to silence her objections and prepare herself to listen to Sam's confession.

Amanda picked up the chair and sat down, carefully adjusting her skirts. She made a point of primly folding her hands in her lap.

"I've never really given you a chance to explain yourself to me, Sam." She studied his expression and hoped her trust was apparent.

"I'm going to believe what you're telling me is the truth. I will put my faith in you, so please, Sam, don't lie. Even if what you have to tell me is horrible, or sad, or seems too awful to share. I'm sick to death of all the lies, and beg you for only one thing. Honesty between us." She glanced away from him. "I'm beginning to see that my life has been a sham. I want to believe in something again, Sam. Please, let it be you."

Sam sat down on the bed again and rubbed his chin. "I promise you, Amanda. I'll try my best to be honest with you." He gave a deep sigh. "But you have to understand, sometimes telling the truth is the worst thing a person can do."

Chapter Fourteen

"Elsbeth Waring was one of the most beautiful debutantes in Massachusetts. Her family was rich, powerful, and well-connected."

Sam wiped a small bead of perspiration from his brow. This was going to be more difficult than he'd imagined. Going back, reliving all the memories he'd tried to put behind him. Re-discovering all the pain he'd worked so hard to forget.

"There wasn't a single reason she should pay attention to the son of a merchant, but one night at a soirée, she flirted with me. She tossed those golden curls and made coy remarks behind her fan. I was young, impressionable, and very quickly became entranced."

Sam closed his eyes, and Elsbeth's face appeared before him. Those flashing blue eyes, the gentle, cultured cadence of her speech, and the way she could make a man feel he was the only one in the room. She was a practiced flirt, and he'd fallen into her trap so quickly it shamed him now.

"My family pushed me to court her. My mother wanted acceptance from the wealthy families, entry into that society. My father dreamed of making business connections and expanding his enterprises."

Sam pushed back a lock of hair that had fallen forward into his face and opened his eyes to find Amanda patiently waiting for him to continue.

"I was simply lusting after the first beautiful female who

had paid any attention to me." His lip curled in sarcasm. "I imagined that somehow I was special and unique. Later on I discovered I was just a naïve and foolish young man."

Amanda's eyes darkened, and he breathed a bit easier. He wanted her to understand, because despite the anguish this was causing him, it was important that she know the truth about him.

"So, I courted her, and Elsbeth allowed me certain liberties. Things I knew weren't proper, but I thought she loved me so much she was willing to cross the line. I learned later I wasn't the first to seduce her, but I was an innocent boy, caught up in the fervor of passion." He grinned. "I'm sure you understand."

She blushed a deep raspberry shade that crept down her cheeks to color her full breasts. The delightful sight brought heat to his groin and nearly washed what he wanted to say from his mind.

He drew his hand through his hair, trying to capture the right words. "So when her father caught us together in a rather delicate situation, I married her."

Amanda's face broke into a grin. "So I'm not your first shotgun bride, Sam? You seem to make a habit of being coerced into matrimony."

Sam stroked his chin and considered her words. "I'll have to think about that, Mrs. Calhoun.

"Anyway, it seemed a reasonable arrangement, and I was satisfied to have a wife I desired. My family was grateful for entry into the circle of the wealthy Bostonians. As for Elsbeth, well, she was the least satisfied with the circumstances of our marriage. But I didn't discover that until much later." Sam paused to take a deep breath. A dull ache squeezed his chest.

"We had nearly a year of happiness, or what passes for it when you're not really paying attention. I was distracted by all the talk of war, and often away from home due to training in the militia. My businesses also took up much of my time. And the need to still carouse with my friends. I was never exactly an attentive husband." He sighed, recalling Elsbeth's screaming temper tantrums and hysterical demands.

"Quite honestly, Elsbeth bored me. She started to refuse me entry into her bedroom, and my physical interest was all that had sustained any relationship between us. She locked her door, and I didn't really care." He shrugged his shoulders. "By the time I left for the war, we harbored nothing but contempt for each other." He stood to stretch his cramping legs. "I was relieved to escape from her and from that hell of a life we'd created."

He paced across the room, pausing to glance down at Amanda.

"I didn't have a very happy marriage either, Sam, but I tried to make the best of things." She glanced away from him. "But I don't think I ever tried hard enough to build any real happiness with Arthur. I wish..."

Sam should have known. Of course, Amanda would understand the circumstances of his marriage. She had already confessed she'd never loved her husband, but simply tolerated the situation with him. Why had he been so afraid to tell her the truth? Amanda understood the farce of a loveless marriage better than anyone he'd ever known. A wave of compassion swept through him for what this brave, sweet woman had endured.

"I abandoned her, convincing myself that going off to war was noble and brave." A lump rose to his throat as the rush of memories engulfed him. "But the blood, the carnage, the suffering and death." He gazed off into space, working to keep the horror from his voice. "There wasn't anything noble or heroic about that."

"I promised myself when I was a prisoner on Belle Island that if I survived, I'd make it up to Elsbeth. I made a vow to do whatever it took to make her happy. I swore to God we'd build a good life together if the almighty would give me another chance." His hands were clenched into tight fists.

Amanda stood, crossed the room, and took his hands into her own. He gazed down at her, and the tenderness he felt overwhelmed him. When had this face become so precious to him? A warm, soft light churned through him, chasing away dark shadows that had haunted him for years.

"You've suffered terribly, Sam. I'm so sorry. I didn't know. Perhaps if you'd told me this before, we—it would be different between us." Crystal tears sparkled in the depths of her emerald eyes.

Maybe it wasn't too late for them, Sam thought, wondering if he should tell her how much he cared for her. He could assure her they could work out their problems and be together. But he'd failed Elsbeth in so many ways. How could he bear the pain if he did the same thing to Amanda?

Besides, he'd taken a vow to the President that he'd protect his assignment and duties as a member of the Secret Service. He couldn't tell Amanda everything.

He touched her cheek gently with one finger. "I managed to survive that hellish prison camp and make my way back to Boston."

His arms circled Amanda's waist. He was grateful she didn't pull away. He needed the comfort of her leaning into him, the soft floral fragrance of her hair. The steadiness and warmth of her body gave him the strength to continue.

"When I finally made it to my parents' home, I was so sick and emaciated; I nearly dropped dead on their doorstep. I was feverish, and it took me weeks to finally regain consciousness. I asked for Elsbeth as soon as I was coherent, but my family kept making excuses for her absence. She was delicate and frail, couldn't visit me yet. Finally, I discovered the truth."

Amanda lifted her chin to gaze at him. He wondered if she understood how hard this was for him. He hadn't spoken of Elsbeth in years.

He swallowed and avoided meeting her eyes. "I was finally well enough to go home. I was desperate to see Elsbeth again, but I found her in our bedroom, hiding from me."

He touched Amanda's hair, stroking the silky softness. Her presence calmed him despite the ache in his heart.

She backed away from him, confusion playing across her face. "Did you appear so different? Were you so changed from the prison camp that she didn't recognize you?"

"She didn't want me to see her, to know what she'd been doing while I was in that Confederate prison." His voice choked with despair. "She was obviously pregnant, terrified about what I'd do to her when I found out."

"Oh, Sam." She traced her forefinger down his cheek, one tear sliding silently down her face.

Sam pulled her into his arms. "God forgive me, but I just wanted to walk away. That damned war had cost me everything. I just wanted to leave, to forget about my family and my responsibilities and start over again someplace else. I wanted to be greedy and selfish."

Amanda leaned her head on his shoulder. "But that's not the kind of man you are, is it, Sam?"

He gave a harsh laugh. "I didn't think so, but it's the kind of man I've become."

Sam leaned forward to inhale the scent of lilacs that surrounded Amanda. It calmed him again, anchoring him for a few moments in reality.

"I told myself I could forgive her anything, after all the horrible things I'd been through. Her deception wounded me like a saber through my heart, but I wanted to try to build a life with her. I'd made a promise to God. If I had enough time, tried hard enough, I believed I could do it. I did try, Amanda, please believe me, I tried."

She clamped her hands on each side of his face, forcing him to look down at her, holding him captive with her gaze. "I do believe you, Sam, because I know that despite everything that has happened between us, you're an honorable man."

Trust and confidence flashed in her eyes. A small jolt of hope surged through him.

"Eventually, I had to go on a business trip to New York. I told her I was going away, and she became hysterical. She grabbed me, begged me not to leave her alone." He shook his head sadly.

"She was having nightmares and slept with a lamp lit. She seemed convinced something horrible would happen to her, that she'd be forced to pay for her sins. I tried to reassure her. I told her that her sister Jilly would stay with her."

Amanda nodded. "She lived with the pain and guilt of her betrayal, didn't she, Sam?"

"Yes, and God forgive me, but I wanted to escape for a few days. I craved distance from her and the daily reminder that she'd been unfaithful to me."

Amanda stepped away from him. "I do understand, Sam. When Arthur was sick and I sat by his bedside day after day, watching him suffer and listening to his ramblings, I dreamt of walking down the stairs, out the front door, and of never, ever returning."

Sam had never before considered how similar their lives had been. They had both endured disappointment and grief before finding each other. He wished he could repair the damage he'd done tohis relationship with Amanda. He wanted their marriage to work. But the truth was a tormenting, ugly thing. And he couldn't consider a new life until he completed his assignment for the Secret Service.

He focused on a spot on the wall over her head, avoiding meeting her eyes and fearing his confession would drive her away forever. His heart beat wildly, as the words forced their way out of his aching throat.

"When I rode back into the yard, Jilly was sitting in a rocker on the porch. She'd been crying, and I knew right away something terrible had happened. When I finally reached the top step, she stood up and slapped me hard across the face. She said Elsbeth had become terrified one night; she'd called out for me, crying and begging for my forgiveness. When Jilly went to get some laudanum to try and calm her down, Elsbeth screamed my name and tried to run down the stairs. She tripped on her nightgown and tumbled to the bottom. She died of a broken neck. At least that was the doctor's verdict. But Jilly accused me of murdering her, of wanting her dead. She told me I'd abandoned my wife when she needed me the most." Guilt and shame settled upon him as he glanced at the floor.

"I didn't stay and take care of her, and I never could forgive her betrayal, so I feel that in some way I was responsible for Elsbeth's death."

"No, Sam, I can't believe you wanted her to—"

"Her sister told me I would burn in hell for what I did to Elsbeth. Maybe it's her curse that's pursued me all these years." He lifted his gaze to find Amanda staring at him. "To be honest, I believed I *was* responsible for what happened. I grabbed two saddlebags and a horse, and I rode away from my past." He took a deep breath, trying to fill his lungs with air. The room felt hot and stuffy.

"I swore I'd wander, try to find a new life for myself. Maybe even some redemption." He leaned forward to kiss Amanda gently on the forehead. "And I promised myself I'd never love another woman, because I was afraid I would fail her in the same way I'd failed Elsbeth."

Amanda gave a deep sigh, and Sam was shocked to see tears coursing down her cheeks. Her small rosebud mouth trembled. She reached for him and clutched him to her in a hug.

"Oh Sam, why didn't you tell me this before? If only..." Her voice trailed off and she wiped away the tears, then straightened her shoulders.

"I'm not about to blame you for a deceitful woman's death, Samuel Calhoun. I don't care what other people believe, and I'm not going to allow you to waste time blaming yourself for a terrible accident. Despite what you think, we all create our own path in life. I don't know all the circumstances surrounding your marriage to Elsbeth, but I believe you tried to take care of her. I also suspect you did so long after you stopped loving her."

A rush of relief washed through Sam. Amanda believed in him.

"I'm tired of the lies, the mistrust, and the anger between us. I want a marriage based on trust. I can't promise to forgive you for everything, at least not right away, but we can make a new beginning with a new pact." She held out one hand, palm face out.

Sam touched his palm to hers, enjoying the feel of her soft skin against his. The heat of her blood warmed him.

She gave him a small smile.

"From now on, we're going to be honest with each other. We don't lie, or even pretend for that matter." A challenge flickered in her eyes. "And we are equal partners in this arrangement."

Sam raised an eyebrow. "Equal?"

Amanda's chin thrust forward and her eyes blazed. "Equal, no secrets and no lies. That's the deal, Samuel Calhoun."

Sam dropped his hand and wrapped an arm around her

waist again. "Is that so? Shouldn't a deal with such strict terms be sealed with a kiss, Amanda *Calhoun*?"

Before she could object, he leaned down and touched his lips to hers. She reacted with surprise, but a moment later she relaxed against him, raising up on her toes and wrapping her arms around his neck. He deepened the kiss, letting his tongue slip between her lips, and she moaned. He didn't need any more encouragement.

His tongue slid into the sweetness of her mouth, exploring, linking with hers in a delicate, erotic dance, then plunging deeply to savor her taste. She was honey and spice. It was a ballet of desire, and blood rushed hot through his body, culminating in a hard thickening between his legs.

He cupped her soft bottom, urged her closer to him, and he was relieved that this time she didn't pull away. Instead, she welcomed his touch, reaching out one small hand to stroke his face softly.

He lifted his lips briefly from hers, afraid she'd demand he step away. He would do so if she asked. He gazed down at her with a sensual hunger tearing him apart. The evidence of his lust pressed eagerly against her thigh; the padding of her dress and petticoats provided no protection against his rampant desire.

"I want you, Sam. I've wanted you since the first moment we met, and the devil be cursed, I can't seem to stop wanting you."

Her words swept away all of his inhibitions. His mouth claimed hers again in a deep, searing kiss. His hands were free to explore her body, to touch, to fondle and caress. She was his to treasure, and despite his need, he had no intention of rushing this lovemaking. It had taken too long to win her back, and all the precious moments of this night belonged to them.

Taking a step away from her, he worked patiently to unfasten each of the black pearl buttons on her dress. His brow knitted into a frown.

"When are you going to discard these widow's weeds, Amanda? I want to see you in bright, beautiful colors. Wear something that will bring out the green of your eyes and do justice to this hair." He ran his fingers through the smooth silkiness of her auburn locks, dislodging the last of the pins.

She threw her head back and gave him a mischievous smile. "I haven't been inclined to discard my dark, sad garb because it's been a good match for my mood lately."

His fingers finished with the buttons, and he pulled the fabric of her gown apart, exposing the soft mounds of her breasts perched above the satin fabric of her corset. Her flesh was a feast for his eyes, and for a few moments he savored the view. His cock grew rigid.

Amanda laughed softly. "I have a feeling that in a very short time, my mood is going to improve dramatically."

Sam leaned down and licked the deep valley of her cleavage, savoring the sweet taste of her skin.

"It will if I have anything to do with it, madam." He trailed kisses up over her shoulder, across her neck, to the gentle curve of her ear. He suckled one earlobe delicately, and she shivered.

He pulled the arms of her jacket free, discarded it, and moved his hands to her waist. Giving her a gentle twist toward the bed, he impatiently unfastened the hooks of her skirt. It fell into a heap at her feet, and Amanda stepped away from the pool of dark crepe fabric. Sam felt drunk with the pleasure of seeing her undress, as if he were sipping a rich, delicious wine.

Climbing upon the bed, she waved a finger in warning. "My turn now, Sam," she said in a husky, sultry whisper.

He stepped close enough to allow her elegant fingers to begin the painfully slow process of unfastening first his silk vest, then the small buttons of his linen shirt. When she finally separated the fabric, her lips rewarded him, moving sensuously across his skin, blazing a trail of fire down his chest, then to his belly.

She looked at him from beneath her thick, dark lashes. Her emerald eyes sparkled while her tongue perched on the edge of lips still swollen from his kiss. When she reached for the buttons of his trousers, Sam stopped her.

"By God, Amanda, if you touch me there, I'll be finished in a moment." He lowered his head and stroked the sweet curve of her breast with his tongue. "And tonight, I want for us both to be well- satisfied."

He briefly recalled what Father Mikelson had said about avoiding the conjugal bed in order to secure an annulment for Amanda, but the fever of desire overwhelmed his senses and drove the thought from his mind.

With a gentle push, he set her back upon the pillows, then with eager fingers unlaced her boots. Flinging them aside, he traced the outline of her small foot before reaching beneath the starched cotton of her petticoats to unroll each silk stocking. It was like unwrapping a beautiful gift, and he wanted to savor every moment.

He tongued the curve on her insole and trailed kisses from there, across her foot, nipping the inside of her ankle, then up the curve of her leg. He lifted her petticoat, cupped her bottom, and leaned forward to discover her sweet, hot core, flowing with the honeyed juices of her desire.

His tongue flickered across the small rosebud of pleasure. She whispered his name as he elicited shivers from her.

He inhaled her female musk and reveled in the taste of her. She was ready for him, he could tell, but the pleasure of the play held him rapt. He wanted to extend the minutes into hours of lovemaking, but he throbbed with a need to plunge himself deeply into her, to feel her tight, wet sheath surrounding him.

He stood and made quick work of his trousers, kicking them aside. She gave him the smile of a cat well-pleased with the bowl of cream placed before her.

"Come here," she demanded, sitting up and letting her legs dangle over the edge of the mattress.

He obeyed, unable to imagine doing anything else. She held him prisoner, with only the chains of passion to enslave him.

When she wrapped her small, soft hand around him, fire exploded in his veins. Before he could do anything but throw back his head and encourage her with a deep, guttural sound, she took him into her mouth.

It took every ounce of self-control to keep from exploding into the pliant softness. She suckled him, and he swore he felt the floor moving in waves beneath his feet. His breathing was ragged. She stroked, fondled, and nearly drove him insane with the pleasure she offered.

Finally, he pushed her tenderly away, gazing down through a haze of desire. "Woman, you surely know how to drive a man out of his mind."

Her green eyes sparkled up at him. She stood and slowly and deliberately removed the rest of her underclothes.

"I'm planning to make you beg for mercy before the night is over."

She took her time unfastening her corset, and Sam groaned. He wasn't sure he'd survive.

Her corset and then her petticoat fell to her feet. Sam envisioned his beautiful goddess standing on a cloud. He'd gladly burn in hell for this night with her, and nothing, no punishment, penance or retribution, would stop him from making love to her.

She climbed upon the bed once more, spreading her legs and arranging her hair upon the pillows. Her gaze traveled the length of his body, her eyes widening at the hard length of his cock, then she gave him a slow, seductive smile.

"You going to stand there all night, Sam, or do you have something else in mind?"

Sam climbed upon the bed, positioning himself above her. "I'm just trying to collect my thoughts."

Amanda ran her fingers up his chest lightly, a tingling path scorching him from her touch. "We've spent too much time lately thinking. Let's concentrate of what we're feeling."

Sam lowered his lips to hers and pushed his tongue into the yielding moistness of her mouth at the same moment he thrust into her. They were both hot and eager, with no pretense of shyness. Their bodies entwined, and there was only the rhythm of their mating and the sweet, pure physical need, which ended in a trembling crescendo as they shuddered, cried out, and climaxed together.

When Sam finally relaxed against Amanda, savoring the sweet moments after making love to her, a flash of conscience jolted him. She'd demanded honesty, and he'd agreed.

But he couldn't tell her the entire truth, because if she knew about his mission to Willow Creek, her life would be in even more danger. He had to protect her, and the only way he knew to keep her safe was to deceive her.

It was a helluva deal, and if she found out he hadn't been totally honest, their relationship would be over.

She dozed beside him. Her face was soft and flushed from their lovemaking. Sam touched her cheek gently.

"I love you, Amanda," he murmured. It was better that she didn't hear him. His love would only bring her more pain and sorrow.

Chapter Fifteen

It was nearly dawn when Amanda nestled closer to Sam, snuggling her head against his hard, firmly- muscled chest to listen to the soft cadence of his heart. His arm wrapped around her, tugging her even closer before he adjusted the quilt he'd pulled across their naked bodies after their last interlude of lovemaking.

Closing her eyes, she inhaled his masculine scent mixed with the primal fragrance of their recent mating. She felt warm, relaxed, and safe.

Sam's lips gently caressed the top of her head. "Thank you, Sam," she murmured.

He was silent for a moment, then chuckled deeply. "You're welcome, Amanda. I'm grateful I could be of service."

She gave him a playful push and leaned on one elbow to gaze at him. He looked well-pleased with himself. His amber eyes glowed with what she might foolishly interpret as love if she didn't know better. Sam had vowed never to love another woman. His heart was too damaged by his experience with Elsbeth to take a chance on being hurt or betrayed again.

"Not for the, well, you know." She gave him another punch when he grinned. "I want to thank you for sharing the story of your first marriage. For trusting me enough to believe I wouldn't judge you for a terrible accident." She drew her fingers gently across his chest. He inhaled a sharp breath, and she marveled that he reacted so immediately to her touch.

The small chocolate flecks in his eyes grew darker. Her fingers continued to tease him, and she moved closer to better gauge his reactions. The quilt slid lower, exposing her breasts. Instead of covering herself, she shifted to permit him a better view.

Her fingers moved upward, delighting in the hard line of his jaw. His teeth clenched when she tickled the outline of his lips.

Sam grasped her wrist and raised an eyebrow. "Ready to play again so soon, madam?"

Amanda sat up, tossing her hair in a playful motion. His hand moved up her arm, caressing one breast, then pausing to stroke her nipple. Ripples of pleasure swept through her. With the lightest touch, he sketched an outline of her womanly shape as though he wanted to memorize each curve and line of her body.

Finally withdrawing his hand, he leaned forward to kiss her. Not with the hot, eager passion of their recent mating, but with a soft sweetness that brought tears to her eyes.

"I've never wanted anyone the way I want you, Amanda. I need you." His voice rumbled with emotion. She thought he wanted to say more, and she waited patiently. She would wait a lifetime for the words she ached to hear.

"But I think we should have some breakfast. I promise," he said, lifting a lock of her hair and curling it around his finger, "there will be plenty of time for us to be together. Later."

A wave of disappointment washed over Amanda. She'd been hoping for other words. At the very least, she wanted him to say he cared for her. Most of all she wished to hear him say he loved her. Yet she knew they were words he couldn't say because of his deep-rooted fear. Her heart ached with the sadness of it, a man so capable of deep, profound love, yet so afraid he would destroy anyone he cared about.

"I'm famished." She adjusted the quilt to cover herself. "Although I confess I'm reluctant to climb out of the warmth of this bed."

Sam dropped the curl he'd been toying with and matched her grin. "Then I'll arrange for you to stay right here, enjoying the luxury of a nap." His gaze lingered on her naked shoulders.

Stretching her arms above her, she gave a deep, contented purr. "That sounds wonderful."

He leaned forward and caressed her bare skin with his lips, creating a trail of fire down her shoulder to one breast.

"I'll have Harriet fix us a tray, and we can have a picnic right here in our room." The chocolate flecks appeared again in his eyes. "You won't even have to bother getting dressed."

Amanda fell back upon the pillows and giggled. "That will save me the trouble of undressing later."

"Precisely my plan," Sam said, climbing from the bed. His lean, heavily muscled body ignited a fire deep within Amanda. Lust and desire. She couldn't tear her eyes from his gorgeous posterior as he pulled on his trousers.

He gave her a devilish grin as he buttoned his shirt. "You are well on your way to becoming a lascivious woman, Amanda Calhoun."

She curled her lips into a satisfied smile. "Then hurry up and get back here, Samuel Calhoun. I'm hoping you'll be able to give me further instruction."

He answered her with a hearty laugh and leaned forward to kiss her. "It will be my pleasure, Amanda, I assure you."

"If you do it right, Sam, it will be a pleasure for both of us."

He laughed again before leaving the room.

Amanda considered her circumstances. She was in love with her husband. Madly, completely, and foolishly in love. Despite all effort to ignore him and keep herself from him, she had eagerly returned to his arms at the first opportunity.

Lifting her eyes to heaven to beg for help, she recognized another truth. Despite all of his efforts to erect a wall around his heart, Samuel Calhoun was in love with her, too. Now she just needed a way to prove it to him.

∞∞∞

Later that day, Amanda considered playing at her game of public disdain for her husband. Her pretense of a chilly, silent meal at noon dissolved the instant Sam grabbed her hand and brought it to his mouth. Nibbling gently on her fingers, he joked about how sweet she tasted, and she dissolved into a fit of laughter.

She knew they were being observed, yet she couldn't bring back the icy demeanor after a blissful night of making love, then sleeping wrapped in each other's arms.

Harriet gave them a warm smile when she came to the table. "It's about time the two of you patched things up." She looked pleased with herself. "I knew you were perfect for each other right from the start. It does a matchmaker's heart good to see folks settle in the way they oughta."

"So you planned this whole thing, did you?" Sam said.

"Well, I figured where there's smoke, there's fire. I mighta helped you two along some, but"—she settled her hands on her hips—"I guess that priest managed to outdo me in the matchmakin' department, didn't he?"

Sam and Amanda joined her in laughter before ordering.

"I'm feeling a little queasy this afternoon. Just tea for me, please."

Harriet stared at her sharply, and Amanda tried to reassure her friend. "I'm sure it will pass soon, but I haven't felt well for a few days." She adjusted the white lace cuffs on her dress. When she looked back up, Sam's eyes reflected concern.

"Perhaps I should try to get more rest."

She nearly giggled as deep red crept up Sam's neck to color the tips of his ears.

"I'll plan to tuck you in early this evening, madam." A lilt of amusement shaded his voice.

Harriet's mouth curved into a smile. "Seems to me you two might have some other kinda catchin' up to do, eh?"

Sam and Amanda dissolved into another fit of laughter. Unfolding the linen napkin onto her lap, Amanda grinned. "I'm afraid we're destined to be a public spectacle wherever we go in Willow Creek, Sam."

"What are your plans when you've finished with the work at the Miners' Benevolent Association?" he asked.

His question caught her off guard. Lately, she'd been living from day to day, almost from moment to moment. She'd given no thought to where she would live or what she would do when her work was finished in Willow Creek. Was he telling her they could have a life together? "I, well..." She blinked in confusion. "I'm fond of Willow Creek. And there's so much to be done here, for the families of the miners and for the town. I guess I'll be staying here for some time now."

He raised an eyebrow at her and shook his head. "Is that what you really want, Amanda? You're a wealthy woman. You could live in any big city, San Francisco or New York. You could even travel to Europe."

His words echoed in her heart. He was talking about her, not them. Is that what he wanted, to be rid of her? "My work here has just began, so I doubt I'll need to make travel plans soon." She decided to be brave. "Would you be interested in traveling to Europe with me, Sam?"

He leaned forward. "I don't know, Amanda. Would you want me to go with you?"

Amanda held her breath. Should she simply blurt out the answer, admit that no place would ever really be home if he weren't with her. Perhaps if she told him how she felt, he'd be honest about his own feelings.

Harriet interrupted the tense moment by bringing their food to the table.

"Do you know how some folks manage to stay happy all the time?" Harriet asked.

"No," Amanda said, "how do they manage to do that, Harriet?"

Harriet wiped her large rough hands on her apron and pursed her lips. "They just up and decide to be happy." She turned on her heel and headed toward the kitchen.

"That's an interesting idea," Amanda said.

"A very simple philosophy," Sam said, slicing his steak and concentrating on the food before him.

They ate in silence, and Amanda wondered if it were possible. Could she change fate, control the elements of chance, and seize happiness simply by telling herself to be happy? Sam interrupted her thoughts.

"Do you think it would work? We could decide right now. Mr. and Mrs. Samuel Calhoun will be the happiest people on God's green earth."

Amanda sipped more of the sweet hot tea. "It sounds like the sort of thing that would require a pact. You know, blood brothers or something. How do I know you'll live up to this vow of happiness?"

Sam rubbed his chin.

"I believe I can be trusted. Haven't I convinced you yet of my honorable intentions?"

Amanda nearly spit out tea at his words. Taking a deep swallow, she tried not to laugh. "Are you the same man who ruined my reputation for money?"

Sam shook his head. "I never said a word about your incredibly imaginative skills in bed."

Amanda warmed. "And didn't we end up getting married in a shotgun ceremony?"

Sam shook his head again. "If I remember events correctly, you were the only one doing any shooting that night."

Amanda raised her eyes to heaven. Lord give me strength, she prayed.

"So, you were just in the wrong place at the wrong time, falsely accused, and forced to marry a crazy woman? Pity. You seem to be stuck with me now." She picked up her cup, but a wave of nausea rolled through her and she set it back on the saucer.

Sam folded his napkin and placed it on the table. Leaning back in his chair, he smiled, and the dimples on each side of his beautiful mouth grew deeper. "There's some that might say I'm stuck with you."

A flare of temper raced through Amanda. She reminded herself that Sam was just teasing. At least she hoped he was.

He reached across the table to grasp her hand in his. Warmth spiraled out from where their palms met, making her feel safe.

"I don't think you're crazy, Amanda." He frowned. "Maybe just a tad too impetuous sometimes. I don't think I've been cursed either."

Amanda's mouth formed a thin smile. "Cursed? Who said anything about being cursed?"

He lifted her hand to his lips and brushed her knuckles with a gentle kiss. "I've been blessed in a thousand ways by knowing you, Amanda. You're stronger and braver than any man I've ever known. You won't back down and you don't give up."

His words weren't sugarcoated compliments designed to turn her head. He admired her, and her shoulders straightened when his praise finally sank into her mind.

"I will certainly try to be less impetuous." She gave a beleaguered sigh. "Although dealing with you can be a trial, Sam. Sometimes, well, I just can't seem to control myself."

Sam flicked his tongue between her fingers and she gave a small yelp of surprise. Heat slammed through her, and she shivered, recalling the many ways he'd found to pleasure her last night.

"I'm counting on that, Amanda. I much prefer a wild wanton in my bed to a sedate civilized lady."

Amanda discovered nearly every pair of eyes trained on her antics with Sam. She yanked her hand back and prayed for deliverance once again. Not that it seemed to do any good. She couldn't resist this infuriating, overconfident man. She was constantly torn by her emotions. She'd vow to stay away from him, only to discover she ached with a need to be near him.

She stood and nearly tipped the chair over in her rush to get out of the dining room. She paused on the steps outside the Parmeter House and waved her hand to fan herself.

"The day's heating up, isn't it?" Sam's voice was calm and composed when he approached her from behind and offered his elbow to escort her.

She studied the azure canopy of sky above their heads. "It would be a lovely day for a picnic, don't you think?"

Sam nodded. "I have to ride out to the willow grove near the river bend," he said. "That's the place I took you that first day, where I..." His words trailed off into the warm breeze.

Amanda gave him a flirtatious smile. "Where you had the audacity to"—she adjusted her hat carefully— "recite poetry to me, Mr. Calhoun?"

Sam laughed, two deep dimples appearing on each side of his face. "I always knew poetry was destined to get me into trouble."

They strolled along the boardwalk, and Amanda enjoyed the gentle peace of simply being with Sam without any conversation. Today they didn't seem to need words. In fact, if they spent more time in silent companionship, they might avoid the too frequent arguments.

She turned to him at the door to the Miners' Benevolent Association and plucked a small piece of lint from his dark frock coat. "I didn't hear an invitation to join you, Sam." She pushed out her lower lip to form a pout.

He grasped her chin gently and brushed his lips across hers.

"If I take you on a picnic, it will spoil me for getting any work done this afternoon," he murmured.

"You don't need to work, Sam. I've heard rumors you married a very wealthy woman and you're set for life."

Sam stepped away from her and shook his head. "She's quite a demanding wench, so I believe I'll earn every penny of those riches."

Amanda didn't release her grip on his lapel and pulled him forward again. Gazing into his amber eyes, she brushed her fingers lightly across his face.

"It's a pity you're forced to labor under such demanding circumstances. I suppose you're too exhausted from all that work to spend a quiet afternoon rolling around on the soft grass." She licked her lips. "Too busy for a bit of fun and frolic."

Sam grasped her around the waist and bent her back, his lips trailing heat down the side of her neck to nuzzle her.

"Promise me something, Amanda."

Her breathing had turned into tiny, little pants and she wanted to push him away, to demand they stop making a scene in the middle of the street. She simply couldn't find the strength.

"What?"

"If I'm ever too busy for a bit of fun and frolic on soft grass in the warm sunshine with you, shoot me again."

His lips came closer to hers, but before he could silence her with a kiss, she giggled.

"You can count on it, Sam."

Then she was lost in a swirl of heat and desire.

Chapter Sixteen

Sam tipped his hat. "I'll be looking forward to our picnic." Leaning toward her, he kissed the top of her nose.

She slanted her head to give him a coquettish smile. "Me, too. And I believe it's my turn to ride Stranger."

Sam backed down the steps. He waved a finger at her. "I don't think so, darlin'. He's a bit too rough for a sweet thing like you. I'll bring Duchess. She's a more suitable mount for a lady."

Amanda stuck out her tongue at him. "Sometimes it's downright boring to be a lady."

Sam turned and strolled down the street, lost in the fantasy of an idyllic afternoon spent in the arms of his bewitching wife.

The sound of her scream tore through the early morning, ripping the air with its mournful wail. Sam stopped breathing. His heart slammed against his chest. Pain clenched his gut, and he turned quickly to head back to the Miners' Association.

If someone had hurt her, he swore he'd tear that person apart with his bare hands.

Amanda stood at the front door, her face ashen. A dark wet stain spread across the skirt of her dress. Both of her hands were covered in blood. Stumbling up the steps, Sam grabbed her shoulders.

"Amanda, are you hurt?"

She was shaking and her eyes were wild with fear.

"Caleb," she whispered, her voice hoarse with emotion. "It's Caleb..." Tears flowed down her cheeks. "Sam, Caleb's been hurt. Badly hurt."

"I'll get the doctor." Sam examined the scarlet stain on her dress and a boulder of fear crashed down upon him. "But I need to be sure you're not bleeding." He pulled her to him and held her for a moment.

When he finally released her, she was sobbing quietly. Sam felt helpless, unable to soothe her, and apprehensive about leaving her alone to check on Caleb. He couldn't rely upon her to summon the doctor. She was too overwrought.

Her face went white, and she stumbled to the edge of the boardwalk, leaning forward. She lost the contents of her stomach. Sam wrapped his arms around her waist, concerned she might faint and tumble over the edge. When she finally stepped back and leaned into him, he didn't release her. She swallowed several times and wiped her mouth with the lace cuff of her dark dress.

"I think he's dead, Sam."

"I want you to sit down here and lean back onto the building." He helped to settle her against the front portico. "I need to get some help, but I'll be right back."

Glancing each way down the street, he swore under his breath. Hell and damnation, any other day there would be folks falling over each other in the street. Today it was nearly deserted. He crossed to the General Store and caught the shopkeeper who was putting merchandise out in front.

"There's been an accident over at the Miners' Association. Caleb's been hurt, and we need the doctor."

Homer Fullerton shook his head and refused to look up at Sam. "I got a business to run, Calhoun. Can't you go get the doctor yourself? He's sleeping it off at Mrs. Holt's place."

Grabbing Homer by the collar, Sam leaned forward, pausing just inches from the other man's yellow teeth and pockmarked face. "My wife has nearly collapsed from the shock of finding that boy. She's covered with blood, and I'm not exactly sure if any of it's hers." Sam released the terrified man. "Now, you go get that nearly useless doctor. I'm going to give you ten minutes to wake him up, pour some coffee down his throat, and drag him over to the Miners' Association." Sam stepped away from the man. "And after ten minutes I'll come looking for the both of you." Menace dripped from his voice, and he let his hand graze his revolver to emphasize the point. "God help you when I find you."

Sam's heart pounded as he crossed the dusty street. He discovered Walter Abbott squatting next to Amanda, trying to comfort her.

Sam nodded at the young man. "Could you go fetch Harriet Parmeter? I need a cool head around here right now."

Walter plopped his brown felt hat back onto his head and took off at a run toward the hotel. Sam dropped to a crouch and studied Amanda's face. She was still crying, but she had a stunned, glassy-eyed look that frightened him. He said her name, but she didn't seem to hear him. Gently, he lifted her chin with one finger, trying to get her attention.

"Amanda, honey?" Her emerald eyes captured his, and the distant, forlorn look chilled Sam to his bones.

"Why, Sam?" Her voice cracked with emotion. "Why would anyone want to hurt Caleb? He's such a nice boy." She stared off into space, and tears continued to roll down her cheeks. "He was just learning to read, you know."

Sam patted her on the shoulder. "I need to go inside and check on him. Will you be okay?"

Amanda didn't respond. Her red lips were bright against the pallor of her skin. She continued to cry, her shoulders shaking, her breasts rising and falling as she took deep, ragged breaths. Sam cursed the abandoned street once more. He didn't want to leave her, but he also worried that if Caleb wasn't dead yet, he soon would be if he didn't get some help.

She finally lifted her head and tried to straighten her shoulders.

"Go inside, and..." Her head fell forward again, and she sobbed into her hands.

Sam patted her arm again, hoping the simple gesture would calm and reassure her, then he rose to his feet and took long measured steps into the shadows of the entryway. Caleb stretched across the parlor floor, surrounded by a large pool of blood.

Sam's stomach wrenched. The substantial meal he'd just eaten threatened to reemerge. Swallowing, he stepped closer. The boy's form was still. Deathly still, and Sam feared the worst. Kneeling down, he forced himself to touch Caleb's back. The boy was still breathing. It was a thin, shallow sign of life, but Sam was overjoyed.

Ignoring the blood, Sam shifted the boy and used the edge of his shirt to wipe Caleb's face. The boy groaned, and a glimmer of hope seized Sam.

"Caleb?" He wiped more of the blood away. "Stay still. The doctor's on his way."

Sam held Caleb in his arms, and memories of other injured men, their bodies torn apart by the cruel weapons of war, swept through his mind. He swallowed the pain knotting his throat and squeezing his chest. He'd seen so many young men die. Dear God, please spare this one, he prayed. Amanda loved this boy, and she had lost so much lately.

Voices echoed in the street, and Sam heard people rushing about. Loud steps pounded on the boardwalk, and several men entered the room.

"I got him here, but it ain't my fault if he's no damned good to you." The shopkeeper shoved the doctor forward.

Doc Potter stumbled in and belched loudly before addressing Sam. "If a body loses that much blood you can't blame me if he dies."

Sam made his voice as cold and heartless as he could manage. "You'd better hope this boy lives. Because if you don't do everything in your power to save him, I'll cut out your liver and hang it on a pole for the vultures to chew on."

The doctor coughed and turned back toward Homer Fullerton. "I'll need hot water, bandages, supplies from my office, and whiskey."

"I can't be expected to hang around here all day long. I got a business to run." Homer tried to back out the door, but Sam stopped him with an angry growl.

"Do what the doc says, and I won't be forced to shoot you."

When Walter Abbott stepped into the room, the shopkeeper grabbed him by the elbow and twisted him around. "We got supplies to fetch, so don't be lollygagging around here. Calhoun would just as soon shoot us as look at us this morning. C'mon and help me and save yourself some aggravation."

Sam gave the doctor a cursory glance before studying the pale white face below him.

"Tell me the truth, Doc, what are his chances?" Doc Potter wobbled a bit, belched again, then straightened his stained frock coat. "I won't know until I can find out where all that blood came from. Do you see a gunshot, or a knife wound?"

Sam searched the length of the inert form. He couldn't see any wounds, just a lot of bruises and cuts on the boy's face. It looked like someone with large fists had punched him repeatedly. Caleb made a low, mournful sound.

"Take it easy, my friend; we're going to find out what happened to you." Sam tried to reassure him. He pointed toward the stairway, giving the doctor a look that held a stern warning.

"Go on upstairs. I know you've been here enough times to remember the way. There are linens and pillows on the beds. Bring some down so we can make this boy comfortable."

Doc Potter looked ready to argue with Sam, then seemed to think better of the idea and headed out of the room.

"Don't." Caleb's voice was thick, the words barely intelligible through his swollen lips. "Mrs. Wainwright."

Sam leaned forward to capture the words. "What is it, Caleb? What about Amanda?"

Caleb's eyes fluttered open. "Don't let 'em kill her."

Blood rushed through Sam's body and congealed into one large ice crystal that suddenly encased his heart.

∞∞∞

Amanda sat on her bed, her teeth chattering and goose bumps crawling across her skin. She couldn't get warm, despite the sunshine streaming through the windows in her room.

The image of Caleb in that dark red pool of blood wouldn't leave her. Caleb, his young body so injured he couldn't move or speak. He was so still, she thought, he must be dead. Though Harriet had assured her Caleb was still alive, the fear that his injuries had killed him haunted her.

Harriet bustled into the room with a tray of food. "Land's sake, Amanda. Let's get a quilt around you."

Her stomach turned over in protest at the smell of the food.

Harriet pulled the quilt from Sam's bed and tucked it around Amanda's shoulders. "I made us some tea, and there were apple tarts just comin' from the oven." Harriet pulled a chair closer to the bed and sat down. "I figured since you didn't eat much earlier you might be hungry."

Amanda grasped the steaming cup of tea and inhaled the aroma. It was chamomile, to calm her shattered nerves. She took a sip but held up a hand to indicate she didn't want any of the fruit tart.

"I'm not feeling well enough to eat, but thank you, Harriet. The tea will help me settle down again, I hope."

Harriet unfolded a linen napkin on her lap and dropped one of the pastries upon it, breaking off a corner to take a bite. "Robert said he'd come and tell us when they figure out what happened. Sheriff Brody is over there now, with Sam." She raised an eyebrow at Amanda. "A woman in your condition can't be sitting here worryin' all day. T'ain't healthy."

Amanda sipped the tea again and nodded. "I know I need to calm down, but the shock of seeing Caleb on the floor, and all that blood." She shuddered, blinked up at Harriet and forced herself to keep the tears in check.

Harriet continued to nibble at pieces of the tart. "Does Sam know yet?"

Amanda frowned. "Sam was there when I found Caleb. Don't you remember?"

Harriet gawked at her, her mouth still wide open. "Not about Caleb, about the little one."

Little one? What was Harriet talking about? Caleb was just a boy, but a tall, strapping boy. Hardly what anyone would call little.

"I'm sorry, Harriet. I seem to be confused. What are you talking about?"

"I'm talkin' about your condition."

Amanda set her cup on the matching saucer and settled it on her lap. She had experienced a shock that morning, so perhaps her mental faculties were not operating at full capacity, because she couldn't understand what in the world Harriet Parmeter was talking about.

Leaning forward, Harriet regarded her from the tip of her toes to the hair on her head. "When was the last time you had your courses?"

Amanda's face heated. Ladies rarely ever spoke of such things.

"I, it was..." When had she experienced her monthly flow the last time? Before she came to Willow Creek, at least that was the last time she could remember. Dawning realization washed over her as a light, joyful feeling bubbled up from deep inside. She peeked down at her stomach with awe and wonder.

"Do you really think?" She looked to Harriet. "Is it possible?"

Harriet nodded. "You'd know better than me of course. But I noticed you don't have an appetite, and that's one sign." She finished off the last of the tart. "Missing your monthly is another. I suspect you're in the family way." She brushed the crumbs from her fingers and gave Amanda a playful wink.

"And since this is news to you, I'm bettin' Sam doesn't suspect a thing." Her eyes took on a warm, faraway look. "That man will make a wonderful father. I've seen him around kids, and he sure does enjoy bein' with them."

"Sam's going to be a father?" A baby? She was going to have a baby. Sam's baby? The prospect delighted yet frightened her. She didn't even know if her husband wanted a wife, and now she was going to present him with a family.

"It might take him a bit to get used to the idea, but once you tell him, I swear he is goin' to be the happiest man on earth." Harriet stood up and shook the crumbs out of her skirts. "I think you'd best lie down for a bit, to gather your strength. Soon as I hear anythin' about Caleb, I'll come up and tell you." She patted Amanda's hand. "And I want you to try to eat somethin' when you wake up." She gave Amanda another wink. "You're eatin' for two now, remember that."

With a sweep of her dark skirts, Harriet left before Amanda could form a response. She attempted to gather her scattered thoughts. She was going to have a baby. How in the world had that happened?

Warming again, she realized she should have anticipated this. She was no innocent virgin. For heaven's sake, she was a widow and a married woman. A flutter of deep and profound happiness swirled through her. She closed her eyes to savor it.

A baby. A small, perfect creature created from her love for Sam. The corners of her lips lifted into a smile, because despite the horrible events of the morning, she now held a precious secret.

The quilt drifted to the floor when she stood up and opened her eyes. Standing before her dressing table, Amanda wondered how long it would be before her body started to blossom and change. Touching her breasts, she visualized a tiny, downy head tucked into her arms, suckling.

The day suddenly seemed brighter, more filled with hope than she'd ever imagined possible. Amanda hugged herself, and pure joy exploded within her. She wasn't barren. In a few months she would give Sam a child, and despite his protests about being unreliable, uncertain, and irresponsible, she knew he was simply afraid.

Sam was afraid to admit how much he loved her, because experience had taught him the things he loved and cared about could be snatched from him by tragedy and loss. But Amanda knew the things he denied himself were the very things he desired most. Stability, honor, love, and a family. These were the things Amanda would give him. A new sense of purpose seized her. She could make Samuel Calhoun very happy, if he could learn to trust her.

She lay down and spread the quilt over her legs, suddenly realizing how utterly exhausted she was. It didn't matter now; she could rest. Tonight would be soon enough to share the news with Sam, and whatever his reaction, Amanda was determined to remain calm and composed. The Calhouns were a family now.

She closed her eyes and whispered a prayer of thanks to God for this miracle in her life. She humbly added another prayer, asking for a miracle for Caleb.

Chapter Seventeen

Sam scrutinized the doctor while he ministered to Caleb. When he pulled a bottle of whiskey from the pile of things Homer and Walter had collected, Sam stepped forward to grab it from his hands.

"You won't be needing that for a while," he said. The doctor yanked it back and glared at Sam.

"It's not for me, you fool. I need it to cleanse these wounds." He opened the bottle and poured the golden liquid onto a clean linen cloth. "If you want to be of some real help, let's get that jacket off him. There's too much blood here to come from the scrapes on his face. This boy has been badly injured, and I need to find out what caused all this loss of blood."

The authority in the doctor's voice shocked Sam. He couldn't remember seeing Doc Potter sober even once these past few months. Apparently, when the man wasn't inebriated, he knew a great deal about medicine. Caleb whimpered and thrashed as they removed his heavy denim jacket. Sam grimaced when he saw the gaping wound near the boy's shoulder. A knife wound, one that looked jagged, ugly, and deep.

"This boy's lucky," the doctor muttered.

"I'm betting when he wakes up, he won't agree with you."

The doctor poured whiskey onto the wound and Sam winced.

"At least there's a chance he will wake up." The doctor sat back on his heels and wiped the sweat from his brow. "Whoever did this was probably aiming for his heart. Caleb must have moved and deflected the blade." He pulled some dark thread from the pile of medical supplies. "I can stitch him up, but he's lost a lot of blood. It'll be nip and tuck as far as him pulling out of this."

Sam stood back and observed the doctor making small, precise stitches to close the wound on Caleb's shoulder. The boy cried out again, but he didn't regain consciousness. Sam was grateful for that, because what the Doc was doing looked painful. His stomach clenched at the sight of the needle piercing skin. He turned away, wiping the moisture from his own brow.

When the wound was closed, the doctor stood up and gave Sam a satisfied look. "He's young and strong, and that's about all he's got in his favor. Do you think we can get him into a bed upstairs?"

Sam considered the boy's long, lanky body and nodded. "He probably doesn't weigh much. I can help carry him up there. Then I'll get someone to stay with him."

Doc Potter nodded. He walked to a basin filled with water and started to scrub the blood from his hands. "No need to hurry on that, Calhoun. I'm going to keep an eye on the boy for a few hours. He'll need some laudanum when he wakes up, and I have to make sure he stays quiet."

The doctor's words stunned Sam. The man had a reputation for leaving a patient as soon as possible, always eager to get back to the saloons and his whiskey. "You turnin' over a new leaf, Doc?"

Potter shrugged his shoulders before wiping his hands. His eyes, though bloodshot, were determined. "Maybe it's time I decided to practice medicine instead of self-destruction." He eased himself onto a chair and put his hands on his knees. "Your wife has created quite a stir in this town. She's been telling folks I'm worthless and good-for-nothing."

Sam rubbed his chin, but didn't answer. Truth be told, he'd thought the same.

"She's talking about bringing a new doctor to Willow Creek." Potter tossed the towel onto the pile of blood-stained linens on the floor. "And I'm forced to admit, most of the time, she's right."

Sam sat down across from the doctor, folded his arms, and nodded. "Amanda has a way of being right that can drive a man insane."

Doc Potter laughed. "I guess you'd know more about that than me." He settled his elbows on his knees and took a deep gulp of air. "But your wife is right this time. I had the opportunity to study medicine at one of the best schools in the country. And despite the rumors about my skills, when I'm sober, I have a talent for healing." He swallowed, and his eyes glistened. "But I wasn't skilled enough to save my beautiful Anna or our baby."

Sam had no words of comfort to offer. What did a man say when another talked of losing the most important thing in his life? How would he feel if he lost Amanda? He remembered Caleb's words. How would he feel when he lost Amanda? She'd have to leave Willow Creek now. Her life was in danger, and Sam knew he couldn't protect her.

Doc Potter shook his head and rose from the chair. "I don't know why I'm spilling my guts to you, Calhoun." He stared at the young man stretched out on the floor. "Other than I want your wife to know I'm going to try to remember why I became a doctor in the first place. I started out with a desire to heal people and do some good in this world. I'm going to attempt to be a real doctor again."

Sam stood to face him. "I'll tell Amanda. She's got the crazy notion that Willow Creek can become something more than a wild mining town. She has dreams of respectability and decency. She talks about building schools and homes and making this a real town."

Doc Potter straightened his shoulders. "Sometimes a good woman can change the way folks think and act. It might be a crazy notion, and then again, she just might be dreaming big enough for all of us."

A flicker of hope whistled through Sam at the Doc's words. Amanda certainly held all of his hopes and dreams. He loved her, cherished her, and wanted her to remain his wife. But telling her would bind her to him, and to Willow Creek, forever. If she knew how he felt, she'd never leave. Most of all, he feared that someday, when he'd been careless and dropped his vigilance, someone would hurt her.

Seeing Amanda lying on the floor in a pool of blood would destroy him.

"Let's get this boy upstairs and into a bed. I think he'll stay unconscious at least long enough for us to move him." The doctor pointed. "If I remember correctly, there's a pretty decent room at the top of the stairs."

"Maybelle's room?" Sam grinned.

Doc Potter flushed and stammered for a moment, then grinned back. "Good Lord, but doesn't that woman have some big. . . ?" The Doc coughed. "Sorry Calhoun, I forget you're now a married man."

Sam just grinned. After they got Caleb upstairs and settled onto the bed, Sam opened his pocket watch to check the time. It was nearly two. How had the time disappeared so quickly?

He remembered his conversation with Amanda that morning and her eagerness at the idea of riding out to the Willow Grove to have a picnic. He slipped the watch back into his pocket. There wouldn't be any delightful sojourns, today or ever again. He was going to tell Amanda the truth about his arrangement with Father Mikelson. After that, he had no doubt she'd leave Willow Creek.

His heart ached. She would leave him. Forever. The first time he caught a glimpse of her face he'd been afraid she could capture his heart. The night she'd discovered him in the kitchen, when she'd talked about loneliness, he'd warned himself to beware of her allure. How could a man protect himself from loving Amanda?

Sam stumbled up the steps of the Parmeter House, admitting he didn't have the courage to face her yet. He settled into a rocking chair on the porch. Lighting a cigar, he enjoyed the smooth taste of good Virginia tobacco. He tapped the end of the cigar against the porch rail and attempted to conjure the words to explain to Amanda why they couldn't be together. They wouldn't come.

Various plans to keep her by his side coursed through his mind. He could retire from the Secret Service, grab whatever cash he could raise quickly, and travel with Amanda. The idea filled him with hope.

Then masculine pride reared its ugly head.

How long would his measly savings support them? Sooner or later, he'd have to rely upon his wife's money. And the thought rankled him. He'd done a lot of things he was ashamed of, but he'd never used a woman's money to survive.

For the first time in years, he was regaining some of his pride. Living off his wife would destroy that.

Then again, he didn't want to give her an annulment and send her away either. Tossing the cigar over the railing, he stood up and brushed his frock coat. It was time. In a few minutes, the decision would no longer be his to make. Everything would depend upon Amanda's reaction to his confession.

Robert waved at him as he crossed the foyer to climb the stairs. "Harriet was with her for a while, tried to get her to eat something and rest."

Sam kept one booted foot on the first step. "We need to take turns sitting with Caleb. The doc will stay for a few hours, but I want to make sure we have a man at the door and someone in the room with the boy at all times."

Robert nodded. "You expectin' more trouble?"

Sam nodded. "I don't think Caleb was the real target. Once word gets out he's alive, I suspect whoever attacked him might try again. We don't know if Caleb recognized his attacker or not, but if he can identify him, that means the boy's still in danger."

Robert lifted the oak divider that allowed entrance into the desk area. "I'll get some men together. There are a lot of miners who like that boy, and they're upset about what happened. I won't have any trouble finding volunteers."

Sam started up the stairs. Each step seemed agonizingly difficult, and he tried again to rehearse what he would say to Amanda. He swallowed when he finally stood in front of their door and fumbled with the key. His fingers felt as thick as the lump in his throat.

Finally, he unlocked the door to step into the quiet late-afternoon shadows stretching across the two rooms. Silence greeted him. The soft rhythm of Amanda's breathing was the only sound in the room. He quietly approached her bed and watched her sleep. He admired her features—the pert nose, the full, luscious mouth that invited his kisses. Soft russet-colored curls had escaped from her chignon to frame her face. She was so beautiful, so precious, and so vulnerable.

How was Sam going to convince her they could never be together, when he couldn't convince himself?

She stirred and whispered a word. *Baby*? Was that what she said? Sam grinned. Maybe she was dreaming about him. He shook the thought away. He turned to walk back into his own room when her voice stopped him.

"How's Caleb?" Her tone was soft, dreamy sounding.

Sam knelt next to her, grasped one of her hands, and tried to make his voice gentle and comforting. "Doc Potter is still with him. He had a deep stab wound in his shoulder and he's lost a lot of blood."

He watched her face go pale, visible even in the deep shadows of the room.

"We won't know anything for a few hours. But the doc says he's young and healthy. That should work in his favor."

Amanda sat up and tried to fling the quilt aside. "I should be with him."

Sam held her in place. "The doc is still with him, and I've sent Robert to find volunteers to keep guard around the clock." He touched her face gently. "You had a terrible shock this afternoon and you need your rest."

She gave him a small smile and leaned back against the brass headboard. "I suppose you're right."

A tremor of concern gripped Sam. It wasn't usual for Amanda to agree so quickly. Was she truly feeling ill? Had the shock of seeing Caleb injured at the Miners' Association affected her so deeply?

"I need to talk to you, Sam."

He took a deep breath and stood, pacing across the room. "We need to talk to each other, Amanda. And seriously."

He twisted on a boot heel and walked to the window, opening the curtains to allow sunlight to spill into the room.

"You have that 'I know what's best for you' tone in your voice, Sam. I'm not as fragile as you think I am." She pulled the covers back again to climb out of bed. "In fact, since coming to Willow Creek, I've discovered just how strong I can be when necessary." She crossed the room to face him, her chin high with pride and her eyes bright with confidence. "I think my experiences here have helped me grow up. Arthur tried to keep me childlike, dependent upon him." She took a deep breath. "And I guess I enjoyed that, too. But I've learned I like being independent and making my own decisions. I appreciate that, even though we're married, you haven't tried to control me." She touched his arm and gave him a brilliant smile.

Sam couldn't resist. He slipped his arms around her waist and pulled her closer. He inhaled her lilac scent and closed his eyes as her soft, curvaceous body molded against him. He'd never love another woman the way he loved Amanda, and the thought made him weak with longing.

He wanted to kiss her, to enjoy the soft petals of her lips opening beneath his. He ached to taste the sweet nectar she offered, but if he did, he'd be lost forever.

He took a step back and inhaled a deep breath. "I've been lying to you, Amanda."

Wariness grew in her eyes and suspicion lit the deep emerald depths.

"But, we promised each other. We said..."

He didn't wait for her to finish the sentence. The words were a painful memory. "I know what I said, but I lied." He raked his hand through his hair. God, he wanted a drink. He should have gone to the saloon to prepare himself.

She crossed her arms and the soft planes of her face hardened. "I think you'd better explain yourself, Samuel Calhoun."

He was backed into the corner, trapped by her dressing screen, the bed, and an angry and perplexed Amanda. He glanced at the window and briefly considered opening it and stepping out onto the roof. Then he could fling himself off and hope he'd be so severely injured he wouldn't need to do this. "I think you should sit down."

"I don't want to sit down, Sam."

He swallowed again and tried to find the words. Finally, he closed his eyes, summoned every ounce of courage he could find, and proceeded.

"I made a deal with Father Mikelson."

"Father Mikelson? What kind of deal could you make with that pious old fool?"

Sam winced and opened his eyes. A frown furrowed her brow. He wanted to pace, but she remained implacable. With her crossed arms and harsh, angry look, moving her wouldn't be wise.

"It was all to protect you and keep you safe. For your own good."

She tapped a toe. "Whenever a man utters those words, my blood turns cold. It means I'm going to hear something I won't like."

He took a step closer, wanting to reach out and touch her, to reassure her. "Father Mikelson knows about the threats against you—that someone might even be trying to kill you."

She gasped, and her lips formed a hard line. She stood silently, glaring at him, before stomping across the room. She kicked several pieces of clothing to the side. "I told him about that in confidence. He's a priest for heaven's sake. He's supposed to keep secrets. He took some kind of vow."

She picked up a silver brush from her dressing table, and Sam imagined it flying toward his head. Instead, she sat down and tugged pins from her hair before roughly yanking the brush through it with no apparent regard for her scalp. He winced at the thought of the pain she inflicted upon herself.

He cares about you. He said he loves you like a daughter."

She snorted and turned to face him. "Love is just a word men use to justify their treachery."

The words wounded Sam deeply. Is that what she thought of him? No, because in all their time together, those were the words he'd kept locked inside. He'd never told Amanda how much he loved her. At least not when she was awake and able hear him.

She turned back to the mirror, but their eyes met in the reflection.

"He knew you were in danger, that you'd been threatened, and that's why he insisted on the marriage. He thought I could protect you."

"How noble of you, Sam. You took a wife you didn't love to keep her safe." Acid dripped from her words. "But, wait. This is the same Samuel Calhoun who planned to seduce a defenseless widow for money." Her smile grew hard and cold. "How much did he pay you, Sam?"

He froze at her words. Fumbling for an answer, he tried to distract her. "Father Mikelson wanted you to be safe and happy."

She stood, hands on her hips, to face him. "Then why did he force me to marry you, Sam?"

He recoiled. "Because he thought he could trust me?"

Her brittle laughter slashed through the room. "Then he's more of an old fool than I ever imagined. Didn't he know you're the prince of lies? Remember Sam, I called you that once before. Truly, you deserve the title."

She slammed the brush down on the dainty lace doily lining the surface of the dressing table and glared at him. "Why did you do it, Sam? Tell me the truth. The truth, if that's even possible, and then I want you out of here."

He considered pleading with her. He could tell her he'd started out wanting to protect her, but that he'd fallen deeply, irrevocably in love with her. He might tell her she was the woman he wanted to spend the rest of his life with, have children with. He could tell her about dreams that the two of them would grow old together.

His heart was shattering within his chest as he realized being with Amanda was what he desired most in this world, and the one thing he couldn't have. He wanted to fall to his knees and plead with her to forgive him, but telling her the truth would bind her to him forever, and lies would send her away. Lies that were necessary for her survival.

Blood moved slowly through his veins. If he'd been submerged in a glacial stream before the spring thaw he couldn't be more chilled.

"Money. Isn't it always money?" He made his voice cold and emotionless. "That and an annulment. He said if I left you alone, didn't share your bed, he'd arrange for an annulment. We'd both be free."

Amanda stared at him, her eyes betraying her shock and surprise. She laughed again, the hollow, brittle sound making him shudder. "Well, Sam. You didn't exactly fulfill that part of the bargain did you?" She pointed to her bed. "I seem to recall I haven't spent all the nights since our wedding alone in this bed. How will you explain that to Father Mikelson?"

Sam's face heated. "I...we..." The truth, that he simply couldn't resist her, sounded feeble.

"Don't worry, Sam." She leaned forward, acting as though she were conspiring with him. "I won't tell if you won't. You can have your annulment and good riddance to you." Her words were clipped and icy as she waved a hand in the air, brushing him aside.

She pointed toward the door. "Now get out, and I don't want

you bothering me again. When the Miners' Ball is over and Caleb is healed, I'll be leaving Willow Creek for good."

Sam hurried around her, anxious to escape her anger and accusations. He was afraid the dark, cold emptiness filling him would bring him to his knees. He grabbed his hat from the bed and stood in the doorway separating their rooms. "I'm sorry, Amanda. I never intended to hurt you."

She had bent over to fasten her boots and he couldn't see her expression. "Just do me one favor, Sam." Her tone was icy.

"I'll do whatever I can to make you happy, Amanda."

She lifted her head and flung the buttonhook across the room. "Hang that door back on the hinges. I still have a gun, and I can't be certain I'll resist the temptation to shoot you again."

He pulled the Stetson down on his head and nodded. "You won't need to worry about indulging your murderous tendencies. I won't be sleeping at the hotel anymore."

He turned and walked out of the room, trying to appear calm and composed. When he finally reached the porch, he leaned against one of the carved newel posts. He remembered crossing this street several weeks ago, telling himself he didn't need to worry about losing his heart to the Widow Wainwright, because he didn't believe he possessed one anymore.

He'd been a damned fool. Today he knew for certain he still had a heart. He recoiled as he realized everything he had treasured with Amanda was lost forever. All those years he'd spent building a wall around his emotions had been useless. A shattering sense of loss overwhelmed him.

He'd just sentenced himself to a future without love. He clenched his fists and fought back against the wave of loneliness that swept over him, nearly choking him with pain. He yanked his hat down over his eyes to hide the tears he knew glistened there.

He stumbled across the street toward the saloon, knowing there wasn't enough whiskey in the world to wash away the heartache he was feeling. He didn't care.

Drinking himself into oblivion was the only way he could think of to get through the night.

Chapter Eighteen

Amanda resisted the urge to throw herself across her bed and weep. She choked back tears and tried to replace the cold, desolate feeling of loss with hot, hard-edged anger.

Lies.

That's all he'd ever told her.

She swept a loose curl back from her face. Her earlier conversation with Harriet haunted her, and tears filled her eyes, threatening to cascade in a waterfall of heartbreak.

She'd never tell Sam about the baby now. Her hands moved to cover her stomach protectively. Maybe the father of her child didn't want a family, but she did. This baby would be the one good thing she could take away from her marriage to Sam.

She unfolded her silk shawl and wrapped it around her shoulders. In a few weeks, she could leave Willow Creek and all the horrible memories. She'd travel to Europe, perhaps to Italy. She'd heard there were places on the Mediterranean coast where the sun was warm, and the air perfumed with the scent of flowers. A rich American widow could easily hide herself in some small seaside town there.

She stood at the doorway to Sam's room and wiped away tears that insisted upon falling. She wanted to bury her face in his pillow, to smell the clean masculine scent of his shaving soap. She wanted to gather some small item to remind her of the man she loved.

She pushed the thought aside. When she left Willow Creek,

she would be the Widow Wainwright again. She wouldn't even give Sam's child his name.

The thought fulfilled her desire for vengeance. Sam wanted his freedom, and she was obliged to give it to him. But he would never know about the child she carried in her womb. Her final act of retaliation would be to rob him of that knowledge. She needed to find Harriet and make sure she didn't congratulate Sam.

Hurrying down the stairs, she waited at the desk in the foyer. No one was about, which was unusual. She gasped when she saw a letter in her mailbox. Bright blood-red ink screamed at her, and she backed away, terror clenching her in a vise that nearly strangled her. She was ready to scurry back up the stairs when she bumped into Mr. Penny.

"I heard what happened to young McQueen. I was hoping there might be something I could do." He rolled the brim of his hat in his hands and avoided looking directly at her.

Amanda twisted around to ponder the letter in the cubby-hole, then turned to find his small black eyes studying her. He grasped her elbow.

"You look a bit pale, Mrs. Calhoun, perhaps you should sit down. You've had a very trying day from what I've heard."

Amanda sat down in a deep upholstered chair and gave Mr. Penny a sharp glance. "What do mean, trying?"

He swallowed hard, and his Adam's apple bobbed up and down. He seemed intent upon destroying his black bowler while he fumbled for words. "The whole town is talking about it."

Amanda's eyes grew wide. Had the news of Sam leaving her swept through town already? Mr. Penny shook his nearly bald head. "They say you were the one who found Caleb." His eyes glittered with something that disturbed her. "That you found him lying in a pool of blood."

Amanda shuddered as she recalled the image of Caleb, pale, wounded, and sprawled upon the floor. Taking a deep breath, she adjusted the shawl around her shoulders and gave Mr. Penny a grim smile. "I seem to be getting used to astonishing events and frightening experiences. My constitution is stronger than you might imagine, Mr. Penny." She stood and lifted her chin, hoping he would see confidence where it didn't really exist. "I need to finalize the arrangements for the Miners' Ball." She took a deep breath. "I've decided to leave Willow Creek soon. Please have all the papers ready for transferring management of the association to the miners within the next week."

Mr. Penny's eyes popped wide. "Will Mr. Calhoun be leaving Willow Creek with you?"

Amanda started toward the door and paused to glance over her shoulder. "I'll be traveling alone for the time being. Mr. Calhoun has business interests to attend to before he can join me in San Francisco. After that, we'll be taking an extended voyage to Europe." She gave him a weak smile. "Our honeymoon."

Before he could ask any more questions, Amanda spun on her heel to briskly walk out the door. That would be her version of events, and Sam could go to hell if he didn't support her. She planned to leave Willow Creek with her pride intact and her head held high. No one would know her heart had been broken and her dreams destroyed. No one except Sam, and he'd made it perfectly clear that the sooner she disappeared from Montana, the happier he'd be.

Sam learned to observe Amanda from the shadows. If she

caught sight of him, she went to extremes to avoid him. He tried to inquire about her, but ugly frowns and cold stares from both Robert and Harriet silenced him. Sam cursed Father Mikelson and his arrangement. He considered resigning from the Secret Service. Several times he'd started to cross the street to the Miners' Association, aware she was there, keeping vigil at Caleb's bedside. He wanted to unburden himself and beg for her forgiveness. The honest, painful truth was that without her, his life wasn't worth living. He'd tell her about the sleepless nights, pacing the lonely rooms above his office, trying to drown his sorrow and loneliness in whiskey. He'd make any promise necessary to win her back.

He'd tell her about the times he fell exhausted upon his bed, only to be tormented by dreams of her. He couldn't sleep, he couldn't eat, and now, he lurked in the shadows, hungry for the sight of her.

He slammed his fist against the wall and grimaced at the crushing pain that slid up his arm. Lately, pain was the only way he could remind himself he was still alive. Most of the time he felt like a phantom, flickering in and out of conversations, drifting through each day, feeling nothing but cold, bleak loneliness.

Amanda's head was bowed as she crossed the street to the Parmeter House. An ugly dark black bonnet obscured her expression, but he knew what he would see if he could catch a glimpse of her face. There were deep shadows beneath her eyes, and the corners of her mouth were drawn sharply down. He'd heard when others expressed concern over her she waved them away, explaining her long hours with Caleb were taking their toll. Yet, she'd hardly leave the boy's side.

She planned to leave town after the Miners' Ball. Gossip said she was going to Europe, and when others questioned him, Sam simply nodded at Amanda's assertion they would be traveling abroad together after he settled details of his business.

In a few weeks, his mission would be over and he'd leave

Willow Creek forever. Father Mikelson would arrange for the annulment, and Sam would get a new assignment. Most importantly, Amanda would be alive and safe.

Sam pondered the box sitting at his feet. He'd ordered a gift for Amanda weeks ago. It had arrived on the stage today, but he didn't know how to give it to her. If he placed it on the steps of the Miners' Association for her to find, she'd discard it. He needed to explain the significance of the gift, the reason it was so important and why he wanted her to have it.

He tucked the box beneath his arm. He could sneak up the back stairs so no one would see him. He still had the key to his room. As far as anyone knew, he worked late each night, attempting to organize his affairs so he would be free to travel on an extended honeymoon with his wife. When the town slept, when even the doors to the saloons closed, he doused his light and climbed the steps to his lonely rooms above the office.

At first light, he made sure he was back downstairs, so intent upon his business he never had time to dine with his wife. She took her meals with Caleb or in her room. He climbed the steep back stairs of the hotel, preparing the words he'd use when he faced Amanda. She hated him. She certainly wouldn't want to accept a gift from him.

He opened the door to his room quietly and stood for a few moments trying to locate her. A soft rustling echoed from the other room, followed by the heavy crash of an object hitting the floor. Amanda cussed loudly and Sam grinned. Her temper was certainly intact. He didn't know if he should be grateful or wary.

Many of her garments were now spread across his bed. He paused to caress the fine lace of a petticoat. It brought to mind the nights he'd undressed her, discarding each piece of lingerie to reveal the soft, satiny skin beneath. Blood surged to his groin and he rose. There was no denying the carnal appetite they shared, but there was more than sensual lovemaking between them. A lancet of regret pierced him. He hated to hurt her. The pain was worse than anything he'd faced in prison camp. His breath caught when her shadow fell on him.

"What the hell do you want, Calhoun?" Poison dripped from her voice.

She stood on the threshold between their rooms. The door had not yet been replaced, but without him in the other room, why would it matter? She was garbed only in her corset, petticoat, and chemise. Sam couldn't tear his eyes away from her, and his cock grew as hard as stone. His mouth was so dry, he didn't think he'd be able to form words.

Instead of blushing and turning away, she pushed her breasts out, set her hands on her hips and tossed her head. "Get out. I told you to leave me alone, and I meant it."

The length of her hair, glowing copper in the late afternoon light, moved in an undulating swirl. Desire ripped through Sam's body like a flood released from the gates. His tongue was thick in his mouth and he grew harder with a hot, sizzling need that flashed red across his vision.

"I have something for you. A gift." Before she could back away he thrust the box toward her. She smiled coldly at it but made no move to take the box away from him.

"A little late to come courting, isn't it, Sam?"

She was different, as if she'd grown into a woman and discarded all of her girlish affectations. She didn't accept the box, but moved with a familiar glide across the room to sit at her dressing table.

"I don't need anything from you, Sam, remember?" She picked up her brush and pulled it through her auburn tresses.

Sam couldn't tear his eyes from her. Her breasts, spilling out over the top of her corset, seemed fuller, rounder than he remembered. She tossed her head again and gave him a long desultory look. The tip of her tongue flickered across her lips, and a sharp stab of desire clawed at Sam. She was teasing him, and damn her to hell, it was working.

"I didn't come to play games with you, Amanda. I brought you something, and we need to talk."

Amanda set her brush down and fluffed her hair. "More's the pity, Sam. You're much more fun to play with than to talk to."

Turning on the bench, she leaned forward, and he caught a glimpse of her ankle when she lifted the ruffle of her petticoat. He nearly forgot what he needed to say. Then he spied the deep cleavage between her breasts and he did forget what he was going to say. The bulge at his crotch was painful and pushed hard against his trousers.

She looked at Sam with a languid, predatory glow in her eyes. "So, talk."

He mumbled and closed his eyes in exasperation. She toyed with him, and he felt green as a boy again.

"Enjoying yourself, Amanda?"

"Actually, yes. I'm enjoying this immensely."

He opened his eyes, threw the box on the cluttered bed, and removed the lid. He held a satin and lace gown out to her. A modest offering for a goddess.

"I ordered this for you, back, well...when we were first married. I want you to wear it to the Miners' Ball tomorrow night."

Amanda's eyes widened and her mouth formed a tiny "o" of surprise. Her gaze moved from the pale green frock to him and back again. What might be pleasure glimmered in the emerald depths of her eyes for a moment, before the cold indifference reappeared.

"That color is not appropriate for a woman in mourning." She dismissed his gift with a brief wave of her hand. "I'll wear black crepe, it's my usual garb."

Sam clenched his hands. "That's what I'm trying to tell you, Amanda. You can discard those widow's weeds. It's time for you to pull yourself out from under Arthur's shadow. You've proven to me and everyone else in Willow Creek that you're a woman capable of making decisions and running a business on your own."

He settled the gown back into the box and approached her.

He forced his hands to remain at his sides, fists clenched, though his fingers itched to stroke her hair, touch the softness of her cheek, and trail down to cup the fullness of a breast. The fragrance of lilacs, mixed with her personal woman's scent, assailed his nostrils, and he struggled for self-control.

"You're a woman to be admired, Amanda Wainwright Calhoun."

She tossed her head and rose to move within inches of him. Her breath was sweet and warm, and he fought to keep his hands off her creamy skin, bare and inviting and within his reach.

"Admired or pitied, Sam?"

He threw back his head and laughed. The sound wasn't filled with mirth though; it rang sad and hollow in the room.

"I pity myself, Amanda. Only a fool would walk away from you."

Her glance flickered across his face, searching. He wanted to cringe at the stark appraisal, but knew he needed to be honest with her.

"I'd never be good for you, Amanda. In a few years, you'd be looking down the table at me, feeling angry and betrayed at being forced to marry a man so unworthy of you."

She took a step closer and Sam nearly stopped breathing. He needed to hold her, to kiss her, to plead with her to make the pain inside him go away.

He closed his eyes, knowing she was going to touch him, and that at that moment all of his composure would dissolve. He prepared himself for the assault on his senses, but instead she turned away.

"So, that's the kind of woman you think deserving of admiration? One who would discard people because they didn't meet her preconceived notions or expectations?" She crossed to the bed and lifted the dress to examine it.

Sam took a deep breath. "I've lied to you and betrayed you. Certainly, you deserve better than that."

With one quick motion, she turned and threw the dress at him.

"Yes, I deserve someone who loves me. That's all I ever wanted, Sam. Someone who could see beyond the widow's weeds, and the mines, and yes, even beyond the money." Her eyes filled with tears. "I wanted someone to see *me*. Was that too much to ask?"

Sam fought the urge to rush to her and pull her into his arms. Instead, he draped the dress on the curve of the trunk near the foot of the bed and took another deep breath.

"People do see you, Amanda. That's why I believe it's time you get rid of all these black gowns and start to show people how beautiful you really are." He raked his eyes over her, from the toes peeping out from beneath her petticoat to the unruly russet tangle of her hair.

"Stop hiding behind Arthur and me. You're intelligent, beautiful, and desirable. Let the world see who you really are, Amanda. You're a butterfly, and it's time to crawl out of your cocoon."

Her face went pale. "How dare you. I'm not hiding behind you, or Arthur, or any other man."

Sam flung the green dress back onto the bed and flipped

open the trunk. He grabbed the first black crepe gown he could find and held it up. "Really? Isn't this a costume? You admitted you weren't really in mourning for Arthur. But traipsing around town in widow's garb reminds people of how sad and lonely you are." He shook the gown in her face. "Even when you publicly declared a marriage to me, you couldn't get rid of your disguise. Isn't that true, Amanda?"

She grabbed for the gown, but he took two steps away. "The poor, pathetic Widow Wainwright, isn't that what you want people to see?"

Tears rolled down her cheeks. "Stop it. Why can't you ever just leave me alone, Sam?"

Sam fumbled in his pocket and pulled out his Lucifer matches.

"People have been leaving you alone all your life, haven't they, Amanda? Is that why you hide yourself away, drape yourself in black, and hope you disappear into the background?"

She stumbled toward him, hands raised into fists prepared to pummel him. She stopped when he lit one of the matches. "What are you going to do, burn down the hotel?"

Sam didn't hide his loathing as he glared at the ugly black dress he held in one hand. "I certainly hope not. I do believe Harriet Parmeter is already quite annoyed with me." He touched the match to the dress and it burst into flame. He opened one of the windows and flung it toward the middle of the street. She brushed him aside to look out the window, then turned on him and smacked him with the palm of her hand. He grabbed her by the wrist and yanked her to him.

"I'll burn every single gown you own before I see you dressed in that crow's garb again. Do you understand, Amanda?"

She struggled, and all the warnings against holding her disappeared as a wave of longing swept through him. With no thought to the consequences, he pulled her into his arms and fastened his mouth to hers with a hard, deep, demanding kiss.

Her struggles ceased and her lips opened beneath the assault. He forced his tongue into her mouth and stroked her with a plunging, exciting rhythm. Her arms circled his neck, pulling him closer, and he dipped his hand beneath the silk of her chemise to find the perfect pearl of her nipple.

All his control slipped as desire seized him. He wanted to fall down on the bed, yank her on top of him, and spread her legs over his hips for a wild bucking ride that would carry them both over the edge to ecstasy.

She seemed transfixed by the motions of his mouth and hand, and finally surrendered. With one swift movement, he tumbled to the bed with her, pulling her down on top of him.

He yanked on the top of her corset, exposing her breasts before he placed his mouth where his fingers had been. She arched her back as he suckled one, then the other.

His hand slid down to the buttons of his pants, and he fumbled to release his erection.

“You bastard,” she whispered, her words rough and angry. “How dare you use me in this way.”

She spun off the bed to stand over him, her arms folded across her breasts and her lips twisting her face into a mask of pain and defiance. “I’m not some cheap whore you can use and discard. I’m your wife. And you either take your marriage vows seriously, Samuel Calhoun, or get out. And I mean out of my life, once and for all.”

Sam struggled to his feet. His body demanded satisfaction, the length of his cock was rigid with a burning need to slide between her legs and satisfy the ache, but her words hit him like a bucket of ice water tossed on his head. He felt off-balance, as if he’d just downed a bottle of whiskey and been in a barroom brawl, all within the last fifteen minutes.

"I'm..." He adjusted his collar and string tie and straightened his clothing, then bowed gracefully. "I apologize, Amanda. I didn't mean to take advantage of the situation." He curled a tousled strand of her hair around one finger. "Just remember what I said. No more of that black crow. You're a beautiful butterfly."

He stumbled from the room and down the stairs, forgetting to sneak out the back. Harriet Parmeter's smile thinned when she spied him making his way out the door.

He couldn't stop to explain. The air in his lungs was hot, making it painful to breathe. The searing agony of losing Amanda again, this time finally and for good, was too horrible to contemplate.

Chapter Nineteen

Amanda picked up her silver brush and sent it flying toward the door where it hit the frame, barely missing Sam. He'd once again walked out on her. "Damn you, Samuel Calhoun!" she screamed, not caring that she sounded like a harridan. "You keep walking away, but you just won't leave me alone."

She tumbled to the bed, throwing an arm across her eyes and fighting to keep from dissolving into tears. Her breasts still ached from his sensual assault, and she was wet between the legs, moist and ready for him to thrust into her. Angry and frustrated that he could so easily arouse her, she struggled to breathe and worked to regain her composure. He was gone, leaving her to pick up the pieces of her shattered heart.

"I won't cry for you, not again." She swore under her breath and wiped a tear from her cheek. "Not ever again."

The man was impossible. He'd recite all the reasons they couldn't be together, and in the next instant, wrap her in his arms and tease her to distraction with his kisses. She sat up, catching a glimpse of the gown he'd given her. She snatched it up and briefly considered taking a match to it and tossing it out the window to join her blazing widow's weeds.

What difference did it make to Sam what she wore to the Miners' Ball? He wouldn't be there, and as far as she was concerned, no one else mattered. She heaved a deep sigh of regret. She could dream of dancing in the beautiful dress, candlelight flickering in those golden eyes, and seeing desire blossom in their depths. But the reality was Samuel Calhoun had once again said good-bye to her.

She tossed the dress to the floor, stood up, and stomped across the room to stare at her reflection in the dressing table mirror. Her lips were swollen from his kisses and her clothes askew. She adjusted the top of her satin corset. Her breasts were fuller, more mature looking.

Turning sideways, she looked for signs of the babe she carried. Her stomach was still flat, and she spread her hands protectively over the spot where she imagined her child slept. "I'll never abandon you, my darling."

Amanda perused her reflection. Was she a butterfly? She scoffed at the idea. She knew she wasn't plain, but she'd hardly call herself beautiful. Yet Sam had said she was that and more. His words echoed in her mind. Strong and capable. The very things she wanted to be, but always felt were so hugely lacking in her character. How did he see those things in her?

And why wouldn't he just leave her alone? She recalled the way he'd looked at her, the gentle softness of his touch and ache of desire in his kiss. Twisting her head to the side, she gathered her hair in one hand and traced the outline of her face with the other. Who was she? Certainly not the woman who'd arrived in Willow Creek so many weeks ago.

That woman had been a shadow, afraid of facing the challenges before her, terrified of the gaping loneliness that nearly consumed her. Where was that woman now?

Sam was right. She had emerged from a cocoon. She'd been wrapping herself in the black crepe mourning clothes so she could pretend life wasn't going to pass her by. Or pretend she didn't care if it did. She shivered at that thought. She cared very much about her life at this moment.

She cared because a new life was growing stronger each day within her. Her future wasn't going to be filled with morning mass, afternoon prayers, and cold lonely nights.

She gathered up the pale green frock. Hugging it to her body, she examined the effect in the mirror. The color brought out the red highlights in her hair and the dark green of her eyes. Sam had chosen well.

The corners of her mouth lifted into a smile. Samuel Calhoun didn't want her to leave, that much was obvious. He might pretend his bargain with Father Mikelson obliged him to annul their marriage, but his kiss told another story.

A surge of power rushed through her. Of course, she needed to contact the old priest and find out what kind of deal he'd forged with Sam. If she knew how Father Mikelson had manipulated Sam, she could convince her husband they needed to stay together.

She gently draped the gown across the foot of the bed and hurried to the dressing table. Locating her stationery, pen, and inkwell, she scrawled a note to Father Mikelson. She finished the note and contemplated who could act as a messenger and take it to the telegraph office. She would normally ask Mr. Penny, but their earlier encounter had left her unsettled. His eyes had been cold and measuring when he'd noticed her looking at the letter in her box. Remembering the cursed missive written in blood-red script, she reached into a hatbox and pulled it out with trembling hands.

Get out of town, bitch, and forget about Willow Creek. If you value your life, you'll leave today. We're watching you. Beware, Mrs. Calhoun, because you live only as long as we allow it.

Amanda crumpled the letter and tossed it back into the box. A cold tremor of fear ripped through her. She wished now she had told Sam about it. He never would have left her if he thought she was in real danger. She could have kept him with her, protecting her and their baby.

But she didn't want Sam as a guardian angel, stuck by her side because he felt guilty and responsible. She wanted him to be her husband, staying because he loved her. And the only way she could accomplish that was to prove to him he couldn't bear to see her leave town. She stretched and yawned. She decided to take a short nap and wait for Harriet to bring her supper.

She'd settle this thing with Sam and make him realize their marriage was destined to be strong and successful. Caleb would recover soon, and the three, no, the four, of them, could build a family together.

Amanda smiled. She felt content for the first time in days. She would fill her life with people who cared about her, and that would be a gift beyond measure.

∞∞∞

Amanda woke the next morning possessed by a feeling of cold, hard determination. She'd given the note for Father Mikelson to Harriet and asked that she telegraph the message to Helena as soon as possible. Hopefully, the priest was already in route.

Dressing quickly, Amanda was eager to be on her way to the Miners' Association. She had many tasks to complete before the ball tonight. She grabbed the bed frame for a moment to steady herself. The combination of her usual morning queasiness and the thought of trying to accomplish everything made her lightheaded.

When she opened the door to the association, she found Margaret Abbott and a crew of miners already hard at work.

"Look at these Chinese lanterns, aren't they just the prettiest things?" Margaret beamed at her. "I feel like a kid again, all excited. This is Christmas and my birthday all rolled into one."

Amanda grinned at her. "You've done wonders with this

place, Margaret. It's beautiful."

Margaret threw back her head and laughed. "The idea of decorating up this fancy house for a big shindig just tickles me to no end." She leaned forward and gave Amanda a wink. "And the other wives can hardly wait to get into the place, just to satisfy their curiosity. I'm looking forward to seeing their faces when they get a gander at that picture of the fancy lady hanging in the kitchen."

"I wish you would have allowed me to remove that painting," Amanda said. "I don't want to embarrass the other women."

Margaret waved a hand. "They'd be madder'n hornets in a stirred up nest if you did that. For most of them, the high point of the evening will be pretending to be shocked to see such a thing. It'll give us something to gossip about for months."

Amanda couldn't keep her eyes from straying toward the staircase and shuddered at the spot still stained with Caleb's blood. No amount of scrubbing could seem to remove the dark blight upon the wooden floor.

"Any change in Caleb today?"

Margaret shook her head and patted Amanda on the arm. "I'm sorry honey, he's still not awake. The doc was here though, and I have to admit, that man seems to have had some kind of revelation or something." She grabbed a brightly painted lantern and held it out to examine it. "He was clean and sober and talking just like a regular doctor. He says Caleb has better color today and his breathing is real normal. He's been sipping that good broth Harriet made for him, just a bit at a time, but enough to know he's gonna come out of this, mark my words."

A wave of relief rushed over Amanda. Worry over Caleb's condition had consumed her for days. She felt guilty that he'd been left alone to face his attacker the morning he was beaten and stabbed because she'd lingered in bed with Sam. If only she'd been a bit more reluctant to frolic with her husband, they might have arrived before Caleb had been hurt.

"You go on up and visit him for a bit, I've got things under control down here." Margaret nodded in the direction of the kitchen. "We got the best cooks in town setting up in there. The folks will surely have a feast tonight, thanks to you, Amanda."

Amanda gave the woman a sad smile. "We should be grateful to Arthur Wainwright. It's his money that's paying for all of this. I'm sorry Arthur missed the opportunity to see how happy he could make other people. I'm learning to never pass up the opportunity for happiness, because you might not get that chance again."

Margaret Abbott nodded. "You got that right, honey. If God hands you dandelions instead of roses, you better learn how to make wine."

Amanda grinned and walked up the stairs. Is that what God was offering her? Dandelions? She wrinkled her nose. Roses would certainly be preferable, but when she considered the humble dandelion, she had to admit it was admirable. The bright yellow flower attracted children who considered them beautiful. The seeds could be scattered with a soft whisper, to carry wishes across the countryside. The deep, tenacious roots couldn't be destroyed or ripped out, despite all efforts one exerted to remove them. Perhaps it was preferable to be a stubborn weed rather than a delicate blossom, destined to need pampering and care.

Lydia Brown nodded to her when she entered Caleb's room. "He's comfortable. We moved him already this morning, and Doc says there's no sign of bedsores."

Amanda stared at the pale young face against the pillow and fought the urge to cry. He was just a boy, and the pain of seeing him so weak and helpless gnawed at her. He had sustained a beating clearly intended for her. "I'll sit with him for a little while, until Margaret needs me." Amanda settled into the maple rocker and folded her hands on her lap.

Lydia brushed at the calico dress she wore and grinned at Amanda. "Don't fret about Margaret. I haven't seen her in such a good mood in years. She's got every available man scrambling to do her bidding and she loves it."

Amanda leaned back in the chair and closed her eyes. "Just come up and get me when you need some help. I'm not feeling well this morning, but it usually passes by noon."

She regretted her confession when she opened her eyes and found Lydia staring at her with certain knowledge shining on her face. "Oh my," she said, before quietly exiting the room.

Amanda bit her lip. What a foolish thing to say to the mother of three children. Now her condition would be a topic of discussion amongst all the women. It was only a matter of time before the gossip reached Sam's ears.

She brushed aside her worries. Before the night was over, he would hear the truth from her lips. She planned to give him the opportunity to choose a life with his family.

She'd give Sam one more chance. If he turned and walked away this time, she'd never let him come back.

The Chinese lanterns stretched across the mowed area, creating a pattern of orange, red, and gold light. The tables were set at angles to each other, and snow-white linen tablecloths covered them. Candles sat inside mason jars, and small baskets of artfully arranged daisies, roses, and ivy decorated the tables. Silver, china, and crystal gleamed at each setting. Sam gave a low whistle at the simple yet elegant design.

He'd stayed away from the Miners' Association all day. Since Walter had been helping his mother with preparations, he served as Sam's spy, returning to the office with several reports. With wide eyes, the young man had described the plans for the Miners' Ball. Pride surged through Sam as he looked around the hayfield that stood behind the Miners' Association. Amanda had created a miracle.

Sam imagined how beautiful she'd look tonight, even if she didn't wear the gown he'd purchased for her. Her auburn hair would be burnished as a thousand small flames danced in highlight. He imagined her laughter, a clear, tinkling sound echoing in the soft shadows of early evening. Her emerald eyes would shine with pride, or at least he hoped they would.

He cursed his pact with Father Mikelson. He'd made a bargain with the devil himself. All of his lofty arguments went sailing out the window like Amanda's dress yesterday afternoon when he considered the reality of losing her. There wasn't enough whiskey in the territory to dull the ache in his heart. Now, more than anything, he wanted to spend the evening with her. He wanted to hold her in his arms and waltz with her, nibbling on her ear while whispering lewd, suggestive comments.

The hard length of his cock jumping to attention reminded him of the long, delightful nights he'd spent making love to Amanda. Exquisite nights he'd never forget, and never have again.

He tossed the cigar he'd been smoking to the ground and crushed it beneath the heel of his boot. He could stand here and torture himself all evening with fantasies or get back to his office and try to ignore the laughter and music that would drift down the street. Tonight would have been the perfect time to lose himself between the legs of one of Mrs. Holt's whores, but they no longer interested him.

Amanda was a rare, unique, and delicious wine, and his palate was spoiled for anything else. When she rode out of town in the morning, his heart would go with her.

Turning to leave, he stopped in his tracks. A vision of loveliness stood before him. Her green eyes studied him as she stepped forward and boldly tilted her face to give him a coy smile. He tensed, a raging hunger sweeping through him. His heart kicked in his chest, and his pants felt so snug in the crotch he was sure the buttons would pop off.

"Leaving so soon, Sam? The party hasn't even started yet."

He swallowed and wondered if he could force any words from his mouth. She had piled her hair on top of her head, and the highlights danced in the light just as he'd imagined. Several long russet curls trailed down a bare shoulder. Her bosom rode high at the lace-trimmed edge of the bodice, allowing Sam to feast his eyes on the creamy skin and deep channel between the twin globes. The dress hugged her full curved figure, the satin wrapping her in an embrace that made him jealous. The simple lines and elegant drape flattered her more than he'd imagined possible. What had he called her yesterday? A butterfly? She was that, and more.

"You've made magic here, Amanda. You should be proud of yourself."

She stepped closer, and the scent of lilacs swirled around him. He inhaled deeply, wishing he had a daguerreotype to capture her image to sustain him through the long, lonely nights of the rest of his life.

"I am proud, Sam." She looked about the outdoor room then regarded him. "I believe you were correct yesterday. I'm stepping out from the shadows and into the light." Her soft strawberry-hued lips lifted delicately to give him a gentle smile. "Don't you think it's time I take control of my own life?"

Sam trembled as she picked a piece of lint from his frock coat. She patted his lapel gently, and the tip of her tongue circled to wet her lips. He wanted to crush her to him, push her to the ground, and caress her until she whimpered, begging him to take her. He shuddered, imagining her legs spread wide, his fingers gliding into her moist center until she panted with her need for him. She was a wanton temptress. He took a deep breath to compose himself. He was too hot, too hard, and too hungry for her; he had to get away.

"I was hoping you would stay and dance with me tonight, Sam."

"You know I can't do that, Amanda." Damn, he wanted to, but he couldn't.

"Can't or won't?" Her fingers caressed the fabric of his coat and found the edge of his vest. She made a path to the gold watch he had tucked into his pocket, and he stood speechless, wondering where her fingers would travel next. She was playing with him, teasing him. Damn it. A hot, molten trail of desire whipped through him at her touch. His cock was hard as oak and his testicles felt like cannon balls hanging between his legs.

With boldness he didn't expect, she swept her hand across the buttons of his trousers to rub him enticingly. Sam was close to losing control, nearly blinded by lust. He grabbed her hand and gave her a sharp look of warning.

"I thought you knew better than to play with fire." He brought her fingers to his lips and kissed them. "After all, you don't want to get burned, do you?"

He suckled the tip of each finger, and she trembled.

"Maybe I'm a moth instead of a butterfly. It could be worth dancing with the flame to experience that wonderful flash of heat."

Her words shocked him and enticed him at the same time. Liquid fire pooled in his belly as he imagined the kind of heat he could generate with Amanda. "You are a temptress tonight, my sweet." He dropped her hand. "And I'm not even going to pretend I can resist you."

He turned to walk away, regretting each step that carried him out of her life forever. If he didn't get away soon, he'd succumb to her wiles and take her right here on the ground. If that happened, he'd never have the strength to leave her again. His honor, his career, his country. None of it would matter.

Her laughter startled him. It reminded him of the soft rustle of birch leaves in the early spring breeze.

"You can't escape from me you know."

He turned to face her, knowing his astonishment must show on his face. "I beg your pardon?"

She lifted one finely arched eyebrow. "Can't you see? You keep walking away from me over and over again. How many times have you said good-bye, Sam? How many times have you strolled out the door, only to discover yourself back to face me again?"

Her question lingered in the air, unanswered. He studied her. She was different tonight. Confident. With the look of a woman who had faced her demons and struck them down, whipping them into submission. He swallowed, aware of the heavy thud of his heart as the blood rushed through his body.

"I believe, for the sake of your manly pride, you have to pretend you don't want or need me."

Sam stared as she lit the candles on the tables. Her skin appeared to be sprinkled with stardust. It glowed in the reflection of the lamps, and he struggled to get his powerful arousal under control.

"I know the truth about you, Sam. I know a truth you won't even face." She shrugged. "It doesn't matter. Despite what you've said, you won't let me ride out of town and leave you forever."

A bead of sweat formed on Sam's brow and he wiped it away

with his forearm. Her words frightened him, because he knew them for the truth.

"Are you so sure of me, Amanda?"

She stepped closer. "I'm sure of me, Sam. For the first time in my life, I know what I want."

She turned to pick up a small bouquet of flowers and inserted one into each arrangement. Was she putting dandelions into the baskets?

"Do you always get what you want, little girl?"

She blinked up at him, turquoise highlights glittering in the depths of her emerald eyes "Up until now, no. I almost never got what I wanted." She continued to work on the flower arrangements. "But that was my own fault. I have always been willing to settle for less. I've let other people make decisions for me, but I know better now."

He was intrigued by her observation. "So, you'll get me because it's what you want."

She brushed at one of the tablecloths and grinned. "I'll get you because you love me as much as I love you. You won't let me go because you know how good our life will be if we're together."

Blood rushed to Sam's head, and he was glad to be leaning against one of the fence posts, because he might have tipped sideways otherwise. "What did you say?"

"I love you, Sam." She lifted her head to give him a dazzling smile. "I plan to stay married to you. And even if you made some kind of foolish agreement with Father Mikelson, it doesn't matter. He should be here by tomorrow morning, and then we can straighten this whole mess out."

His heart slammed against his chest. The hot urge to take possession of her dissolved in the face of her confession. Amanda loved him.

Before Sam could form a response, she lifted her gaze to greet someone behind him.

"Hello Margaret and Walter. The yard looks just lovely. You did a wonderful job."

Sam moved aside to make way for two members of the Abbott family. He knew better than to start an argument with Amanda now. It was going to be a special evening for her, and he didn't intend to spoil it. And the shock of her words had hit him hard, like someone swinging a two-by-four at him. He needed to think about this and find a way to convince her they couldn't be together, despite the fact that they loved each other.

Damned if he knew how he was going to do that, because he was having a hard time convincing himself.

"I'll talk to you after supper, Amanda. You're right. There are things we need to sort out." He turned and stalked toward the front gate.

"Don't worry, darlin'. I'll save a dance for you!" Amanda yelled after him.

Sam yanked his Stetson down on his head and fumed. He slammed the gate closed. He'd done it now. It was apparent that Amanda had gone stark raving mad. His emotions were in turmoil, with her confession that she loved him creating confusion and a jolt of happiness no amount of good sense could subdue. A tremor of hope surged through him, along with a sure knowledge that after tonight, his life would never be the same.

He would be back later tonight, and he'd tell her the whole truth. He'd admit who he really was and beg for her forgiveness. He loved her, and once he told her, he'd never stop saying it over and over again.

A patch of light glided up his backbone and he stopped, trying to figure out what was happening to him.

He was happy. Really and truly happy.

"Well, I'll be damned" he said, laughing as pulled his hat down on his head. He strolled down the street whistling, and he didn't care if the good citizens of Willow Creek thought he was crazy. To hell with them all because he was a man in love.

Chapter Twenty

Amanda contemplated the yard filled with people having a wonderful time. Old, grizzled miners pumped their arms and stomped their feet, dancing to the tune of the small band playing on the wooden stage at the edge of the yard. Tables were loaded with fried chicken, ham, trout baked in a cream sauce, potatoes covered with butter, rolls the size of a man's fist, and creamy coleslaw rich with mayonnaise. A side of beef slowly roasted over an open pit. Other tables were covered with pies, cakes, and puddings for dessert.

Music, laughter, and conversation floated over the men who worked for her. Their families gathered around, laughing, dancing, and eating a prodigious amount of food. With a deep sigh of contentment, Amanda realized her struggle to give these good hard-working folks a night of fun had been worth the cost.

She had arrived in Willow Creek afraid of the challenges she faced. Tonight, she was proving she could follow through on her plans and her promises. She lifted her head with pride when yet another couple visited her table to offer their thanks and express their appreciation.

Harriet gave her a motherly pat on the arm. "You've made a lot of folks very happy, Amanda." There was a note of concern in her voice. "I just hope you haven't sacrificed your own joy doing it."

Amanda tried to muster a smile. It was growing late, and Sam still hadn't returned to finish their conversation. Maybe she'd been wrong, and he was more than willing to watch her leave town, and him, forever.

"Look at young Abbott kick up his heels. He's such a shy, quiet thing, who knew he could dance?" Harriet pointed to a couple twirling around the dance floor. "There'll be a bunch of girls setting their caps for him tomorrow."

Walter lifted his partner into the air, eliciting a delighted squeal from her. A group of young women standing on the side giggled behind their hands.

"He's a nice young man, and I hope he finds someone who understands that beneath the quiet exterior, there beats a good and loyal heart."

Amanda continued to enjoy the sight of the members of the gathering filling and then refilling plates. A keg of beer sat to one side, around which a large boisterous group gathered. The musicians took a short break, and her foreman, Lyman Abbott, stepped forward.

"Folks, we all know who we have to thank for tonight's shindig. But it ain't only for the vittles and the beer that we're grateful." A general roar of approval thundered around the yard and Lyman nodded. "But we are grateful for those things, to be sure. We owe a great deal to our boss-lady, Amanda Calhoun." This time the roar of the crowd was deafening.

When the people finally settled down, Lyman continued. "She came to town to help us, and since her arrival; we've got much to be thankful for. But we got even more good times ahead of us. We'll have new homes, a school, and a hospital by next year. And by God, we're gonna have a real church, too!"

Several loud complaints punctuated the applause. Lyman raised an eyebrow. "There are quite a few of you what'll need the confessional on Sunday after the hijinks you pull on Saturday night."

Laughter followed, and Lyman raised his glass mug and nodded in the direction of Amanda.

"To a long and prosperous life. May your husband adore you as much as we do, and may all your children be happy and healthy."

A lump formed in Amanda's throat at the affection and respect these people demonstrated for her. She was indeed a fortunate woman.

When the crowd settled down once again, she stood up and raised her own glass of cider.

"I want to thank all of you for your help in making the Willow Creek Miners' Benevolent Association a success. When I arrived in town, I was terrified that I could never live up to the promises I made to Arthur on his deathbed."

There was silence as the people waited for her to continue.

"I thought I was coming here to help some people who worked for me. I never realized how much this experience would teach me about myself."

A rush of warmth flowed through her at the smiles on her friends' faces.

"I want to thank you for helping me to gain strength, to believe in a higher purpose for my life, and to show me that by working together, our children can prosper and be happy."

The yard erupted into a joyful cacophony. Amanda moved through the gathered throng, accepting hugs, warm handshakes, and kind expressions of gratitude. She arrived at the back door to the Miners' Association with tears in her eyes. Ducking into the dining room to wipe away the evidence of her emotions, she was surprised to find Mr. Penny seated at the table. He jumped quickly to his feet and removed his hat.

"Begging your pardon, Mrs. Calhoun, but I've been waiting for you."

Amanda frowned at her agent. "Waiting?"

"Your husband asked me to come by and get you. He said there was something important he needed to talk to you about. He told me it was private, and that he'd would prefer to meet you down the street." He sniffed at the boisterous crowd in the lighted yard. The music was starting up again.

"I think he wanted privacy, you know, to talk." Penny rolled the brim of his bowler in his bony hands and stared at the floor. "He said to bring you over to the livery stable as soon as I could find you."

Amanda was confused. She'd been waiting for Sam to return to the Miners' Ball all evening, and she was disappointed to learn he wouldn't be joining the festivities. She gazed out the window, then from the corner of her eye she caught an odd glance from Mr. Penny. It was unsettling, this sense of unease when he was around. When she returned to Helena she would find him another position. "Let me grab my wrap and we can go and meet Mr. Calhoun."

She draped the silk shawl around her shoulders. She couldn't fathom why Sam would want to meet her at the livery. Unless he intended to surprise her with a new horse. But why on earth would Sam give her a horse? Perhaps it was to confirm to her that their dream of building a life together could be real. They approached the faded gray barn that housed the blacksmith and livery, and she quickened her step.

Mr. Penny only opened the door a thin slice, then he quickly ushered her through it. The interior of the barn was dimly lit by one lantern, and the pungent, earthy odor of horses, manure, leather, and hay assailed her. She blinked several times, trying to adjust to the dim shadows. She frowned when she discovered the form of a man lying supine, his arms tied behind his back, curled into one corner near a stall. When she turned to find Mr. Penny holding a revolver aimed at her, she gasped. "I..."

A tall man clothed in a buckskin jacket emerged from the darkness. His cold, hard expression frightened her. He seemed strangely familiar, and Amanda shivered when she noticed the rifle he held in his hands.

"Got the bitch, eh? It sure as hell took you long enough, Jacob."

"She was enjoying her own party; it was hard to drag her away." Mr. Penny snickered. "They were all toasting her, telling her what a great job she's done." The other man made a nasty sound deep in his throat. "She's done a great job of spending her husband's money, that's for sure. Miners'Association be damned."

He glared at Amanda. "You shoulda left town when I told ya to."

"I don't understand," Amanda said. "What do you want? Money?"

"Get up there." Mr. Penny made a motion with the gun for Amanda to climb onto the seat of the buckboard.

The other man laughed before he kicked at the bound man lying at her feet. "I was hoping we'd be able to capture that good-looking husband of yours, too, but I guess we're lucky we got this Secret Service fellow instead."

Amanda tried to control her emotions. She stood with one foot on the metal step of the wagon, her heart racing and her hands sweating.

"What would a Secret Service agent want in Willow Creek? Who are you? Why have you brought me here?"

The man threw back his shoulders and stepped close enough to Amanda so she could see the fine, hard pinpoints of hate in his eyes. Amanda shuddered and returned her foot to the dirt floor of the stable.

"I'm Jack Pruitt, one of the miners who paid Calhoun to run

you outta town." He spit on the ground. "Now that we know the truth about him, we're sure he never intended to humiliate and get rid of you. He's a damned Secret Service Agent, too, and once we deal with you, he's goin' to disappear."

The man on the floor moaned. Jack's face went hard and his mouth formed an angry sneer. "You didn't kill him, Jacob." He aimed the rifle at the man he'd identified as an agent of the government. "I never can trust you to do anything right."

Amanda's head swam. Mr. Penny was part of this? What did they plan to do with her? Their conversation was confusing and frightening. And just who was Sam? If what they said were true, she knew nothing about her husband. She wondered if Samuel Calhoun was even his real name.

"If you shoot him it's gonna bring every man in town running over here to see what's going on!" Jacob Penny warned.

Jack glared at Amanda. "I warned you to get out of town."

"Are you the one who has been sending me those threatening letters?" Terror ripped through her gut, making her queasy.

Jack laughed, but there was no good humor in the sound. "Not only did I send you those letters, but I'm the one who carved up that boy." His eyes went darker and harder. "'Course, I was hopin' it would be you at the whorehouse. I had me some fine plans." His gaze rolled over her slowly, pausing to focus on her breasts. Amanda's stomach roiled and gooseflesh prickled her arms. He laughed again, the noise harsh and ruthless. His eyes were bloodshot and empty of any emotion except hatred. She shivered despite the warmth of the night. Her teeth chattered and her mouth was dry.

"When I finally get rid of you, things around town will settle down. I'll have to kill that husband of yours, too, but everyone will think the two of you left together."

"Get her in the damned wagon before someone misses her."

Mr. Penny's voice was louder and more strident than Amanda had ever heard before. He was glancing nervously at the door.

"And if I won't comply with your demands?" Amanda made no effort to do as she was directed. Her legs felt wobbly, and she worried they'd give out beneath her at any moment. It took every ounce of courage she could muster to keep from dissolving into hysterical tears. She sensed she needed to remain calm, at least on the outside.

She needed to form a plan. And she prayed Sam would be at the Miners' Association now, searching for her.

Jack Pruitt pointed at the man on the floor. "Then he dies. We didn't have much luck with getting rid of that kid who works for you, but believe me, my technique has improved since then." He pulled a long bowie knife from a leather pouch at his side. "I've been practicing."

Amanda swallowed against the nausea in her gut. She'd been right about Caleb all along. He'd been attacked because of her. She recognized the agent on the floor. It was Robert Holcomb. Her heart nearly stopped; she couldn't be responsible for the death of the man, even if she didn't understand how he was involved in this mess. "I'll do whatever you want me to do, but please, don't hurt anyone else."

Jacob shoved her toward the wagon. "Get up there, on the seat. Keep quiet, and maybe I won't carve this man up like a holiday turkey."

Amanda pulled herself up the side of the wagon until she finally settled onto the seat. The horses shied and took a step, and the wagon lurched forward.

"Get up there, Jacob, and make her grab those reins. I'll open the door. Be sure to keep that gun trained on her. She's a tricky one."

Mr. Penny followed directions, holding the pistol carefully

aimed at Amanda's stomach. She had an urge to fold her arms over herself protectively, imagining what a bullet could do to her unborn child. Instead, she took up the leather traces.

Giving a click with her tongue and a shake of the reins, the team swept through the doors of the livery stable and out into the darkness of the night. The sounds of the Miners' Ball echoed at the end of town, and she knew most people were gathered there. The saloons were nearly deserted tonight. Jack Pruitt had planned this well. With all the excitement, it would be hours before anyone missed her.

Her mouth was dry as tumbleweed on a hot summer day, and she worked to keep tears from flowing down her cheeks. She realized she'd never see Sam again. He'd think she simply walked out of his life. Maybe he'd be relieved she was finally gone for good. She didn't think he'd come in search of her.

Jack climbed onto the buckboard. They paused just outside the livery stable. "Let's get goin', Jacob. The sooner we get her to the mine, the sooner we can get rid of her for good."

The team continued down the street, and they were nearly at the outskirts of town when Amanda turned to take one last look at Willow Creek. A man was running after them, shouting her name.

A muscle twitched in Jacob Penny's cheek, and she slapped at the reins and tried to move the team faster. She recognized the voice, and she knew Sam was intent upon catching up to them. Amanda turned again to see his long legs stretching to cover the distance between him and the wagon.

Jacob was hidden in one corner, and Amanda was sure that in the darkness he wasn't visible.

"Go back, Calhoun. I want to escape from you and this stinking town forever." She recognized the shrill note in her voice. It was fear.

They edged into the inky blackness scattered at the fringes of Willow Creek. Sam continued to call her name, and her heart pounded in her chest. She prayed he wouldn't reach them, knowing his fate would then be fatal as her own.

"Amanda—" He panted, catching the edge of the wagon and hauling himself up into the back. He struggled to catch his breath as he pulled himself to his knees. "You were right. I couldn't let you ride away and out of my life. I love you, Amanda."

Tears slid down her face as she choked back a response. Why had he waited so long to utter the words she'd been waiting to hear? Now it was probably too late. A horrible sense of doom swept over her.

Jack Pruitt stood up, gripping the back of the seat. He aimed his rifle at Sam's heart. "Now, ain't that sweet? Since it appears you two don't want to live without each other, how about if I arrange for a double funeral?"

A look of shock, then horror, crossed Sam's face. He reached for the revolver at his side, but Jack's words stopped him.

"It would be just as easy to put a bullet in you now, Agent Calhoun, and toss you over the side of the ridge."

Sam's hand shifted away from his gun, and Jack ordered him to toss the weapon into the back of the wagon. He settled down into a crouch, a grim look of satisfaction on his face.

"I've been keepin' my eye on you for a couple of weeks, Calhoun, and I've got to admit, you're a bigger fool than I ever imagined."

Sam leaned back against the side of the wagon. "Because I waited so long to tell my wife how I really felt about her?"

Pruitt laughed and shook his head. "Who the hell cares about that sorta thing? No, Calhoun, you're a fool because you had one of the biggest fortunes in Montana at your disposal, and from what Jacob has told me, you haven't spent a cent of it."

"I once told my wife I didn't give a damn for that money and it's still true." He glared at Pruitt. "Haven't you ever found anything more important than wealth?"

Pruitt's lips settled into a thin, harsh line. "The only folks who can say that are the ones who have more than enough." He gave a bitter laugh. "But soon, very soon, I'll be richer than those railroad tycoons back east. When the U.S. goes to the silver standard, I'll be selling my stockpile for more than gold. Me and my pals will be the ones wearing fancy clothes, with servants and grand houses."

Sam braced one leg up against the side of the wagon and draped an arm across his knee. Amanda knew he was working hard to control his temper. She had to trust Sam because he was the key to getting out of this predicament. Sam would take care of her.

The dark shapes of trees rushed past them, blending into the night. The road was rough, and Amanda began to recognize the direction they were taking.

She gritted her teeth at Mr. Penny. "Are we going out to the Silver Slipper Mine?"

Laughter cackled behind her, and she turned to see Jack grinning in the pale moonlight.

"It will take folks a long time to figure out where you are, and by the time they do, I imagine it'll be too late.

"Are you going to leave us out here, then?"

Jack ignored her question. In the silence, Amanda tried to steal another glance at Sam, but he was silent now, too, leaning back against the sideboards.

It was nearly an hour before they arrived at the mine. The buildings were outlined against the inky black sky. Stars shone above them. There wasn't a sound, because Amanda had declared a holiday and given everyone the night off. Now that she thought about it, the suggestion to do so had been made by Jacob Penny.

The horses slowed. They entered the yard, and Mr. Penny indicated she should bring them to a halt. Jack stood and ordered Sam out of the back of the wagon, then jumped down behind him. Sam hurried forward to assist Amanda as she climbed down, but Pruitt shoved the rifle between them.

"Leave her be."

Amanda's toes touched the ground, and a sharp pain bloomed across the side of her cheek and she heard a ringing in her ears. Her knees melted beneath her and a small scream of surprise escaped her lips. She tumbled to the earth and into a pit of darkness.

Chapter Twenty-One

Sam could barely control the urge to jump forward and wrestle the gun from the bastard who'd hit Amanda with the stock of his rifle. His rage was a live, angry, hot beast that curled through him, making his heart beat faster. The thirst for revenge was thick bile in his throat.

He moved forward and knelt down to carefully lift Amanda. When she stirred in his arms, he pulled her closer. He tried to wrap himself around her, providing protection and refuge by shielding her with his body. She cried out, and he whispered her name gently.

His wife needed to be his first priority, so he'd have to be patient and cautious. It was difficult to wait for an opportunity, but he hoped their captors would make a mistake. Sam would make sure it was their last.

He tried to ignore the ugly bruise forming on the side of Amanda's face. He worked to make his smile comforting. She shivered, then a single tear slid down her cheek, and he gritted his teeth. The more Amanda suffered, the harder it was for him to remain calm. If he didn't figure out a way to disarm the men holding them hostage, Amanda could die. Fear chilled his blood, and his heart banged a wild beat in his chest.

He had to quiet himself and remember his training. He couldn't let his emotions take over.

"Throw some water on her and wake her up." Pruitt's voice was high pitched and demented.

"You do that and I'll strangle you with my bare hands, I swear it." Sam's voice echoed in the darkness.

"You make big threats for a man with a shotgun aimed between his eyes." Pruitt hung back, just out of arms' reach. Not that he'd drop Amanda to chase the son-of-a-bitch. Pruitt was obviously so deranged he didn't know what he was doing. The cruel glint in Jack Pruitt's eyes told him there would be no dealing with these two.

"Get away from him, Jack. Let's just do what we came for and get back to town." Penny's voice was sharp.

Pruitt ignored his companion, then moved closer, reaching out to slap at Amanda's face. Rage percolated through Sam's body. He carefully leaned Amanda upon one arm, and with one quick push, he sent Pruitt spinning backwards onto the stones beneath their feet.

Jacob Penny stepped forward, his beady eyes dark with hatred, a thick line of spittle dripping from his mouth. "Get back." He cocked the pistol he held tightly, and Sam closed his eyes. He waited for the smashing pain that would signal his death.

"Jacob, don't you dare kill 'em. I want to do it," Pruitt roared.

Sam opened his eye to find the two men huddled together, the gun still trained on him. "Move on into the mine, twenty paces." Jacob Penny gestured with the barrel of the pistol. "I want to see you move past those timbers at the entrance."

Sam gathered Amanda into his arms and she opened her eyes. She gave him a quizzical smile, and a few moments later her memory seemed to return. She twisted to look at the men standing in the dim light of the lantern.

"What's going on, Sam?"

"I'm not sure." He kept his voice low and even while he carried her farther into the mine. His steps took them past the square-set heavy timbers at the opening that formed the head-frame. They were nearly twenty feet into the mine when he settled her back upon her feet. "Can you run?" His words were a husky whisper.

"I think so."

"Good, when we get past this next cross cot, we'll be in near total darkness. I want you to gather up your skirts, hang onto my hand, and run. Run like your life depended upon it."

Because it probably does, Sam wanted to add. But they were still close enough to the mine entrance that he didn't want to take the chance of alerting their captors to his plan.

"Stop right there," Jacob Penny demanded.

Not a chance. Sam knew the pistol was still trained on his back, but he would use his body to shield Amanda from the bullets. He could buy her some time to find a hiding place in the mine. With any luck, she could escape and stay hidden until morning.

"Now," he urged her. "Run."

Amanda took off, and the thud of her boots scrambling on the dirt floor echoed through the tunnel. Sam followed close behind her, his arm stretched to hold her hand. He waited for the blast of the gun.

Instead, he heard the sound of laughter. When they were farther into the tunnel he stopped, pulling Amanda flat against the wall with him. He listened carefully to determine if they were being followed. The light at the entrance to the tunnel didn't waver.

"Run all the way to hell, because that's where you're headed anyway." Pruitt's voice carried a ruthless tone. "This mine will be your grave."

The cold edge of fear brushed Sam's spine. He wasn't helping them escape, he was sealing their fate. The crazed man's laughter rang through the dark stillness of the mine shaft.

"What is he talking about?" Amanda trembled as she stood flat against the damp wall.

"I'm not exactly sure, but darlin', do as I say." He leaned down to kiss her on the top of her head. "I love you. God forgive me, if we manage to get out of this mess, I'm going to say it so many times each day you'll get tired of hearing it."

Amanda lifted her face to him. "Those are words I'm never going to get tired of hearing, Samuel Calhoun."

Sam quickly leaned down and touched his lips to hers. Then he gave her a nudge. "Run, darlin'. Keep to the edge of the rail and run like the devil is on your tail." It wasn't far from the truth, if his instincts were correct; in a few moments all hell was going to break loose.

"Sam, there's just one thing. I've never told you this, but since I was a child, I've been—afraid of the dark." She grabbed his hand and started running again.

He heard her breathing heavily and he worried about something appearing in the tunnel—a shovel, a bucket, the edge of the rail, anything that would trip her up. Running in the darkness was a dangerous ploy, but his battle-honed senses warned him there was real danger if they lingered near the mouth of the mine.

"I can't"—Amanda was slowing down— "go on much farther."

"Keep going as long as possible." His own lungs ached with the exertion of breathing the thin air. "Keep going."

Sam looked back over his shoulder. The total darkness behind them was a sign they'd either made some progress, or their captors had left the mine.

He bumped into Amanda and reached out to make sure she didn't fall. "I can't." Her words sandwiched between gasps for air.

"Not much farther, just walk if you have to." He gave her another nudge, then stood in the darkness, waiting. There was a low, thin hiss. He craned his neck to capture the sound. It was familiar, yet he couldn't quite place the noise. Dawning realization suddenly hit him, and he turned to yell a warning to Amanda.

"Get down and cover your head." He took one step toward her as a flash of light illuminated the dark chamber. A deafening sound followed the brilliant flash. Sam hurtled through the air as dust, rocks, and gravel swirled around him. He tumbled to the ground, recognizing the acrid smell of dynamite. His head was thick, clouded, and his lungs felt as if he would never again be able to take a breath.

He was dying, and his biggest regret was that he now had so much to live for. Damn God for his ironic sense of humor. He only hoped that by some miracle, Amanda had escaped the force of the blast.

The burning in his lungs subsided, and he heard a voice in the darkness.

"Sam?"

It was thin and plaintive. He wasn't dead yet, and apparently neither was she.

"Here." He was numb, unable to move, and now incapable of even calling out to the woman he loved.

"Sam?" The voice was closer now, and he heard the crunching of steps. Amanda could move around, so she was in better shape than he was. Finally, a hand touched his shoulder.

In the space of a few moments she was beside him, her voice panicked as her hands traveled across his body. It was going to be a pleasant death, for that much he should be grateful. His last memory would be of Amanda's gentle, loving touch.

“What’s wrong?” The words were thick, barely audible in the darkness.

He heard her take a deep breath. “It’s...” Her voice was sharp with panic. She took another breath. “Are you in much pain?”

He thought there was a great weight on his right leg, but other than that, he couldn’t really feel anything. “I don’t think so.”

“I want you to lie still.” She sounded gruff as a general ordering an army to battle.

Sam grinned, but knew she couldn’t see his expression in the thick darkness. “I can’t move, darlin’. I think there’s something sitting on my leg, pinning me down.”

Her hands moved across his body again, and he decided that if God’s humor was ironic, at least he was taking the memory of Amanda’s touch to the grave. There were worse things to remember in the final moments of your life.

“It’s one of the timbers.” His head began to ache, and the clouds seemed to be disappearing. He noticed a pressure across his entire lower body.

“I can’t move it.” Her voice carried an edge of hysteria.

“Stay calm, darlin’. If you panic, neither one of us is going to make it out of here.” Sam searched for a well-spring of strength and found enough to move one arm and reach out for her.

Her head settled upon his chest, and tears seeped into the fabric of his shirt. “I love you so much,” she whispered.

Her words caressed him. Sam realized he didn’t want to die in this dark tunnel with the woman he loved weeping by his side. Damn the cruelties of life, but he had every intention of living.

“I love you, too, Amanda.” He stroked the softness of her hair, wrapping one silken curl around a finger. “And I don’t plan to end my days down here."

She lifted her head, and he knew she was struggling to see him through the inky blackness. He wished there was a light. His entire being ached with the need to see her face.

"Search my pockets."

She did as he directed, and within just a few moments he heard the sound of a Lucifer match being struck. A pale light illuminated Amanda's terrified expression.

She leaned forward, looking at his right leg, then she tried to mask the concern that swept across her face.

"How bad is it, darlin'?" His words felt thick in his mouth as the clouds returned to obscure his vision.

"It's bleeding, but not badly. I'm going to tear off some strips from my petticoats and wrap them around your leg." The match fizzled and they were once again plunged into darkness. Fear clawed at him at the sound of fabric ripping. He would have to depend on Amanda for help. He should be the one taking care of her.

He floated in and out of consciousness as she bandaged his upper leg, but he struggled to keep his focus.

"I need you to do something brave." His words were measured, still an effort to produce. "You have to go get help."

Her strangled sob was the only reply. He waited for the words to settle in so she could absorb them.

"I'm not brave, Sam. If I were brave, I never would have let you walk away from me in the first place. If I were brave, I would have believed in you. I should have known you would never intentionally hurt me. But I'm a weak and foolish coward."

She dissolved into tears again, and although the sound broke Sam's heart, he let her cry. She needed to wash away the pain of this night.

Finally, her sobs dissolved into hiccups. "I should have trusted you, and now I think I know why you couldn't tell me the truth. You're not who you say you are Sam, and even though I should hate you for the lies you've told me, I can't seem to find anything in my heart but love and regret."

"I promise, darlin', when we get out of this mess, I'm going to tell you everything. But if we're going to make it, you've got to get out of here and get some help." A sharp pain ripped through his leg.

"I don't have any choice, do I?" she whispered.

He wished he had words to reassure her, but there weren't any. It was going to be difficult, but Sam needed to send her into the endless darkness of the mine shaft, because it was the only way she might be able to survive.

"No." The word echoed in the silence. He didn't want to ask this of her, but she was right. They didn't have many choices.

"You have to try to find a way out." He coughed and the effort produced a deep, aching pain in his chest. "If you follow the rails, there's an air shaft. You need to stay to the right." He took a moment to capture a breath. "Keep to the right at every turn and you should find it. Go up, never down."

"I can't leave you." Her words were sharp, and she bolstered them with a gentle caress. He brought her delicate fingers to his lips to kiss them.

"You'll save my life if you do this." He didn't want to frighten her, but she needed to hear the truth. "I can't feel anything below my waist, and I can tell you from my experiences in the war, that's not a good thing."

She touched his face lightly before leaning forward to place her lips on his in a kiss filled with all the sweetness and promise he could desire. He prayed his thanks to God that if it were his last, that it should be so tender and filled with love.

"I'll get help. I've finally captured you, Samuel Calhoun, and I'll be damned if I'm going to let you escape from me this time."

She rose to her feet, and he admired the way she marshaled her strength.

"Save your matches for the stopes, those are the bigger chambers. If you're lucky, you'll find a miner's lamp in one of them."

"Close your eyes, Sam. Rest if you can, and I promise I'll come back for you."

"I'll just be waiting right here for you, darlin'." He laid his head back, exhausted from the effort of talking.

He listened carefully. Slowly, her steps drifted farther and farther away. He was completely, totally alone. It took all of his strength to keep from calling out to her, to bring her back to his side. He closed his eyes and tried to pretend that dying all alone in the darkness didn't matter. He had put on a brave face in front of Amanda, but now that she was gone, fear tripped in and sat down beside him. One thought kept him from dissolving into terror.

Amanda had promised to come back for him, and he knew she was a woman who kept her promises.

∞∞∞

The tunnels seemed endless. Amanda felt she'd been journeying through them for days. Yet they continued to stretch out, dividing into different directions and wandering deep beneath the ground. At each intersection, she turned right, making sure she maintained her direction despite the absence of light. If she became really confused, she lit a match. But she was careful not to waste the precious reserve of Lucifers.

She heard the skittering of small animals, and fear raised the hairs on the back of her neck. Soon, she recalled childhood tales that made the darkness even more terrifying. Tales of horrid trolls who labored deep beneath the ground, ancient dragons and caverns filled with the ghosts of pirates protecting their plunder.

She kept her pace steady and even as possible, working to stay in the center of the tunnels by stretching her arms out straight at her sides. Twice she stumbled against a piece of equipment left in the tunnel and fell. Her hands were scraped with cuts from tumbling over a pick, yet she'd been grateful she hadn't found the sharp edge piercing an arm or leg. A shovel had bruised a shin, but it was nothing compared to the pain she knew Sam was enduring.

Finally, in one of the larger stopes, she found a copper miner's lamp filled with oil and with a complete wick. The small treasure was precious as the jewels and gold she had imagined. The thin flickering light gave her hope.

She stumbled on, nearing exhaustion, but always remembering Sam. Her sweet, infuriating, beloved, Sam. She tried to keep the fear from overwhelming her as she thought about him lying, hurt and in pain, far behind her. She had to keep searching, because she had never let him know the true extent of his injuries. She didn't want him to know how badly he was bleeding.

She swore once again when she found herself at a split in the tunnels. How far beneath ground did these shafts extend? She could have sworn she'd been climbing up for the past half-hour, yet there was no sign of daylight. No indication of the air shaft Sam had been so sure existed.

She didn't want to consider what would happen if she couldn't find a way out. She wasn't sure she could locate Sam again, and she didn't want to be forced to sit and watch him endure a slow and painful death. She shuddered at the thought, her stomach twisting at the reality that she could wander these tunnels for weeks and not be found.

She should have told Sam about the threats against her, but she'd been too proud and too angry with him. She'd wanted to prove she didn't need him, when now all she could think about was how much precious time they'd wasted arguing.

If she lived and Sam didn't, how could she explain to their child that they'd been too pigheaded to settle their differences and be honest with each other? How could she live her life, knowing what a fool she'd been?

She shuddered and tried to imagine a different scenario. Her life was going to be filled with love and happiness. She would have a family, build a life with Sam, and never once take any moment of wonder and joy for granted again.

Please God, she begged. I know I've wandered from the path, but I need your help. The prayer became a guide for her, one step after another. She stopped and sniffed the air. It seemed warmer, fresher smelling. There was a noise and she cocked her head to capture it.

Hello. She thought she heard someone calling out in the darkness.

Was that it? She struggled in the direction she thought the sound had come from but was greeted only with dark silence. Was she losing her faculties, imagining voices that existed only in her head?

"Hello."

She wasn't delirious or insane. That was a human voice, and despite the fact that it might be her captors trying to find out if they'd survived the cave-in, she didn't care.

"Here," she screamed, her own voice startling her as it echoed down the long, lonely tunnels. If it was Mr. Penny and that horrid Jack Pruitt, she hoped they'd shoot her and get the agony over with. "I'm here."

"Mrs. Calhoun?" It was a male voice.

"Yes, I'm here. Keep calling me and I'll answer." She heard steps moving closer, then a thin light shone at the end of a long tunnel. "Here," she yelled as loudly as she could. The light grew brighter, and she nearly fell to her knees, sobbing in relief.

Three large men appeared in a glow of lantern light. "Mrs. Calhoun, are you hurt?"

Strong arms prevented her from collapsing to the ground. She recognized the faces of several of her miners, including Margaret Abbott's husband, Lyman. Her heart lifted with hope and she closed her eyes in gratitude that one prayer had been answered. She'd found help, and now they could go get Sam. She recalled the blood she'd seen on his leg and swallowed the huge lump in her throat. Even in the darkness, she knew he was badly hurt.

"Thank God we found you." A rough tenderness laced his words. "We thought you'd been killed in the cave-in."

She grabbed him ferociously by the collar. "Sam's hurt. He's back in the tunnels. We've got to get back there and get him; he's hurt badly, Lyman."

He patted her gently, and pointed at the other men. "See if you can find him, I'll get her out of the tunnels and bring more men."

A sudden panic rose within Amanda, making her voice thin and plaintive. "No, I've got to take you back to him." She struggled to make them understand. "It's so far back, and I can't even remember..." Her voice trailed off into a sob.

How would she be able to find Sam? There had been so many twists and turns to get here. A wave of despair rolled over her. It wasn't fair. She didn't want to live if Sam was going to be left all alone in the darkness to suffer a solitary and painful death.

She turned from Lyman and tried to push her way through

the men. "Follow me. I think I can find him."

Gentle hands grasped her by the shoulders. Lyman Abbott's eyes told her he understood how much she was suffering. "We know these tunnels better than anybody else in Willow Creek." His tone reassured her. "We won't give up 'til we find him, but you've been through a hell of a night from the looks of things." He gave her another gentle pat. "Margaret is waiting up at the office, and she's worried sick over you. Half the town is up there."

Amanda shook her head in confusion. "Half the town, I don't understand."

Lyman grabbed her hand and pulled her with him. "We got time enough to tell the tale after we find your husband. I figure he's at Grand Central," he said to the others. "Head down there, and I'll bring a crew back with me."

Amanda's confidence returned at the foreman's tone. "They'll find Sam, won't they?"

"We'll find him, ma'am, don't you worry about that."

Amanda turned and continued up through the narrow tunnel toward a shaft of light at the top. What was left unsaid was the possibility that they'd be too late. When they found Sam, he might already be dead.

Chapter Twenty-Two

Amanda halted at the entrance to the mineshaft, gazing at the streaks of early dawn edging the still dark sky, and inhaled deeply. She never imagined the rush of fresh air filling her lungs could feel so good.

"Amanda. Oh, praise the Lord, she's alive." Warm arms captured her and she was pulled toward the ample bosom of Harriet Parmeter.

The comforting aroma of fresh baked bread and apples surrounded her, and Amanda felt some reassurance. When Harriet finally released her, it was only to be grasped by Margaret Abbott.

"Honey, we've all been so worried about you," Margaret said.

"Let me through, dad-drat-it, you women can have your hen party another time. Let me see if she's been hurt." Doc Potter shoved his way through the gaggle of women surrounding her.

His appearance shocked Amanda. He wore a spotless white shirt with a new black frock coat. His hair and beard were trim and clean. His boots gleamed in the light from the torches that surrounded the tunnel entrance.

"Doc?" Amanda couldn't keep the astonishment from her voice. "Is that really you?"

He bustled around the women as he threw her a disgusted look. "Of course it's me, did a rock land on your head and knock you senseless, woman?"

Amanda shook her head. "I don't think so, but if you're sober, maybe I am hallucinating."

"I am sober, and it's all your fault." He pointed a finger at Margaret. "You and that interfering, meddling woman. She's been following after me and lecturing me about demon rum until I finally gave in and stopped drinking just so I could shut her up and get rid of her."

Margaret Abbott never flinched. "I saved your soul, you old fool, and you know it." She settled an arm around Amanda's waist. "You can't examine her out here in front of the whole dang town." She pulled Amanda toward a large log building sitting in the center of the clearing. "Come on, dearie, we need to get you warmed up."

Amanda leaned on the woman, taking comfort from her words and the warmth of her body. She was grateful for the concerns expressed by the other women, but the respite was brief. Sam was still injured and lost underground. Her heart beat quickly, and she trembled as she recalled the dark stain of blood she'd seen oozing from his injured leg. She looked down at her skirts and the sight of bloodstains made her stomach heave. She was grateful for the arms of the other women to steady her.

They entered the log structure and someone scrambled to get her a chair. Within minutes a blanket was draped around her shoulders and a cup of hot, steaming coffee placed in her hands. She sniffed the rich aroma and wrapped her hands around the enamel cup to warm them.

Amanda savored the feeling of being warm and safe again. How foolish she'd been, taking so much for granted. She'd never really appreciated things like being free to move about, having friends who cared about her, and the love of a good man. She would never see another dawn without whispering a prayer of thanks to God for sparing her life last night. Finally, she lifted her head and found Doc Potter towering over her.

"Are you hurt or bleeding?" His tone was gruff, but there was real concern reflected in his eyes.

Amanda shook her head and took another sip of her coffee.

"Have you, um, experienced any effects from your condition?"

She could swear the man was blushing.

"No. I fell and scraped my hands and knees, but otherwise I'm not injured." She tried to keep her voice calm and controlled as she lifted her gaze to plead with him.

"But Sam's hurt." Her hands began to shake and she set the cup on the table next to her. "He was bleeding and there's a large timber on his leg." She worked hard to keep a sob from escaping. "He told me he's lost the feeling below his waist."

Doc Potter leaned back on his heels. "Was the blood gushing or oozing?"

Amanda wrinkled her brow, trying to remember. "Oozing, I guess. Seeping slowly." She shivered despite the blanket draped around her.

He nodded. "And this timber, did it appear to have crushed his leg or pelvis?"

His words were beginning to terrify Amanda as she considered how gravely injured Sam might be. Harriet patted her gently on the arm and shot an angry look at the doctor.

"Why don't you get on down in the tunnels and take a look at Sam yourself." There was a note of disgust in her voice. "Quit pestering Amanda. Hasn't she been through enough tonight?"

Doc narrowed his eyes at Harriet. "I expect you think I'm too much of a coward to go down there, don't you Harriet Parmeter?"

Harriet waved a hand in his direction and scoffed. "I could give a hoot about you, old man. Go straight to hell for all I care, just leave this poor woman alone."

The doctor lifted his head and squared his shoulders. "I'll show you women that I'm just as good as the next man." With that he stomped out of the room.

Harriet shook her head. "Damn fool men, can't figure out why we have to put up with such nonsense."

Amanda touched her friend's hand. "He's only trying to help, and I appreciate that he's not drunk." She looked out the window and into the early dawn light, which outlined the buildings of the Silver Slipper Mine in russet and orange. "I think Sam will need all of his skills when they bring him up. His injuries are serious." Tears filled her eyes and she stifled a sob.

Harriet patted her shoulder. "Sam will be all right. That man is strong as an ox."

Amanda wiped the tears from her cheeks and tried to return her smile. "And stubborn as a mule, sometimes." She sniffed.

"I don't understand how you managed to find us out here. Mr. Penny and a man named Jack Pruitt kidnapped me and forced me into a wagon." She shivered and her voice trembled. "Sam thought I was leaving town and he jumped into the wagon to stop me."

Margaret dragged a chair across the room and sat opposite Amanda. "We had a surprise for you. We planned it for after dinner."

Harriet jumped in. "But of course, I had to go get a second helping, and I guess that's when that sneak Mr. Penny told you something that convinced you to go with him."

Amanda nodded. "He told me he'd been sent on an errand for Sam." She felt sheepish. "He told me Sam was at the livery stable and I foolishly followed him out there."

Both women nodded. "There wasn't any reason for you to suspect him, and I guess we should have warned you," Harriet said.

"But Caleb wanted to tell you himself, because he thought you'd be more likely to believe him," Margaret added.

"Caleb?" Amanda lifted her head. "He's conscious again?" Her heart quickened a beat.

"He's back to his own self, just as sweet and good a boy as ever." A motherly note of pride brightened Harriet's voice. "Eatin' you out of house and home I suspect. But we were plannin' to bring him downstairs to surprise you, when that Mr. Penny spirited you away before we could prevent it, or even warn you."

"Warn me?" Amanda's head swam. The women took turns telling the story, and she had never felt so worn out and tired before in her entire life.

"Caleb told me it was Jack Pruitt that jumped him at the Miners' Association that day." Harriet folded her arms across her breasts. "That's one man who can dance at the end of a rope and may he rot in hell." She spit on the floor.

Amanda frowned. "Caleb?"

"Jack Pruitt," Margaret said with venom in her voice. "Of course, that nasty little sneak of an agent can join him, too."

"Vengeance shall be yours, ladies. They've both been arrested and taken to Helena for their trial."

All three women jumped at the sound of the man's voice. Father Mikelson stood in the doorway, his head nearly touching the top of the wood frame. Dawn's light bathed him in gold, and Amanda shuddered at the image he presented. She imagined a stained-glass window with the archangel Michael streaking across it, heading to earth to exact vengeance.

The priest cleared his throat. "I beg your pardon, ladies, but I must speak with Amanda." He took a step closer. "Alone. Her message was most urgent."

Amanda stood up, wrapping the blanket more tightly around her to keep from shivering uncontrollably. Her fear for Sam wiped out her anger at the manipulations of the old priest. She didn't have any more time for arguments.

"I have something important to discuss with Father Mikelson, if you could give us a bit of privacy."

Both women rose quickly, but Amanda stopped them with a wave of her hand. "Did you find Robert tied up in the livery stable?"

Harriet nodded. "He's got a giant lump on his head, and I think he's feelin' mighty low about being tricked. He'll be real happy to find out you've been rescued."

"I'm grateful he's not seriously hurt." She said, waiting for the door to close behind them.

"You've been meddling in my affairs, again, haven't you, old man?"

The priest avoided making eye contact and paced across the room. He deposited his thick wool overcoat on the chair, but he didn't sit down. His fingers combed through his silver hair.

"I know you're angry with me, Amanda." He turned his blue eyes toward her. "I want you to know I did everything in order to protect you."

"Protect me?" Her voice was incredulous. "You have never, ever considered what I want or need. You've manipulated and controlled me, but God knows, you have never cared anything about me or my happiness. How could separating me from the man I love, the father of my child, protect me?" Amanda took a deep breath to steady her nerves. A band of sorrow wrapped around her chest, making it difficult to talk.

Shock hit the older man's eyes like a thunderbolt. He slumped to the chair, his head dropped, and he folded his hands together, the thin skin looking pale and fragile.

“God knows I have loved you as if you were my own child since you were just a little girl.” He finally lifted his head, and sadness painted the features of his face with grim remorse. “I wanted to spoil you, indulge you, and I never, ever wanted anything but happiness for you.”

Father Mikelson rose and paced across the room to a window. The early morning light warmed the leaves of the trees just beyond the glass. Birdsong filled the air outside, as the creatures of the sky sang to welcome the sun.

“I asked Sam to protect you, and he agreed to serve as a bodyguard. He hated that you’d been forced to marry him, and he wanted to release you from your vows.”

Amanda sat down, her body aching to her bones with weariness. “You made an arrangement with Sam to have our marriage annulled.” Her lower lip trembled, but she couldn’t seem to make it stop. “Why would you do that, Father?”

The old man’s face crinkled, and he suddenly looked old and exhausted to her. He coughed, and Amanda saw tears turning the bright blue of his eyes a shade paler.

He looked down at the floor. “I thought I was protecting you, Amanda. I never should have interfered, because after talking to Sam the night I forced the two of you to get married, I knew he loved you.” He lifted his head slowly. “Maybe I thought if I bargained with him, he’d stick around and the two of you would find a way to work things out.”

Amanda nodded. In a way, the priest had been right. She couldn’t blame him for trying to protect her. She reached out to gently pat his hand.

A clamor ensued outside in the yard and the door swung open. “We need the priest; they’ve just brought Sam up from the tunnels.”

Father Mikelson rushed to get out the door. Amanda covered her mouth to stifle a scream. If Sam needed a priest, that could only mean it was too late for a doctor.

She stumbled out the door of the cabin, oblivious to the bright early-morning sunshine. A group gathered at the opening to the mine shaft, and their grave faces and silence terrified her.

Several of the miners who had brought Sam up to the surface made a space for her. Sam was stretched upon the ground, covered by a woolen blanket. There was a dark, shiny spot where he had bled through the fabric. Amanda bit hard on the knuckle of her fist to hold a scream within her throat. His face was so pale, it appeared to be carved from alabaster.

She fell to her knees, barely able to breathe. Tears trickled down her cheeks despite her effort to hold them back. She grasped Sam's hand in her own and whispered his name over and over, like a litany. His skin was so cold, his body so still, she felt her world spinning sideways as an icy numbness seized her.

Doc Potter was on the other side, ordering the women behind him to rip their petticoats into strips for bandages. His leather bag was open at his side.

Amanda tried to rise and join the other women, but a firm hand gripped her shoulder. "Never mind that," Father Mikelson said. "Stay here and talk to him."

Tears rolled down her cheeks, and she wanted to put her hands to her face and sob out the great piercing sadness that was shattering her heart. Sam was going to die, and she had never told him about their child. It was so unfair, and she knew that she would never be able to forgive herself for withholding the truth from him. An aching loneliness washed over her at all the love she'd squandered because of her foolish pride. Her heart had cracked in two.

Doc Potter drew the blanket aside, and she flinched when she saw Sam's torn and bleeding flesh. The doctor poured alcohol on the wound, and her spirits lifted for a moment when Sam swore and twisted with the pain.

"He's still alive," she whispered, a jolt of hope gripping her.

The doctor gave her a desolate look. "He's lost a lot of blood, and this leg is broken."

Amanda tightened her hold on Sam's fingers. "He's strong, and I know he wants to live."

Doc Potter shook his head. "I won't give you false hope, Mrs. Calhoun. I've seen wounds as bad as this on the battlefield. There's not much chance he's going to make it."

Amanda laid her head on Sam's shoulder and let the tears flow freely. Several of the men stepped back, giving her a little privacy to say good-bye to her husband.

There were so many things she had left unsaid. So many promises they'd made to each other and then broken. She regretted the lost time, the harsh words and arguments. They'd spent their days so angry at each other that they had squandered their only chance at happiness. She'd never love any man as much as she loved Sam. The enormous sadness within her broke loose like water surging over a dam, releasing a flood of tears. She felt a hand gently stroking her hair and lifted her gaze to find Sam's clouded, pain-filled eyes staring at her.

"Don't cry darlin'. I never could stand to see you cry."

Amanda took a deep breath and tried to steady her voice before she spoke. "I love you, Sam. I wish I could have been a better wife to you, and that I'd been kinder and more understanding. I wish..." She couldn't go on. She dissolved into great gulping sobs.

"None of that matters now, darlin'. I've loved you since that first night I met you." He gasped. "I tried to keep from giving my heart to you, but it's no use. You were right last night. I never could really let you go." He closed his eyes. "We belong together."

Amanda gazed down at Sam with all the love and tenderness she could muster. Pain was etched deeply onto the pale surface of his face.

She could give him one last gift before they said goodbye for eternity. She swallowed and worked to make her voice steady and strong.

"We're going to have a baby, Sam."

Ebony lashes fluttered, and his amber eyes opened wide. He stared at her, incredulous, before his face split with a huge grin.

"I'll be damned." He winced, and it appeared that speaking was causing him a great deal more pain. He grinned again.

"That's wonderful news, darlin'. Promise to stay with me, right here by my side." He coughed. "I believe I can get through this." He closed his eyes and drifted off.

Amanda licked her lips and took a deep breath. "I promise, Sam. I'll be here with you every moment. I need you, Samuel Calhoun. If you dare to leave me, I swear, I'll come right down to hell and battle old Beelzebub himself to get you back." She gently placed her lips to his and sealed that oath with a kiss. His mouth was cool and tasted salty.

He opened one eye to give her that infuriating, lazy, lopsided grin. "Just one more thing, darlin'."

"Yes, Sam?"

"Tell me why you're so all-fired sure that if I do die, I'm going to end up burning in hell."

Epilogue

"I see that very familiar glint in your eye, Sam, and you can just forget about it."

Amanda raised one leg in the bath and gently soaped its length. She felt Sam's gaze on her, his amber eyes shaded with gold as they filled with desire. She should have known better than to arrange her bath here in their bedroom, but the house was so crowded with company today, it was the only place she could find some privacy.

"There isn't time."

"I won't take long, I promise." His voice was a sexy, inviting drawl, and the familiar heat washed over her.

She should be embarrassed that she could respond so quickly to her husband's passion, but instead she felt a tremor of excitement.

"The other guests will be here at noon." She dropped the soap to reach for a length of linen toweling to dry off. Rising from the scented warmth of the hip bath, she started to rub her body with the towel.

The flare of desire in her husband's eyes banked to a raging flame.

"I hope you're not going to make me climb out of this bed and come over there to grab you, woman."

Amanda flirted with him, fluttering her lashes like a brazen hussy, and grinned.

"With that bum leg of yours, I could easily escape."

Sam threw back the covers and brought both of his long, muscular legs to the floor. The jagged scar on his right thigh bore testimony to the ordeal they'd survived over a year ago in the mine shaft.

"I'm getting stronger everyday, madam, so I wouldn't count on getting away so easily."

She crossed the room to lean forward and touch her lips to Sam's mouth, the kiss deepening, her tongue thrusting and parrying against his. His hands moved to squeeze the smooth mounds of her buttocks and she sat on his knee rubbing her soft, moist slit against him.

"Woman, you're torturing me."

"Heavenly torture," she murmured. "We've got a busy afternoon, but a long night to look forward to." She delighted in the way they fit together so perfectly. And the way their carnal appetites matched just as well.

"You never cease to amaze me, darlin'". His hand gently kneaded her soft flesh, and there was admiration in the tone of his voice.

"Amazing Amanda will be my stage name when I join the circus." She laughed as his tongue slid into her ear and he tickled her.

"Why would you need to do that? Isn't there enough excitement here in Willow Creek?"

She stroked the side of his face playfully. "Things seem to have calmed down a bit around here lately, don't you think?"

He twirled a strand of her hair around one finger and gave her a lazy grin. "Hell, darlin', it's been months since you've tried to shoot me, anyone has attempted to murder us, or I've set something on fire. I guess we've settled into being old married folks."

Amanda wrinkled her nose. "Do you really think so, Sam? She gently rubbed his chest with one hand. "I would hate for people to think we're boring. Since you broke up the plot the other mine owners were hatching to profit from manipulating the supply of silver, this town has been downright tedious."

A deep laugh rumbled in his chest. "With all the excitement of the new houses for your miners, our ranch, and a baby, I doubt you've had time to become bored." He patted her gently on the bottom. "But I suspect if we don't get some clothes on and get down to the willow grove for our son's baptism, Father Mikelson will come barging in that door searching for us."

Amanda giggled. "Imagine being caught by the priest in the middle of the day in our bed, naked. That should stir up some interesting gossip."

"Our reputations might never recover from such a scandal."

Amanda took a deep breath, savoring the image of her husband's hard, smooth body. Her fingers gently traced across his skin and she marveled at the warmth, the heat he produced.

She shrugged. "We're already legendary. It's probably not a major leap to becoming notorious."

Sam shook his head sadly. "We might consider poor little Ethan. He *will* have to grow up in this town."

"Everyone adores Ethan. He's the most perfect baby ever born."

"Spoken like a very proud mother."

Amanda tossed hair as she grabbed her undergarments.

"And who was the one boasting that his baptism day will be the biggest celebration ever held in Montana territory?"

She tied the ribbons of her petticoat, then wrapped her corset around her full rounded curves. She struggled to fasten the front and frowned at Sam.

"Having a baby certainly creates havoc with one's figure."

Sam pulled himself off the bed to stand in front of her. "In my eyes, you're the most beautiful creature on earth. There isn't a soft curve"—his fingers brushed against her breast—"an angle, or a line that isn't perfect on your body."

She stepped into his embrace, leaning forward to place her head against his chest to listen to the steady cadence of his heart. "Will you always love me, Sam?"

He lifted her chin gently with one finger and gazed into the depths of her eyes. She could see the chocolate highlights flickering in his gaze.

"I promise to love you with every inch of my being, for every moment God allows us to be together. I've learned to live each day as if it were my last, because someday...it's gonna be."

"I never imagined I could be so happy, Sam. When I first met you, all I could think about was how much I wanted you. It terrified me that my sensual hunger could be so consuming." She studied the smooth, chiseled line of his jaw carefully. "I thought such desire was sinful, and that I would be destined to burn in hell for eternity in penance for my carnal lust."

Sam laughed. "Don't you think a lifetime with a devil for a husband might be enough penance for a good woman like you?"

Amanda smiled. "I thank God every day that you managed to lure me off the path of the straight and narrow." She gave him a playful look. "If being bad feels this good, being good couldn't be much of an improvement."

Sam laughed, the deep rumble in his chest comforting her with its sound. His mouth covered hers and she closed her eyes, allowing contentment to wash over her.

Amanda had learned to cherish her life with Sam and their son, Ethan. Every day was a precious gift from God, and she promised herself her life would be filled with all the happiness she could find.

And she knew better than anyone that a promise kept was one of the most powerful forces on earth.

The End

Special Bonus Short Story

A Winter Welcome

"She's a fine figure of a woman, Sam. I will say that."

Samuel Calhoun nearly spit out his cigar. Robert coughed, and tried to hide his grin at his friend's response. He'd likely shocked Sam with the comment, because while Calhoun was a great admirer of the female form and known to dally with a woman once in a while, Robert was more subdued when it came to romancing the ladies.

"I was beginning to think you were beyond any interest in the fillies," Sam commented as he sipped his black coffee.

Robert leaned his chair back and considered the lady serving a weary group of travelers on the other side of the dining room. She brushed back a curl that fell into her face before pouring the exhausted looking woman at the table a cup of coffee.

"I own up I ain't no man whore." Robert said, never taking his eyes off the mature, voluptuous woman as she swirled though the dining room.

Sam laughed. "Nope, I don't believe I could ever accuse you of that. Far as I can recall, you hardly ever visit the sportin' gals, which maybe ain't natural but I've learned to live with your peculiarities."

Robert snorted. "Particular ain't exactly the same as being peculiar. I don't fall in bed with every calico queen we stumble across just to ease an itch. I guess it takes more'n a scrap of petticoat to hold my interest."

Sam nodded. "A man of high ideals and exacting standards. I admire your principles, Robert." He raised his coffee cup in salute. "Wish I could say I'd emulate your behavior, but I try not to make promises I don't intend to keep."

The woman waiting on tables sailed across the room. Her dark brown eyes sparkled as she lifted the coffeepot and nodded at the men. "Can I interest you gentlemen in some more?" Her cheeks were bright red spots of color, and the heat of bustling around the room made the dark black hair sprinkled with silver highlights curl around her friendly face.

"What's your name, darlin'?" Sam asked.

She quirked an eyebrow at him and dimples appeared at each corner of her shapely mouth. "I'm Harriet Parmeter, the proprietor of this hotel. And if you're askin' so's you can come courtin'—don't waste your time on pickin' flowers for me." She leaned toward Sam and winked. "I'd rather have some good whiskey instead!"

Both Sam and Robert roared at her spunky response as she poured their coffee then whirled to the table next to them. They watched as she chatted with her customers, brought orders from the kitchen, whisked dirty dishes off the tables and then set them for new customers.

"It appears she's in need of some help," Sam commented.

Robert blew on his coffee, lifted his gaze to watch Harriet Parmeter for a moment then shrugged.

"Appears so."

Sam was silent, then nodded. "An extra pair of hands around this place would be a big help to Mrs. Parmeter. I expect she'd be willing to take on some help, if the offer was put to her right."

Robert sipped from his cup slowly and took his time as he considered his partner's comment.

"I s'pect so, what with the town growin' and her business bein' brisk, especially on a night like tonight. Everybody for miles around wants to be in town for the New Year's celebration." He put the four legs of his chair back onto the floor. "Mayhap I'll go ask the lady about employment."

Sam didn't have time to object as Robert scraped back the chair and rose to his feet. He slipped through the door of the kitchen with a silent, easy gait.

Harriet Parmeter leaned into the oven of the cast iron stove and Robert was met by her round, shapely bottom as she balanced herself to remove a pan. He stopped to take a deep breath. In his opinion, a woman's ass was one of the loveliest sights on God's green earth. If the woman was a full-figured and mature creature, the pleasure was intensified a thousand times for him.

Harriet straightened, turning to put the skillet of cornbread on the table behind her. Her eyes opened wide and a strawberry blush crawled up from her ample bosom to tinge her cheeks when she noticed Robert standing behind her.

"Ya nearly scared me outta my skin, Mister." She made a noise of disapproval. "Customers ain't allowed in the kitchen." She snapped a linen dishtowel in his direction. "Scat! Get yerself back in the dinin' room and I'll be out shortly."

Robert shifted from foot to foot and held his hands behind his back. He wasn't good at talking, that was Sam's job. But if they were ever going to succeed at their new assignment, he'd have to find a job that gave him access to miners, travelers and gossip. The dining room of a hotel seemed like the perfect solution. Not to mention the establishment was owned by Harriet Parmeter.

He nodded. "Beggin' your pardon, ma'am, but seein' as how you're so busy and all, I was wonderin' if you'd have a job for someone like me." He swallowed, reluctant to look away from the soft brown eyes staring back at him.

Harriet frowned. "I ain't got no horses to buck-break or cows needin' to be punched. Most of what I need done around here is emptyin' slop pails, scrubbin' floors and haulin' wood." She sniffed. "All the men I've hired have run-off soon as they got a poke for minin' or somethin' better came along."

Robert nodded. "I understand, and I ain't plannin' on stayin' in these parts much beyond next spring. But I could be a good help 'til then."

Harriet was quiet as she put her hands on her hips and sized him up. He blushed as her gaze swept down from the top of his head to the toes of his boots. He wondered if she was going to ask him to open his mouth so she could see his teeth. He almost neighed and fought the urge to stomp a foot.

"You might do, if you ain't afraid of hard work. I can't pay much but I'd give you a room to sleep in and three good meals every day."

Robert nodded. "That sounds fair."

"What about your handsome friend out there, he lookin' for work too?"

He shook his head. "I'd say he's more interested in searching for business opportunities."

Harriet snorted. "Gambler?"

"Sometimes," Robert answered. "But he's got some education and a bit of money. "

Harriet grabbed a knife and started slicing the cornbread. "What's your name?"

"Robert Holcomb," he said as he removed his woolen coat and started to roll up the sleeves of his linen shirt. "I'll just start washin' up in here right now if you don't mind."

Harriet loaded a tray with plates and balanced it across her arm. "I ain't gonna argue with you, Robert. We got a dinin' room full of hungry folks in town for the big doin's tonight and I believe in makin' hay while the sun shines." She slipped out the door.

Robert took a tin pan to the reservoir of hot water on the stove and filled it. He returned to the sink and pumped some cold water in it, then grabbed the bar of soap and rubbed it in his hands. He could hear Harriet's bright, cheerful laughter through the door, and he smiled. So far, he'd seen no sign of a Mr. Parmeter, and he felt a jolt of awareness that hit him without warning. If Harriet wasn't a widow, it was going to be a real temptation to rein in his desire to make her one.

It was many hours later, after washing a ton of dishes by Robert's estimation, that he slowly climbed the stairs to the room Harriet had assigned him earlier in the evening. Despite the late hour, the street outside was still filled with the celebration for New Years. The Chinese rockets had been lit hours ago, but men were shooting off their guns as they yelled out their greetings and stumbled through the streets.

There were a lot of drunks out there, Robert concluded, and not being a drinking man, he had no desire to go out and join them. His bed was looking pretty good right about now. He might not be able to fall asleep, but he could get his boots off and stretch out.

"Get your hands off me you son-of-a-bitch, or I'll give out a yell that'll bring the roof down."

Robert paused when he recognized Harriet's voice coming from one of the rooms at the end of the hall.

"Ain't nobody gonna hear you with that racket out in the street," a deep voice drawled. "You know you want it, woman, so stop fightin' me."

It was all the reason Robert needed to dash up the stairs.

He could hear a crash from behind the door and then a muffled thump. He didn't bother to knock; he kicked at the door and stumbled into the room.

A man lay sprawled across the bed and Harriet Parmeter brushed crockery across the pine floor with her foot. She looked up as Robert stood in the doorway with his gun drawn.

"Damn drunks cost me more in pitchers than they're worth!" She turned to glance at the man and then shrugged her shoulders. "I'll charge him an extra dollar tomorrow for the trouble."

"You can put that gun away, Mr. Holcomb, no need to shoot anybody tonight." A smile played across her lips. "I do appreciate you comin' to my rescue though —you're a regular hero, ain't you?"

Robert blushed as she closed the door behind her before leaning back against it. She seemed to see him, really see him, for the first time since he'd walked into the kitchen.

"You worked hard tonight and I never heard a word of complaint," she paused to consider him more, "no cussin' neither, which I sure appreciate."

She stepped closer and Robert didn't move. He could smell her cinnamon, coffee and honey scent and he inhaled deeply. She smelled like warm bread from the oven, sitting by the fire with spiced cider comfort. Harriet Parmeter smelled like home. Her rosy lips formed a sweet smile and his heart thumped against his chest.

She lifted up on her toes to grasp his chin gently. "Happy New Year, Robert," she whispered before putting her lips on his. He felt frozen to the spot, as if the howling North wind had brought a blizzard into the room. He was too surprised to respond; too afraid she'd pull away from him if he so much as grasped her around the waist to pull her closer. Finally, she leaned away from him, a flirt of a smile on her lips and a sparkle in her eyes. She turned to go to her room.

Robert felt like his boots were stuck to the floor. He needed to say something, but his mind was blank. She stood outside her room, and he finally found his courage.

"Mrs. Parmeter," she turned with one hand on the brass doorknob. "I believe we're in for a special New Year," he paused to look down at his feet, knowing his neck and face were probably red as a ripe apple. He finally looked up to see a delighted smile on her face. "I... I appreciate you taking me on and giving me work," he said.

She cocked her head at him like a curious crow sitting on a fence post. "There's more to you than most folks can see, Mr. Robert Holcomb, it's gonna be interestin' to figure you out!"

When she finally closed the door to her room, Robert grinned. "If you only knew, Mrs. Parmeter," he said softly as he passed her room, "if you only knew."

The End

About the author...

A love for American History drew Deborah to the field of education and she holds a teaching degree in Social Studies with an emphasis on American History. This explains her interest in the American Revolution, the Civil War and Westerns. She resides in a small town near the Cascade Mountains in the Pacific Northwest. She's the winner of the Molly Award for the most Unsinkable Heroine for Sinclair Redford the heroine of *Beneath A Silver Moon*. She's received the Open Book Award from Pacific Northwest Writers, the Stella Cameron Award and was named Librarian of the Year in 2009 by Romance Writers of America. She loves writing about strong, smart women who aren't afraid to challenge the men they love. She's employed by one of the busiest library systems in the U.S. and believes in the power of books to change lives.

Visit her at http://www.debschneider.com

Facebook: Deborah Schneider

For more about her paranormal and steampunk books written as Sibelle Stone,

Visit http://www.sibellestone.com

Thank you for taking the time to read, "Promise Me". If you enjoyed this book, please review it at the website where you purchased it. Authors rely upon reviews not only to help us sell more books, but to become better writers.

www.ingramcontent.com/pod-product-compliance
Lightning Source LLC
LaVergne TN
LVHW091118080826
845145LV00008B/1963

* 9 7 8 0 9 9 9 1 9 4 7 0 6 *